Acclaim for Alice Adams'

AFTER THE WAR

"With its deliberately breezy tone and style and multiple crises, the novel is an unabashed page-turner, a kind of *Peyton Place* for college graduates or—as other commentators have remarked of Adams generally—like gossip with a good friend. . . . Like a gardener who doesn't overwater the plants, or a benignly indifferent mother, Adams is attentive to each of her creations but gives each its head; she lets them all fly free of her control while appreciating their idiosyncrasies. Her mix of old-fashioned storytelling with a modern sense of the elusive perplexities of identity makes for an unusual combination, and one not easily replaced."

—*The New York Times Book Review*

"Imagine God as a small-town gossip and you'll get the feel of Alice Adams' eleventh and last novel. . . . [It] excels in evoking a nearly lost world."

—*Los Angeles Times*

"Lovely, tender, and just a little hokey, like that moment just before the birthday candles are blown out."

—*The New Yorker*

"As always, Adams' strength is her fine, elegant language and the attention she pays to the minutiae of every day living. Like Jane Austen, she stays close to her characters and weaves intrigue out of their interrelated and complex life stories."

—*San Jose Mercury News*

"*AFTER THE WAR* arrives posthumously and with quiet grace, as though Adams knew faithful readers would need comforting after she died. . . . Steering a path between gothic and folksy, Virginia-born Adams gives us a clear-eyed view of a South in transition, a view that doesn't pander to accepted stereotypes. At the end of her life, she could scarcely have done her birthplace a better service."

—*San Francisco Chronicle*

"Alice Adams succeeds with *AFTER THE WAR* in creating a sustained plot as rich as her evocative setting and complex characterization."

—*Boston Sunday Globe*

"Adams has pulled off a graceful tale about romance and racism. And she surprises you by the end with her carefully drawn characters. You can't quite guess who turns out to be a true friend, or not quite the bigot, or who proves more caring or sassier than you might have originally believed."

—*Newsday*

"Adams is a genius at affectionately tweaking the stereotypes of a Southern gentility struggling mightily to understand the ways of the world. . . . Highly recommended."

—*Library Journal*

"Tender, funny, and touching: a fitting close to an admirable career."

—*Kirkus Reviews*

"A copiously but relevantly detailed tapestry of small-town life during a time when the world beyond Pinehill is changing at a rapid rate."

—*Booklist*

"Reading this posthumous novel is a bittersweet experience. On the one hand, it's wonderful to be back in the Southern town of Pinehill, and to enjoy Adams' inimitable prose and her calm intimacy with the characters introduced in *A Southern Exposure*. On the other, it's a pity to realize that we'll never know what future lives Adams had planned for these vibrant individuals."

—*Publishers Weekly*

ALSO BY ALICE ADAMS

Careless Love

Families and Survivors

Listening to Billie

Beautiful Girl (stories)

Rich Rewards

To See You Again (stories)

Superior Women

Return Trips (stories)

Second Chances

After You've Gone (stories)

Caroline's Daughters

Mexico: Some Travels and Travellers There

Almost Perfect

A Southern Exposure

Medicine Men

The Last Lovely City (stories)

Alice Adams

After the War

A novel

WASHINGTON SQUARE PRESS
PUBLISHED BY POCKET BOOKS
New York London Toronto Sydney Singapore

A Washington Square Press Publication of
POCKET BOOKS, a division of Simon & Schuster, Inc.
1230 Avenue of the Americas, New York, NY 10020

Published by arrangement with Alfred A. Knopf,
a division of Random House, Inc.

ISBN: 0-7434-2222-8

First Washington Square Press trade paperback printing December 2001

10 9 8 7 6 5 4 3 2 1

Cover photo by Barry Marcus

Printed in the U.S.A.

FOR DEREK C. PARMENTER,

A TRUE REAL FRIEND

Part One

1

BY mid-August, in the third summer of the Second World War, heavy and relentless heat had yellowed all the grass and almost all the flowers in the little college town of Pinehill, in the middle South. Cynthia Baird, an actively unfaithful Navy wife, contemplated the limp petals that lay beneath what had been a beautiful display of roses, massed blossoms of gold to pink to white—although she was not thinking of roses, nor actually of the war, but rather of her lover, Derek McFall, the famous war correspondent. Derek, who was tall and blond and not in love with her, not at all. Cynthia thought too of her husband, Harry—Captain Harry Baird, USN, now in London—but less often than she thought of Derek; Harry and wartime London, as well as the war itself, were vague to Cynthia, as they were to most of the rest of that town. People there were more aware of the state of Cynthia's lawn and her flowers, of their own lawns and flowers, than of the terrible but distant war. If they had known about Derek and Cynthia, they would have given that some thought, and much talk, but so far they did not.

In the town's view Cynthia was still a transplanted Yankee, from Connecticut; over five years now but her Yankee ways and those of Harry were still remarked on, in Pinehill. And the trouble with the lawn and the flowers was that the Bairds were hardly there in Pinehill anymore, since Harry went up to Washington to work for the Navy, and then was sent off to London. They actually lived in Washington—Georgetown, of course; there was a rumor about Cynthia going to law school in Georgetown, but she gave that up, of course, when Harry went to London. Abigail, their daughter, came down to Pinehill more often than they did during the Georgetown days, but she did not do any gardening chores; she came to stay with her friend Melanctha Byrd, and they both went out with a lot of boys. Abigail had always been independent—"a regular Yankee child, always does pretty much what she wants to, always has."

But now Cynthia lived mostly in Pinehill, and it was too bad that the garden looked so pathetic, especially today: Cynthia was having an important party that she said was for Abigail, and for Melanctha too. The girls were both going up North to college in just a few weeks, Abigail to Swarthmore, a Quaker place that had boys as well, and Melanctha to Radcliffe, the girls' part of Harvard.

What gardening got done at the Bairds' house these days was done by Odessa, the maid. Odessa actually lived at the Bairds', sort of, in the out back—"real nice of Cynthia to take her in like that, but sort of Yankified, wouldn't you say?" In any case, Odessa had enough to do just keeping the house in shape, not to mention certain problems of her own: a wandering husband, Horace (too bad: Horace was a wonderful gardener, just terrific with flowers, but he'd been off somewhere all summer); a daughter in trouble at the defense plant—Nellie, Odessa's only child, and no one knew just what kind of trouble, but they had their own ideas.

But the garden was nobody's fault, not Abigail's or Odessa's, but probably the Lord's. Or the war's, like everything else.

Odessa's husband, Horace, was actually in the Navy, in the Pacific Ocean. He was overage but he looked young, and he'd lied about his age, and Odessa saw no point in telling anyone (no one white) where he was, and she never had, not even Miz Baird, who had treated her good. But she sorely missed him, and all she got were little notes sometimes that Horace got some man there with him to write. She didn't even know just where he was, but sometimes on the radio she heard these Japanese-sounding names, Okinawa, Hirohito, and talk about boats and battles, and she was scared, just plumb dumb scared, and not a single thing she could do about it, and not a person to tell. And then Nellie: some white folks' crazy talk about a union over to the plant, which would end up getting her fired, Odessa knew. Some crazy students from over to Hilton. Every time the phone rings in the house, which is not too often these days with them all off somewheres, Odessa was mortally afraid of terrible news: Horace, or Nellie, or even Mr. Baird, off in the Navy too, though not with the same uniform at all that Horace wears.

Cynthia was not looking forward to her party. For one thing, it was planned as a by-the-pool party, and she might not hear the phone from the pool, and Derek might call; all day she has had a strong sense of the imminence of Derek. Odessa will be up at the house to answer some of the time, but there's all the food to bring out, and more glasses and fresh ice—always something. Odessa could all too easily not hear the phone. Really smart of me, Cynthia thinks, to be waiting like a sixteen-year-old for a phone call—congratulations, dumbbell—and a phone call from a man who doesn't even love you, he says. She frowns and tries to concentrate on what's to be done.

Sliced cold ham, a notch up from the usual cold fried chicken, and a cold green rice salad, two notches up from potato salad. Odessa's beaten biscuits, locally famous, and Odessa's fresh peach ice cream. Divine.

A nice lunch, the problem being that she doesn't really care for any of the guests—except of course for the two girls of honor, her own dearest Abigail, who actually has been a considerable pain in the butt, of late, and dear Melanctha Byrd, who at times looks so unnervingly like Russ, and who seems unhappy, poor child. And no wonder, with those great big breasts almost weighing her down—just like her mother, poor SallyJane. Does Melanctha drink too? Well, probably not yet. But she'll always have trouble buying clothes.

Cynthia herself, a former Vassar Daisy Chain girl, is tall and thin, is made for clothes—as salesladies have often told her. And Abigail, an inch less tall and a tiny bit heavier than her mother, could wear almost anything if she cared to, but she does not; she does not give a fig about clothes, she wears any old thing and gets by with it because she is so young, and pretty, really (if she'd only do something about her hair).

But the person Cynthia surely does not want to see, who always makes her uncomfortable, is James Russell Lowell Byrd, father of Melanctha. Russ, who was once a famous poet and a playwright, now just writes screenplays, sometimes—he was the true reason that Cynthia and Harry moved to Pinehill in the first place: Cynthia wanted to meet the poet, she loved his words. And a few years later it had happened, they had had the affair that she had always had in mind. Which had been terrific, in its way, but all that is left of it now is social embarrassment. Discomfort at seeing each other. Russ must feel it too, she is sure, along with guilt; it happened so soon after the death of SallyJane, his wife, mother of Melanctha—poor SallyJane with the overlarge bosom, who drank too much and then died of the shock treatment they gave her for depression. Now Russ is married to Deirdre, who used to be the most beautiful girl in town, and who had a little boy with Russ before they were married, and now has a little baby girl, unaccountably named SallyJane. Cynthia sighs, and she thinks for the thousandth time, I will never understand the Southern mind, not in any way.

Cynthia does not want to see Russ, nor her supposed best friend, Dolly Bigelow (Dolly is just too idiotic, some of the time)—nor Jimmy Hightower, another "dear friend," a former Oklahoma oilman who with Russ's help wrote one bestseller. The person she would actually like to see is Esther, Jimmy's wife, who is in New York now doing something with Jewish refugees.

She was glad, Cynthia was, that none of the grown-ups have chosen to wear their bathing suits. They're mostly too old and too fat, a lot of them. Dolly Bigelow is very plump, and her husband, Willard, too; Deirdre Byrd is truly fat (could she possibly be pregnant again? Russ has this crazy thing about birth control: SallyJane told several people that, and Cynthia had what you might call firsthand knowledge). Curiously, the men looked better than the women did: Russ looked really okay (all that time at Hollywood swimming pools, probably), and Jimmy Hightower's exactly the same as always. Cynthia thought then with a pang of guilt and longing of Harry, so trim and elegant in his Navy things—and then of Derek, so very tall and thin, in his belted trench coat, with his pipe.

By mid-afternoon, no one had really drunk too much

except Deirdre Byrd; she did not seem exactly tight, but Cynthia had observed her: lots and lots of gin-and-tonics, there in the waning sun, in the warm smell of grass and flowers and chlorine. Dolly Bigelow had also been aware of Deirdre's drinking, and Cynthia had observed Dolly watching Deirdre. Dolly and Cynthia viewed each other with equal parts of suspicion and affection.

Dolly suspected that a while back there was something going on between Cynthia and Russ Byrd, not long after SallyJane died. About the time that Dolly and Cynthia opened that little store, with some things that Odessa had made along with things by white ladies too, from out in the country. The store didn't work out too well, and probably if they'd've kept it, the war would've finished it anyway. But: Cynthia and Russ. How could a thing like that have come to any good? Lord knows Dolly was no prude, but she really didn't hold with married folk carrying on, you're supposed to keep the promises you made in church. Russ Byrd is a handsome man all right, but then so is Harry Baird, especially now in his naval uniform. How many handsome men does Cynthia need—what is she, some kind of a nymphomaniac? Besides, Dolly never had what you might call evidence, just a hunch from their ways of looking at each other, of saying each other's name.

"This is just the best rice salad I have ever tasted," Dolly said to Cynthia. "You sure have taught Odessa a thing or two," and she smiled, very sweetly.

Cynthia suspected that as usual Dolly was wearing falsies inside her dress, and for what, for whom? Certainly not foggy Willard, her boring husband, who taught Greek and Latin at the local college; she doubted that Willard had had a sexual thought in his head or anywhere else for fifteen or sixteen years, which was how old their younger boy was. She smiled back at Dolly as she told her, "I made it myself, actually. But I'm sure Odessa could have done it better."

Cynthia believed that in some private and half-conscious way Dolly had it in for Odessa, and not just because Odessa was "colored" and Dolly was a Southern woman; it was more personal than that. As though Odessa was not really "Negro" enough for Dolly.

Unlike the lawns, the rest of the garden and the planting around the pool have done well. Flowering sweet-smelling privet thrived, and the lilac bushes that Cynthia, missing New England, insisted on. Next spring they will bountifully, beautifully bloom—assuming that we're all here next spring, thought Cynthia, who was not at all sure what she meant. Nothing to do with the war, probably; she did not think that Hitler would win in Europe and then come over here with his Blackshirts and Storm Troopers and concentration camps. Although some people seemed to believe just that; Cynthia's friend Esther Hightower seemed to believe it. But Cynthia's sense of impermanence had more to do with the fragility of personal connections, specifically her own: with Harry, who was doing God-knows-what in London, and with Abigail, her very own and only daughter, always so independent, so intelligent. And now off to Swarthmore, so far away, difficult to get back from there, what with wartime transportation.

And then there was Derek, with whom anything at all could happen, or, just as possibly, nothing.

Russ Byrd was leaving for New York tomorrow, and then for Hollywood, on a plane. Marvelous, the flights they have these days, he thought, remembering terrible drives back and forth across the country, ten or so years ago, with all the children fighting and poor SallyJane trying as best she could to control them. And he was always thinking then of Deirdre, who sat beside him at this moment, now his wife. Still a beauty but now she weighed too much, and tended to drink. Russ wondered if there was something in himself that brought that out, some germ he carried. Was it all his doing that SallyJane too got fat and took to drink? And then there was his daughter, Melanctha, sitting across the pool in a pretty blue flowered suit that hid those breasts, thank God. SallyJane's breasts. And his face. No wonder the poor child is confused.

In a movie, a long shot could take in Melanctha, across the pool, and Deirdre, her dark curls that now were touched up a bit. And near Deirdre's long white delicate feet was their own baby girl, his and Deirdre's, whom Deirdre unaccountably had named SallyJane. Still less accountably the baby was the dead spit of dead SallyJane, to whom she was in no way related.

So much for genes, Russ thought as he shook his head to refuse cheese biscuits from his hostess, Cynthia Baird, to whom, today, he had not paid much attention. She was beautiful still, with her green eyes and long blond hair—but could he ever have thought he loved that woman, with her sharp tongue and Yankee ways? (Well yes, he did, he loved her wildly for a couple of weeks, or months, a few years ago.)

Genes do not mean a thing, he thought, it's all in the name. And Adam's task of naming the animals was every man's task. SallyJane the baby looked like SallyJane the woman, his wife, because of that name. And his attempt to change the name of SallyJane, his wife, to "Brett" probably was what made her crazy, finally. And maybe her spirit has come back to haunt him in this round golden baby, this new SallyJane. Who has the disposition that SallyJane, not Brett, was meant to have; she was sweet and peaceful and loving, and always loved.

Melanctha was named by her mother, the original SallyJane, although most people assumed that it was Russ's idea, it being a "literary" choice. A lovely book, Russ thought, the best of Gertrude Stein, whom almost no one had read, although some of them knew the book was about a colored girl, and they used to tease his poor daughter: "named for a nigger," although that word was strictly forbidden. SallyJane/Brett had read the book and she loved it; she was the one who made Russ read it. Deirdre splashed her feet in the water; playfully she splashed Russ, who pretended not to feel it.

Jimmy Hightower, the once very successful Oklahoma oilman, then best-selling (one book) novelist, and now, he would have said, lonely bachelor (he hopes temporarily), misses Esther and his daughters, especially Esther. His brilliant beauty. His *wife.*

He could probably write another book, but he really doesn't want to, not at all. Things were so different when he wrote that first one: he had just come to Pinehill, and partly because Russ Byrd was there, Russ, the famous poet-playwright. And, as he had hoped, he and Russ had got to be friends, or whatever they were, and then Russ helped him with his book, and his book was a big success. Those were the facts, the story, but underneath was another story, one that Jimmy certainly did not write about, even if he was certain how it went. But for starters, he and Russ were not exactly friends anymore, and Russ was not really a poet-playwright anymore, but a sometime screenwriter. And Russ's wife SallyJane was dead, and he had this new wife, Deirdre, who used to be his girlfriend. And Jimmy's wife, his beautiful Esther, was living in New York.

Jimmy did not really understand a thing that had happened, or was happening, any more than he or anyone understood the war.

Abigail thought that this typical grown-up party was really one of her mother's dumber ideas, although generally Cynthia was much better than the other mothers around. Certainly nicer than Archer and Billy Bigelow's mother, that awful little Dolly; or poor Betsy Lee, with that dopey Irene for a mother (Betsy's father had died, some folks said, while he was drunk and off necking that silly Dolly, which is what he usually did when he was drunk). And Deirdre: a long time ago, when Abby and her parents first came to Pinehill, Abigail and Deirdre were sort of friends; they used to take walks in the woods together with Deirdre's little brother, Graham (who later everyone said was her son, by Mr. Byrd, whom later she married). But now they are not friends, and Deirdre is just like all the other grown-ups, drinking too much, and fat. Cynthia at least stays thin and she doesn't drink a lot; she just gets silly, sometimes.

But how can she even get silly, how can she think of anything else when her husband, Harry, Abigail's father, is off in London, in danger, in the *war*? Abby is frightened for her father; it is something she should never think of, and yet she thinks of it all the time. Terrible things that could—not impossibly—happen to Harry, in London: bombs and fires, midnight invasions by German soldiers, all shouting and stamping boots and shooting guns and tanks killing everyone in sight. All the Americans there. Harry. The whole U.S. Navy and the Army too.

Those were her darkest, blackest midnight obsessional thoughts. Another, only slightly less terrible, was that Harry would fall in love with some English lady, someone tall and thin with rose-petal English skin. Good at riding and gardening, cooking roast beef and puddings, all those English things in novels. Harry could fall madly in love with this English woman, and they could kiss a lot, and neck, and end up going the whole way, actually doing it. And then Harry would be more in love than ever, he'd forget all about his wife and his daughter, and never come back to them but just stay in England, maybe sometimes inviting Abigail to come and visit, by ocean liner or maybe a plane. But the idea of sailing or even flying did not cheer Abigail much. The thought of Harry living over there was much too terrible, almost as bad as Harry dead.

And then: suppose we didn't win the war after all? Suppose Hitler won, beat our Navy and Army, and Mr. Roosevelt?

Melanctha Byrd, sitting on the edge of the pool, her bare feet cooling in the water, imagined falling in. How cool, how lovely it would be, all over her body. And then into the silence Melanctha heard (probably everyone else there did too) the overloud, still girlish voice of Deirdre, who was saying, "Derek McFall? But I knew him, he went to Pinehill

High one year. He was really cute, real blond and tall, with this accent, from somewhere up North. New England, somewhere like that. He was nice but not one bit friendly. A lot of the girls had these real big crushes on him, but he would never ask them out or anything. He played basketball real well but he kept pretty much to himself, and got terrific grades."

"And then he went to Hilton and played more basketball and got straight A's there too." Melanctha's father, Russ, said this. He always knew everything, or else he said he did.

"Well, I think he's the best correspondent we've got in this war," said Jimmy Hightower. "He's always done his homework." Jimmy went on to talk about this Derek McFall, whom Melanctha of course had heard on the radio, seen pictures of. "He's even more impressive than Murrow," Jimmy said.

Several grown-up voices from all around the pool disagreed with Mr. Hightower. Including Russ's. "For my money, or what's left of it," said Russ, "I'll take Murrow. There's something too, too Vermont about McFall. Too Yankee."

Cynthia Baird sounded mad at Russ as she said, "Oh come on now, Russell." (Is that what she called him, always?) "I can't stand this professional Southerner stuff. And what on earth do you mean, 'too Vermont'?"

Deirdre interrupted all this to say, "And if our little baby SallyJane had've been a boy, we would've named her Derek. I mean him. I always said that, didn't I, Russ? And I was thinking of Derek McFall, the very same one. Russ, didn't I always say?"

"You sure did, darling," said Russ, in his softest, meanest voice.

Oh God! to be away from all these people, these grown-ups with their preening, knowing Southern voices, their drinks and their silly quarrels. Their secret kissing, their necking behind everyone's back, thinking nobody knew. God, how she hated them all, but soon she would be away, far away. In Boston. In Cambridge, Mass. Melanctha thrilled to those names.

". . . home for Thanksgiving?" Archer Bigelow, beside her, was anxiously asking.

Thanksgiving? In a blind way, she looked at Archer. "I really don't know," she told him, untruthfully; she had already promised Russ and Deirdre that she would. Pullman tickets were bought, hard to come by these days.

Suddenly, into another heavy heated silence, no one talking, no breeze to stir the leaves, from up at the house came the sound of the telephone. Very loud, everyone could hear it.

Cynthia and Odessa reacted instantly; simultaneously they both rushed toward the house.

Cynthia was going too fast, though, in her flimsy green sandals. She skidded on the gravel path and slid to her knees. Looking up, unhurt, for a second she saw Odessa's terrified face, and she knew that the terror was not for her, but it had to do with the phone, whoever, whatever. But why? It must be, must be Derek, for *her.* Or just conceivably Harry, somehow wangling a cable call. Can Odessa possibly be that worried about Mr. Harry, as she calls him?

Getting to her feet, not hurt except for a little stinging on the palms of her hands, Cynthia followed Odessa, who had turned again and was racing for the still loudly ringing phone.

And then Cynthia heard Odessa's voice, very clear. "Yes'm.

Yes'm." And then a pause during which Cynthia just stood there, outside the kitchen door. Unable not to listen, although by now she knew that the call was not for her.

"Unh-hunh. It *you.* I might've knowed. You think call from California *free?*" (A longer pause.) "That so? That true? You telling me *award?* Well now, that just mighty fine. *Mighty* fine. Horace, you done me proud. And yourself too. You a fine man, you know that? You all right now, you tell me true? You not hurt? Yeah, we do that." She laughed, a small rich intimate laugh. "You get on home, you hear?"

By the time Cynthia walked into the kitchen Odessa had hung up the phone and was just standing there, brown and radiant, shiningly happy. She seemed to feel some explanation due, or maybe she simply wanted to tell her news. "That Horace, he in the Navy, San Diego, in California. Say there been an accident, and he pull some mens out the water. Horace always did swim real good. And they give him some kind of a prize. Some medal. The Navy do—"

"Odessa, that's wonderful! How terrific—oh, I'm so pleased—"

Cynthia took both Odessa's hands in hers, saw tears on Odessa's face, and then moved to her, gave Odessa a tight warm hug. But then she had no idea what to do, and she had in that instant to abandon a momentary impulse, which was to lead Odessa back down to the pool to announce the news, to celebrate, to make toasts. But Odessa would hate that, what a totally bad idea. Instead she said, "Odessa, wouldn't you just like to go rest for a while, in your room? Please, I can handle the party. Abigail can help me, and Melanctha."

"Oh, no'm, I jus' keep on—"

"No, Odessa, please—isn't there something you'd like to do? I mean—"

For a moment they stared at each other, helplessly, lacking a common vocabulary or common habits.

But Odessa seemed to read at least good intentions from Cynthia. She told her, "I truly like to go to church now, just for a little?" She glanced at her watch (the watch that Harry gave her, and Harry also taught her to read the time from). "I just make it," Odessa said, "and Nellie be there, I tell her."

The Negro church is less than half a mile away, since this house that Cynthia and Harry bought from Deirdre (the house that Russ bought for Deirdre, long ago) is in a "bad" neighborhood, near "colored people." Still, Cynthia asked, "You want me to drive you? It's so hot. Come on, I will."

"Oh, no'm. And I be back, time to help you with all the cleaning up."

"Odessa, please. I can handle it. Really. Please stay as long as you want."

They were standing there staring again, caught in good intentions, when the phone rang loudly—again.

Cynthia became decisive. "I'll get it, you go on." And then, to the long-distance operator, "Yes, this is Cynthia Baird." And then, "Oh—Derek!"

"Well, I caught you at home." His quick, harsh laugh. "I was wondering," he said. "Any chance of your getting over to Hilton at Thanksgiving? Turns out I have to be down there, some goddam award. It's what they call their Homecoming Game that weekend. How're you fixed for gas—got enough coupons?"

"Oh sure, I think I could arrange that." Cynthia heard her own careless, light laugh, even as she thought, I'll steal some coupons if I have to, or get some black-market gas. And thinking too, I'll take him the Scotch I've saved (not letting herself add: saved for Harry). Thinking: Whatever did Russ mean by "too Vermont"? His voice is ravishing.

"Well okay then." Businesslike, efficient, thrifty Derek, though it's been less than three minutes. "Okay, I'm glad you can make it. Or you think you can. We'll be in touch."

Only then, walking slowly back down to the pool, did Cynthia think of other things that she did not say to Derek: Suppose Abigail wants to come back from Swarthmore, or, suppose Harry gets a sudden leave home for Thanksgiving?

But she was then struck with a stronger, compelling thought: For God's sake, she thought, what's important at this moment is Odessa—this is Odessa's moment, and everyone should know.

And so she paused at the end of the path to the pool, and standing there she clapped her hands for attention—an unlikely gesture for Cynthia, who is generally shy (for a Yankee).

Unlikely too are her first words, when she has everyone's attention. "You all, listen," she says, with a tiny laugh; Cynthia never says "you-all."

"This terrific thing, we just heard. Odessa's husband, Horace, he's out in the Pacific, in the Navy, and he saved a bunch of men's lives. He's getting this medal—Odessa's so proud—" To her own vast surprise Cynthia's voice broke off, choked by tears.

Looking up, though, she could see the faces of her friends, and though they all spoke at once she could hear them.

"Well! That Horace! How you reckon he ever learned to swim so good?"

"Mother, that's wonderful, that's just great!" (Abby, of course.)

"What a great story."

"You could make a movie out of that one, Russ."

"There'll be no holding Miss Odessa now. She won't do any work for any of us."

"Him either."

"Couldn't we take up a collection and buy her a congratulation present?" That last, from Melanctha Byrd, was answered by a total silence, some shifting of feet.

Until Cynthia said, "Melanctha, what a good idea, you're terrific."

But Melanctha had already turned away, in tears.

2

IN Cambridge, during the first weeks of college, in September and October, Melanctha experienced the heady, extreme, and slightly unreal joy of a person reborn. Or, a person restored to her rightful home, the place where all along she was meant to be. At home, back in Pinehill, everyone knew her; they knew who Russ was and what had happened to her mother, SallyJane, her depression and the shock treatment that had killed her. And they knew all about Russ and Deirdre, and all about Russ's poems and his plays and now all this movie stuff. But here in Cambridge no one had ever heard of Russell Byrd, or any of that awful old family story; of course they hadn't, they had more important families of their own.

And all over Harvard Yard, and spilling out onto Harvard Square, there were hundreds of the handsomest young men that Melanctha had ever seen. All around the hooded subway entrance and the Coop, everywhere, in that exuberant wartime fall, men in every variety of uniform, including the old classic Harvard garb of gray flannels and tweed, white shirts and striped ties. So many men, all so handsome and desirable, that at first for Melanctha the faces blurred.

At last a few faces began to separate out, certain men

whom she saw repeatedly and especially noticed. There was one of the Navy officers she saw everywhere, so handsome, with straight blond hair and blue eyes. And a boy about her age, in a V-12 sailor suit, but tall and dark, with curly hair a little like hers (too curly, too much hair). All busily walking along, all preoccupied with the war? Although sometimes they seemed to be giving her certain looks.

Ben Davis, Abby Baird's old school friend, the Negro boy, said to be very handsome now, was supposed to call her but he did not. Of course not, he was a football star, as well as handsome.

In one of her classes, Phil. A with Mr. Demos, she was seated next to a nice-seeming (but too young) boy from Connecticut, Tom (or Ted; she couldn't quite read from his notebook) Byrington; seating was alphabetical. Later she observed or maybe imagined that he was trying to read her address from her notebook, which she usually carried so anyone could see, if they wanted to. And a few people, mostly very young guys, did call her, and they went out for beer at the Oxford Grill, or a movie at the University Theatre. Nothing exciting, not even any good-night kissing at the doorstep.

She was not attractive enough, Melanctha decided, not for those older officers. She needed new clothes, and she wrote to Russ saying that the weather up there was cold. A lie: it had been a balmy, golden fall. Russ sent her a check for two hundred dollars: he must have been drunk. And a letter. "Deirdre tells me I'm not a very good father, so let me try to make up for it a little. Besides, I'm being atrociously overpaid by Mr. Goldwyn." Why did Deirdre even have to know? Melanctha considered tearing up the check and sending it back in fragments, but then did not.

She went in to Boston on the subway, to Chandler's and

Stern's and then out to Peck & Peck, on Newbury Street. She came back with so many bulky packages that she felt silly on the subway. She had bought a good tweed suit and some sweaters and a black silk dress, but not a new formal for the dance at Hilton, where she was supposed to go with Archer Bigelow at Thanksgiving.

A couple of times in the Yard or around the Square, she had seen a tall, handsome medium-dark Negro boy, and at those times her vulnerable heart had leapt up and she thought, Ben Davis, Abby's friend. But he was supposed to call her, after all, and she couldn't exactly run up to him and ask, "Are you Benny Davis?" Suppose he wasn't, he was just some other Negro boy, but he knew Ben Davis, and of course he would know why she thought it might have been. Melanctha found this small fantasy infinitely troubling, embarrassing. As though she had actually done that: rushed up to this handsome Negro and said, "Are you—"

One night in Whitman Hall, the buzzer sounded; someone answered and then yelled out, "Byrd, line one. Melanctha!"

This time it could be Ben Davis, she thought irrationally.

A man's voice, or a boy's, but deep, and deeply Southern. (Or was it someone pretending to be Southern? Boys she went out with had done that, to tease her.) "Miss Melanctha Byrd? This here is Miss Melanctha?"

Not Ben Davis; he wouldn't talk like that. She said, "Yes."

"Well, I'm what you might call a friend." A laugh, at which Melanctha began to feel an unaccountable fear.

"We've sure looked each other over, you and me," the voice went on. Was he drunk? He sounded a little like Russ imitating someone more drunk and more Southern even than he was. But of course it wasn't Russ.

"And I just wanted to tell you"—the man paused, did he

almost laugh?—"tell you that you've got the greatest pair of boobs that I ever saw. Tits like that, well—Melanctha, are you there?"

In the faintest, smallest voice Melanctha breathed out, "No," as she hung up the phone. Clutching her robe around her as closely as possible, she somehow got back to her room; she closed the door and pushed a chair up against it. She got into bed and she lay there, wholly terrified. Disgraced. Mortified and embarrassed beyond all reason, or recall.

He could have been anyone at all. Any of those faces, those eyes that have met her eyes. *Anyone.* It was that that Melanctha found so terrifying. She did not see how she could walk across the Yard again.

She decided that she would, after all, go home for Thanksgiving. Maybe she could get so sick that she would never have to come back. Never hear that voice again, that horrifying voice that she might not even recognize.

At the Deke House, in Hilton, on football weekends, in those bright electric days, the major event was the post-game, predance party. The house then was packed with Dekes and their dates, and a few old grads, who generally did not bring their wives. The air, what air there was in that overcrowded room, smelled of bourbon and cigarettes, a few cigars; the powder and perfume of girls, and boys' anxious sexy sweat. And noise: laughing and shouting, and people trying still to talk above all that. And somewhere a record playing "Tuxedo Junction." And from down in the basement, what was called the Rebel Room, came more shouts, and a wilder noise of yelling—rebel yells.

Melanctha, watching and feeling herself apart from all

that, although she was actually laughing and talking and drinking bourbon, at the same time distantly observed that all the girls in the room, in their too hot fall tweeds and pale cashmere sweaters—they all have perfect pancaked skin and small pearl teeth, small breasts and smooth blond hair, almost all of them. Except Melanctha, with her father's hopeless dark curly hair and her mother's breasts (did her mother get horrible phone calls, ever? No wonder she drank and went crazy).

Melanctha has beautiful legs; all the boys say her legs are great and even some girls have said it. Melanctha doesn't understand: what could be so great about legs, anyway? People don't touch each other's legs, as far as she knows. It's not like breasts or skin.

This particular party, along with celebrating the big Homecoming Game, was to welcome a special old grad, a Deke: the famous news correspondent Derek McFall. There in town for a speech he was going to give tomorrow, in the new Graham Memorial building. On postwar problems or something like that. Melanctha has seen pictures of Mr. McFall, seen him in newsreels—usually in his trench coat, with his collar turned up, and smoking cigarettes or a pipe. Good-looking, for someone his age: very tall, with straight blond hair. Deirdre claimed that she knew him in high school, but Deirdre could have got his name mixed up with someone else's, especially since she was drunk when she said it—making such a big deal of it, of knowing Derek, at that awful party by the Bairds' swimming pool in August.

But at some point, looking across that crowded, smoky room, Melanctha thought that she actually saw Derek McFall, with a pretty blond lady who looked a lot like Mrs. Baird, Mrs. Cynthia Baird, from Pinehill. Abigail's mother. (Once, Melanctha saw that Cynthia Baird out in the woods with Russ; they were kissing, so absorbed in it they never saw her.) But that was probably someone else across the room.

Although Melanctha did not exactly use the word "hate" in thinking of her father, did not explicitly think, I hate my father, she did hate him. His presence to her was unendurable, almost, and she watched him continuously, meticulously: his deep dark and blue eyes, his huge hands gesturing clumsily in the air, his slow warm dishonest smile, pretending to like all the people who loved him too much.

A horrible-looking man, maybe older than her father, even, with his cigar all wet in one hand and his glass of bourbon in the other—this man came up to her, standing much too close and breathing everything into her face, and he spoke right at her: "I just wanted to tell you, honey, that you're the prettiest, sweetest, freshest young thing in this room, and don't let anybody tell you different, ever. Those other gals, they're faded, and jaded—faded and jaded, now there's a good one, ain't it? We live over to Winston-Salem, we're all in big tobacco over there, and don't get back to cheer the Tarheels but about once a year. But you're so young, little honey, I'm not sure you're even old enough to be here!"

Melanctha smiled, hiding her teeth as she has learned to do (as she hid her breasts with big sweaters), and wishing him dead, *this minute.*

"You from around here, sweetheart?" His breath was violent as his big red face leaned toward her.

"No. Pinehill."

"Oh, Pinehill. Well, now—" His face was redder yet as he leaned still closer, until quite suddenly in slow motion, seemingly, he had toppled to the floor—shoving against Melanctha on his long way down. She clutched her breasts (had he meant to touch them?) and gasped aloud at the color of his face, the paralyzed remains of his grin—as people all over the room turned to look, the record stopped, and several girls screamed.

"Someone call an ambulance! He's passed out, he looks terrible! No need for an ambulance, the infirmary's right there. Does anybody know who he is? Is he anybody's daddy? Sick! Drunk! Is anybody here a doctor? Is there a doctor—?"

Archer Bigelow, Melanctha's date, who had come with her from Pinehill, appeared beside her, his face spotted with acne (being in college had wrecked his skin), tall and thin and chivalrously concerned. A Deke pledge. "Oh, Melly, whatever—? Oh, you poor darlin'—"

Melanctha thought several things at once, a bad tendency she had; she was almost always confused. The oddest thought was that Archer sounded a lot like his mother, Dolly Bigelow, whom Russ, Melanctha's father, did not like. Another was that she hated being called Melly, and Archer knows that; it sounds like that dopey woman in *GWTW*. Another thought, which is less a thought than a vision, a quick hot dream—she thought of kissing Archer (probably) later, pushing and twisting together, parked somewhere in the dark, in Archer's car.

She thought and felt all that, as yet another stern voice within her demanded: You wished he was dead, that old man—did you kill him? Mean bitch. Mean Melanctha. Wicked girl.

To drown out that last voice, she said to Archer very loudly, "I'm all right, really I am. I just need another drink." And she smiled up to him.

As it turned out, some old grad in the room who was a doctor pushed through the crowd and squatted down beside the fallen man. The doctor said, "He's just passed out. Hey, help me get him out of here."

Archer, because of a weak leg, did not go over, but five or six big husky Navy boys did, and the still unconscious man was carried out and across the street to the infirmary, which was handily right there, on the corner opposite the Deke House.

Where, still unidentified, he was pronounced dead of unknown causes—but among them booze. When his billfold was found at last, dropped and trampled on the Deke House floor, it turned out that he was someone very important in Winston-Salem, in the R. J. Reynolds Company. Big tobacco.

The dance was held in the gym, which was called the Tin Can, now lavishly filled with flowers, giant pink and white roses everywhere, and rich loops of satin ribbon. No one could call it a tin can now.

At one end, the big band was up on its stand, all the men in cream-colored suits and dark green ties, not quite right with the decorations but never mind, the music was marvelous, everyone thought, throbbing with trombones and trumpets, and aching violins. And everyone was out there dancing now, the most beautiful small powdered blondes in white chiffon or pink satin, and tall handsome smooth-skinned boys, though some were drunk, just barely on their feet. In tuxedos or dress uniforms, mostly Navy, which everyone knew was the best.

Melanctha, although she was wearing her aqua taffeta, with wine-colored velvet bows (a leftover high-school dress), still felt herself merged with the crowd. She was part of the beautiful dancers; she was what she saw.

And she was merged with Archer, a part of him, as they danced very slowly, beyond the lights. It was possible not to think about the terrible phone call, in Cambridge, or the old dead drunk in the Deke House.

Was Archer drunk? Was she? Melanctha had no way of knowing, although she had known Archer all her life. But not in this way, this sexy-dancing way.

At some point, Melanctha thought that she saw Mrs. Baird—again, with that tall famous Derek McFall. Not dressed for a dance, still in their football-cocktail party clothes, tweeds and sweaters; they could not be chaperons, if that's who it really was. Cynthia Baird in her New York–looking red tweed suit, Mr. McFall in dark gray flannel; he carried his dark felt hat. But when Melanctha looked again they were not there. If they ever were.

Softly breathed, persistent rumors, like smoke, circulated through that room, among the dancers—concerning the old man who died.

He had never been a Deke, and had no business at the party there in the first place. He had wanted to be a Deke, but the only bid he got was from the Sigma Nus (far down the desirable list in anyone's reckoning).

He had given a million dollars to the Sigma Nu House, for redecoration, and had just strolled up to the Deke House to check out their shabby furniture.

His wife was a Reynolds, maybe a distant cousin of R.J., and that's how come he had got so high up in the company.

He had four daughters—two at St. Mary's in Raleigh, one at Sweet Briar, and one at Sophie Newcomb—but no sons. No Dekes anywhere in the family. So it was funny, sort of, that he should die there, after all.

He was not really dead when they got him to the infirmary, and he said he wanted to leave a million dollars to the Deke House, which he had thought was in shocking shape.

Rumors about the war were even fainter, and less persistent, and they too had the sound of gossip, mostly—people moving about, taking trips: someone going to Italy, to London, or Pensacola, Biloxi, or, close to home, Fort Bragg. Even the words "overseas" or "Pacific" had glamorous, exotic sounds, though with slight—and thrilling!—overtones of danger.

Archer parked his car, after a long bumpy ride that seemed to be through woods—tall black trees on either side, trees part of the night—and jolting ruts. The car was really Russ Byrd's car, James Russell Lowell Byrd's big Hollywood Cadillac, loaned to Archer for the night; Archer's brother Billy had the family car, a Buick, but did Russ do that against the wishes of Deirdre, his wife—so generously loan his big expensive car to Archer, who might have got drunk, the way boys do?

They were parked in a thicket of pine boughs and honeysuckle vines, a cave, with no visible stars or sky.

But when Archer's hand went down her skirt and reached up slowly, started stroking her leg (her leg!), and then went on up, Melanctha squirmed and reached for the hand, to push it away. She had to: suppose he touched the hot wet that she knows is there? Revolting! He would know how disgusting she is, and not even want to kiss her anymore, much less to be in love.

He whispered, "But, honey, I want to so much—"

"Oh, no, I can't—"

He removed his hand, and after a pause he whispered into

her ear, "I respect you for that, Melanctha. And I love you too—"

She was right! He didn't even want to touch her there, not really—and no one would, if they knew.

Melanctha suddenly felt very drunk—"I'd better get home," she whispered, thinking of the long drive back to Pinehill, with nothing to say.

Melanctha woke the next day, back in Pinehill, in her own bed—in a state of more consuming shame than she could bear. She could not, could not, *could not* face anyone—not Archer, who had spent the night at the Bigelows' house, with his parents. She could not face her father or Deirdre, her brothers and that baby. No—no, never—all those faces in Harvard Yard, all over the Square. One of whom was the one who had called her and said that about her breasts. Whoever that was—and she vaguely knew that he could have been anyone, or *everyone*—that person might know about wetness too, it may have something to do with breasts, maybe everyone with big breasts (*too* big breasts, that is, not like Rita Hayworth, Ann Sheridan)—maybe all huge-breasted women are disgusting in that way.

All the way back from Hilton to Pinehill, Melanctha had pretended to be asleep, so that when they got to her house she could just get out and go inside, as though still half asleep. No need to say, I'll never see you again—go away.

And since some of them, her family, must have heard her come in, no one would think it was strange that she would sleep almost all the next day.

Although she was not asleep. She was lying there in the cold smoky gray November light. She would never be able to sleep again, probably. Her head ached as it never had before, her mouth and her throat were dry. She wanted to throw up, but she could not—she was much too sick to do anything, ever.

That old man, the ugly tobacco man who came up to her at the Deke House, the man who died—that man haunted Melanctha. She saw him still, so clearly—not remembering, but seeing. He was there, he was permanently there, within her brain. She saw the pores in his big red bulbous nose, she smelled his aggressive foul breath. She thought, He can't be dead, I can see him still, and smell him. Half-consciously she felt that he and the man who had called her in Cambridge were the same; they were the terrifying Other, whom she might stay in bed forever to avoid.

She closed her eyes, but quickly opened them again: what lay behind her eyes was far too dangerous. She was visited then, as she lay there, by a curious wish; she wished that Odessa were there with her, not necessarily lying beside her, warmly, in the large bed—but just there in the room. Odessa could comfort her and make her safe, Melanctha thought, and then she thought, This is crazy, Odessa has never even worked here, what's the matter with me? I am truly crazy.

Until at last she slept.

3

"I DON'T fall in love," Derek told Cynthia after making love to her for the third or fourth time that night, in the Carolina Inn. In Hilton. Naked, propped up on one elbow, he lit a cigarette, and continued, "I never fall in love. I'm not a romantic like you, I try hard for realism, I think. You're very beautiful, your beauty pleases me enormously—and in a sexual way you please me, terrifically. Your skin, and all your tastes, really marvelous. And I like you, I think you're interesting and funny, I like some wit in a woman. Also you're nice, that's important. But none of that means 'in love.' Or not to me it doesn't. If I didn't see you again I'd be very, very sorry, but I wouldn't die, I wouldn't even think of dying." And then, moving closer, he said, "Now come on, Cynthia, don't look so hurt. Even in this light I can see your hurt. For Christ's sake, try to take it for what it's worth. Which is quite a lot, in my book. It just isn't 'love,' it isn't some wailing horn off in the distance. Some bad music. The very idea of that kind of love makes me nervous. When you say you love me, I feel scared."

"Could I have a cigarette?" Cynthia too was propped up on an elbow, the top sheet modestly pulled up to cover her breasts. Her nightgown, her best black lace (Harry loves it), was wadded in a corner of the room. (Derek: "Black lace! Cynthia darling, what on earth do you think we're doing?" She wasn't sure, but obediently she discarded the gown.) She had not thought she looked hurt, she thought she had smiled with pleasure and, yes, with love, but since she was in fact more than a little hurt, very likely it was true, she did look hurt. He said that he doesn't love her: how could she not be hurt? She said, "Thanks," and drew on her cigarette. She said, "I'm not hurt. Really."

Disregarding her, Derek continued. "I'm a realist. A practical man. You notice I've never married? I know myself pretty well, and I'm not good husband material, although"—he laughed to himself—"who knows? I might be better in some nice sensible marriage than as a so-called lover."

Cynthia felt a cold drop in her spirits: Did he mean that he knew someone he wanted to marry "sensibly"?

He went on talking. "But I know you don't want to marry me, you know you're better off with Harry. Besides, he might be a war hero, and you couldn't divorce a hero. But seriously, we both know that in your way you're perfectly happy with Harry. In your way you're a practical person too, that's one of the things I like. You just have this large itch for romance—in which you're not exactly alone, of course. But sometimes I wonder, why me?"

She managed to laugh at him. "You're fishing," she told him. "In very shallow water."

He too laughed, briefly and modestly. "Oh, well, you could do worse, I know. But you're so romantic about—everything. A man like Russ Byrd, didn't he used to be a poet? Wouldn't that be more your style? A romantic poet?"

Cynthia would have very much liked to say, I tried that. I was in love with Russ Byrd, my crush on him was really why

I talked Harry into moving down to Pinehill, and we finally had this big love affair, Russ and I. All of that is the absolute truth, is what she would have liked to say, what she would have said if she were the modern, sophisticated woman that she tried to see herself as. Sometimes. But Cynthia could not say all that (although she had a dim sense that Derek would have liked it if she did); she only laughed softly, Southern style, and she told him, "I'll think about it."

She also would have liked to go to sleep, all the drinks and then so much strenuous love have exhausted Cynthia, but as she hardly needed to remind herself, both drink and amorous activity had an opposite effect on Derek; he became energized, intensely communicative. He could talk all night, and sometimes he almost did. Cynthia had learned not to listen but to doze; an occasional murmur took care of Derek's response requirements.

Dozing, then, she thought of Harry, and the unreality to her of his life in London. He wrote often but very briefly, little V-mail letters, and he had never had the gift of putting his own voice into letters; his were dry, almost formal. Harry's letters could be from anyone to anyone, Cynthia thought. She sometimes felt that she was hearing from some other man, some "naval officer" in "wartime London." She tried to imagine the sound of sirens, the crowds in air-raid shelters, but they remained for her as abstract, as unreal as newsreels. Harry signed off always saying, "I miss you, I love you," but even those words seemed not to get through in a personal way; they too were abstract, anonymous. The Harry that she most readily recalled was actually the Harry Baird from a long time ago, whom she fell so wildly in love with, and sneaked off to see on her weekends home from Shipley; her father liked him but her mother disapproved. (Her father, a proud, intelligent "self-made" man, a highly successful engineer, may have seen something of his own early self in Harry, the ambitious charmer from Westerly, Rhode Island—from, as Cynthia's mother put it, "no background.") Cynthia easily remembered Harry from back then, the sexiness of all that kissing in cars, late at night. Worries about coming in late with her lipstick gone and twisted stockings, not to mention certain possible smells and stains that Cynthia would only remember too late, at the door. Then, sneaking upstairs, for a short time she would be successfully quiet, until she would hear, *Cynthia, why are you taking a bath at this hour?*

Oh, I just felt like it.

May I come in?

As though she could say no to her mother, in her pin curls and unstained pink chenille robe.

Cynthia crazily tried to hide herself in the clear, clean water, to hide beneath bubbles—when another voice intruded, and recalled her to the present, to *now:*

Derek. "Cynthia, have you gone to sleep? Come on, you can't be tired." But he laughed.

Outside their wide-open window, the November night was windy and black. Still not entirely awake, Cynthia saw dark torn clouds entangled in the branches of tall and leafless trees, and an edge of moon. She thought how in London it was already tomorrow, and Harry was—but she could not imagine Harry, or London. Or the war.

Unlike Harry, Abigail wrote long, infrequent letters that were very much in her own voice. Often they arrived just as Cynthia was telling herself that she must not call, she must not intrude on Abigail's new, busy, and apparently very happy college life. But Swarthmore, near Philadelphia, seemed so very far away from Pinehill.

"New York was terrific," Abby most recently wrote. "I went up with Susan Marcus, this really neat girl I wrote you about. Her brother goes to Swarthmore too. Her parents live down in Greenwich Village, near Washington Square, on West 11th Street. The neatest apartment, really huge! Her father does something in Los Angeles in the movies. He knows Russell Byrd, isn't that amazing? He asked me if I knew him too, when I said I was from Pinehill sort of, and so I said of course I knew Mr. Byrd, and Melanctha. Susan's mother is really pretty and she works full-time for Russian War Relief.

"They took me to this play, *The Voice of the Turtle,* that I thought was pretty dumb. I can't stand that Margaret Sullavan, so phoney, I don't care if she is an actress. And all that stuff about being a professional virgin—no one talks that way. We wanted to see *Watch on the Rhine* but we couldn't get tickets."

At which Cynthia had chillingly wondered: was Abigail herself still a virgin? She had not before, in a conscious way, thought about her daughter, Abigail, making love. The idea made her extremely uncomfortable.

"But the Marcuses are all so nice," Abigail continued. "They didn't like that dumb play either, even if they said it did get great reviews. Mr. Marcus said Margaret Sullavan is not at all his favorite actress, but then he wouldn't say who was. I don't think he likes Mr. Byrd very much, but I don't know why. He is what you would call *très discret.* Did I get the accent right? They've invited me to come back for Thanksgiving. Will that be all right with you? I hadn't really planned on coming home then. Had you?

"I haven't heard from Dad for a while, but I guess he's okay. Sometimes I think about sneaking aboard some boat to get over to London to see him, but don't worry, I won't do that (probably).

"Benny Davis is supposed to come down to see me, or he might come to New York at Thanksgiving. He seems to be changing his mind about medical school. He's not sure what he wants to do. Me neither! The Marcuses have a lot of Negro friends, Susan told me, so it would be okay about Benny coming. A lot of their friends are Communists, Susan said, but they never want to join, and now after the Hitler-Stalin pact they're glad they didn't. You don't hear a lot of stuff like that in Pinehill, do you?"

All that, so much in Abby's voice—and then not another sound from her for a month or so. Sometimes Cynthia had to practically sit on her hands to keep from telephoning—or she called someone else, some hyper-chatty person like Dolly Bigelow, who she knew would keep her on the phone for at least an hour, at the end of which the temptation to call Abigail will be gone.

Or to call Derek. Although at times she thinks, Why shouldn't I call him? Why is it that women have to wait to be called? It isn't fair, I'm a person, just as much as he is. Even if he is more famous and busier. I don't see why I can't call.

However, whenever she did give in to that impulse to telephone Derek, he was usually not available. Or if he was, his tone was discouraging, polite—though sometimes barely so, and certainly surprised, but never truly pleased.

But: Abigail and Benny Davis, old friends reunited as adolescents? It would be so like Abby to fall in love with—to marry a Negro boy, with no thought of certain later trouble, places they couldn't go, and children—

Derek interrupted this alarming line of thought with a surprising question: "Over in Pinehill, do you by any chance know a woman called Deirdre Yates Byrd? She must be related to that poet. She wrote to me and said she remembered me from high school, that solitary year I spent in Pinehill—"

"Deirdre? Of course I know her, and she's married now to Russ Byrd. But before that she had this little boy, Graham, and she tried to pass him off as her brother but he was the dead spit of Russ, honestly—"

"Oh, that Deirdre." Derek laughed at her, gently. "I do think I remember her. A knockout drop-dead beauty, right? So beautiful I had to avoid looking at her. In her letter she accuses me of never speaking to her. Jesus, if she'd had any idea how I felt. The lone Yankee, I could hardly stand it. Does she still look like that?"

Aware of a flash of jealousy, Cynthia told him, "Well, not exactly. She's put on a little weight, of course—" And then, judiciously, "She still has the most ravishing skin, and those eyes. She and Russ have a darling little baby, named Sally-Jane, that was Russ's first wife's name, and the weird thing is that this baby looks just like her. Like the first SallyJane, I mean."

"Cynthia, please, my dear, don't give me this Southern Gothic stuff. I'm strictly literal. I keep telling you that."

But Cynthia had suddenly and completely fallen asleep, into a dream of Pinehill, and Russ. And Harry.

So that she did not hear Derek, who said in a speculative way, "I should see her again, that Deirdre—"

. . .

Earlier, as they stood on the outer edge of the party at the Deke House, watching those much younger people, all so excessive—in their drinking, their smoking, their extreme good looks (most of them) and good clothes, their intense lusts for each other—Cynthia had been feeling very old, dry and remote. And she had thought then, in a rarely objective, distant way, Why don't they all just pair off and go and make love somewhere? Just do it a few times, and then maybe all change partners, and do it some more. Slake all that excruciating desire, and learn that none of it really matters (does it?). Go ahead and *fuck,* she thought (she who had never in her life used that word aloud), get it over with. Instead of heading out to cars and parking somewhere and torturing yourselves, with frustration, and shame, and worry. And *mess*—one way or another you'll get home all messed up.

She saw so many perfectly beautiful girls, with their lovely pure skin, translucent young eyes, their shining smooth long hair just perfectly curled at the ends. Their soft loose pastel cashmere sweaters. Perfect pearls.

But Cynthia would like to say to them, to all those girls: Wash all the pancake makeup off your beautiful faces, it isn't good for your skin, no matter what Max Factor says about it. And your lipstick's too dark, it looks black in this light, and those stiletto-heeled shoes, with such sharp pointed toes—you'll ruin your legs, and your feet. (Oh, how ridiculous she was becoming! Is this some terrible jealous inner voice?) Who do you think you are? she asked herself; some teenage advice columnist? The only person you could possibly say these things to is Abby, and she doesn't dress like that, or do all that to her face—and if I did she'd answer, Do you think you're a lawyer?

Telepathically, perhaps, in any case it is startling—Derek chose that moment to ask, above all that noise, "Why didn't you go to law school, after all? After being accepted—Georgetown, wasn't it?"

A question to which there was either no answer at all—or one that was extremely long, rambling, and introspective. Neither literal nor historical. And so Cynthia chose the first alternative, and told Derek, "I just don't know." And she added, with a very bright smile—oddly, remembering at just that moment that she too was wearing pancake and very dark lipstick—"I may yet." And then thought, Oh God, now I'll sort of have to.

The boys, for the most part, looked even younger than the girls did, in their dressed-up dark gray flannel suits, white shirts, and ties—except for the ones in uniform, which somehow had a certain aging, sobering effect. Cynthia stared at a very tall, fair boy in Navy dress, a very confident, *very* attractive boy, who was probably twenty years old—and who was probably, Cynthia realized with a certain wry despair, the dead spit of Derek at that age. And at my age, she thought—am I on the verge of a phase of younger men? And her terrible next thought was, To these boys I'm a middle-aged woman, and they're right, I *am* middle-aged, this is probably the middle of my life, and I'd really better find—something. Thinking then, But I have Harry, and Abby, and, for the moment, Derek.

Just beyond the tall fair boy, the young Derek, was a dark girl who looked even younger than the rest. A girl with long thick curly dark hair; a thin girl, with oversized, out-of-proportion breasts. Who must be, who *was* Melanctha Byrd, with a boy whom Cynthia also thought she recognized. Had they seen her? She moved a little farther from Derek, farther into the crowd, which might hide her—but just as she did so a large man walked up to where Melanctha stood, lurching a little; clearly drunk, he bent over Melanctha in what seemed to Cynthia a threatening way.

She whispered to Derek, "That girl over there, see? The one with the bosom? That's Melanctha Byrd, Russ Byrd's daughter, and that drunk old man's scaring her. Can't you sort of haul him off her?"

Derek peered, and turned back to Cynthia, his smile ironic. "That drunk is Bobby Higgenbottom, big tobacco man. He's married to a Reynolds, and they're our sponsors. Christ, all I need is an altercation—"

They were both staring across the room, in time to see Mr. Higgenbottom suddenly fall forward, across Melanctha, and then fall down to the floor. The crowd around them moved back, and then a few of them surged forward to help, Derek now among them.

Cynthia, standing back and watching, saw Melanctha clumsily embraced by that boy she was with, who was Archer Bigelow, one of Dolly's boys; that's who it was, of course.

". . . doctor? Is there a doctor?" Several people called that out, and then apparently there was a doctor, and then the old tobacco man, the drunk (and the sponsor!), was being carried out.

Derek, back at Cynthia's side, grabbed her arm (less gently than he could have, Cynthia felt), and began to propel her ahead of him, hurrying through the crowd—people just coming in, some from another post-game party, in another house, some already formally dressed for the dance, and others who were also leaving. "Coffee shop," Derek was muttering. "Infirmary's just across the street. I'll leave you there while I check it out and make a couple of calls."

"In the infirmary?"

Witheringly: "Of course not. In the coffee shop. You can start eating while I go up to the room and call, and then I'll join you. After *I* go to the infirmary."

The cafeteria–coffee shop was crowded too. Everywhere, that night of the big Homecoming Game, was crowded. But Cynthia recognized no one as having also been at the Deke House party—especially not Melanctha. Unreasonably, Cynthia had feared a closer encounter. This group was a combination of the dateless-on-Saturday-night solitaries, with their books and glasses, their pride and their wistfulness (some of the girls were extremely pretty, which they did not yet know), and other kids from other parties. Most of them had drunk too much, somewhere, and the harsh cafeteria lights were cruel on over-made-up, imperfect skin.

Cynthia got up, she asked for and found the ladies' room, where despite the crush she managed scrupulously to clean her own face, to re-makeup.

When she got back to her booth, fifteen or twenty minutes later, there was the club sandwich that she had ordered; it had seemed safe, she had forgotten how soggy toast could be.

And, a couple of minutes later, there was Derek, who said, "He's dead. Higgenbottom. Christ, poor old jerk." He laughed. "They said they didn't know I was a reporter anymore."

"Poor Melanctha."

"Who? Oh, that girl with the bosom." He grinned, and then, possibly in response to a sensed stiffness in Cynthia, he said soberly, "Scary for her, I'd imagine." And then he said, "Okay with you if we check out the dance for a minute? One whirl around the floor?"

"Not in these clothes—"

But with another, much more personal grin, Derek was already saying, "Of course I'd much rather go right off to bed."

Then why don't we? Cynthia did not say.

All the girls at the dance seemed to wear chiffon, they floated in layers of chiffon, some dresses enhanced with ostrich plumes, softly waving in the vibrations of music, of everyone dancing.

She caught a tiny glimpse of poor Melanctha, somewhere far off, in a terrible aqua taffeta dress. Looking drunk.

She shivered, said to Derek, "Why don't we go back to the Inn, and go to bed?"

Which was finally what they did.

4

THE Marcuses, Susan and her parents, Dan and Sylvia, and her brother, Joseph, went off to a benefit concert, something to do with Russia—and so Abigail and Benny Davis sat alone, somewhat stiffly, in the Marcus living room, brightly facing West Eleventh Street, the relatively quiet Village traffic, bare trees, and a wan November sun. Abby, somewhat shy by nature, was feeling exceptionally so: Benny, her old—her oldest—friend had become an entirely new, almost adult person, no longer a boy but a man, and so handsome that Abby was not quite sure they could still be friends. Her father was the only good-looking man she knew whom she really liked, and beside Benny he would be, well, nothing; just an okay-looking middle-aged middle-sized white man. But Benny—Benny was like a sculpture, a dark bronze statue, so tall and muscular, his face so perfectly molded, with that smooth high brown forehead, huge very dark eyes with those sweeping lashes. And his smooth strong mouth. Looking like that, could he also be interesting and intelligent? Abby was dubious. With scant experience to go on, she had already concluded that superior men were not the handsomest ones, unless you counted Mr. Roosevelt, and he was so old, and could never have been as movie-star drop-dead handsome as Benny was. Benny was better than a movie star, really: Clark Gable was ugly, with those big flapping ears. And not the kind of ugly that Abigail liked; she liked Susan Marcus's brother, Joseph, who was skinny and thin-haired, nearsighted, with glasses and bad posture, and looked brilliant, which he was, everyone said so: a sophomore at Swarthmore, a physics major with plans to go to MIT—if the Army didn't want him; he thought they would not.

Still, though bedazzled by and mistrustful of his looks, Abby tried to get back to being old good friends with Benny—without resorting to anything obvious like "Remember when . . ." (Although she would have liked to remind him of the time they switched around all the compounds in the chem lab, in their Connecticut school, because they hated the teacher, Mr. Martindale—just before Abby and her parents moved down to Pinehill.)

The room in which they sat, the living room, was crowded with souvenirs of Mexico; Susan's parents had often travelled there, and the whole house was jammed with trophies from those trips, gaudy baskets and silver masks, painted pottery and puppets, skeletons and dancers—and pictures, oils and watercolors of bright fruit and dim cathedrals, of women in lace and flowers, of men either bare-chested, sweaty, or wearing various uniforms.

Looking around, after one of their several conversational pauses, Benny said, "I don't know, sometimes I don't much think I want to go to Mexico."

Abby laughed, feeling easier. "I know what you mean, but there must be some stuff to do there, other than shop?"

He laughed too. "It doesn't look like it, does it? I wonder what was here before."

"I can't imagine. I don't know where else they've been. They travel a lot, I think. Or they did before the war."

"You and Susan are friends down at Swarthmore?"

"Yes, I hadn't met her family before. She's talked about them a lot, of course." She added, "I'd really wanted to meet them. I had sort of met Joseph, at college. But the parents, they sounded so—so not like mine. Or anyone in Pinehill." She asked, "Your parents are still in Connecticut?"

"Yes." He hesitated, then told her, "It's interesting, and sort of ironic, what happened to them. My father's father, my granddad, was a slave, and came North by the Underground Railroad, and got work as a blacksmith. I guess he was good at it. Anyway, it seems like he saved some money, and he bought a plot of land. About an acre. One of the first Negro men to own land in Connecticut—you can imagine how proud he was. And my dad was too. So, all the time he was working as a janitor, and if you remember we were not exactly rich, my dad hung on to his land. Even during the Depression. And then it turned out that my dad's little acre was exactly where the Navy wanted to build a base. My dad said no, even when they offered him a lot of money, and then they offered more, and more and more. They probably thought he was this terrific businessman, when he was really an innocent. A sentimental, stubborn old colored man. But at last they offered him this pension, with the money. A pretty good income for life, and then if he dies it goes to my mother, plus enough cash for a house. So my mom worked on him too—and there you have the story of my folks, this sad little colored couple. My dad still thinks he made a big mistake—selling out, he calls it—and they argue. In their little vine-covered Connecticut cottage."

"What a wonderful story!" Abby added, "They must be really pleased with you?"

"They're not so pleased about me not going to med school." Benny made a grimace that Abby remembered: his bad face. He added, "You know, to them a teacher isn't much. They knew too many in the public schools. They don't see much between that and a college professor, which is where I'll probably end up."

Abby had been intensely interested both in what Benny said, this good story about his parents, and in watching his face as he spoke. Despite the extreme good looks of this tall man that Benny had become, the boy that she once knew and had liked so much and felt so comfortable with—that boy seemed to emerge, and Abby began to feel some of the old ease and comfort, and the sheer pleasure of being with Benny. She was smiling as she asked him, "What turned you against med school, finally?"

"Oh, a lot of stuff, really. The time it would take, for one thing. Plus the money."

"I've been sort of thinking about med school for myself," Abby told him. Astounding! This was a distant, unformed plan that she had barely voiced to herself, and certainly not to any other person.

"I'm really impressed," Benny told her, and then he smiled. "Think you can manage all those chem labs? You won't mix up the compounds?"

They both laughed, remembering Mr. Martindale, their hated old chemistry teacher and their youthful trick.

Feeling so easy and familiar with him then, Abby was sorry that the Marcuses were getting back at any minute, that they were all to go out to dinner. With so many people, she and Benny wouldn't get to talk much anymore. In a hurried way she asked him, "You never got around to seeing my friend Melanctha, did you?"

"No, actually I thought I'd call her next week. You know, after I'd seen you."

"Well, there's this problem. I mean, she's not there anymore. Something terrible happened to her up there. She won't even tell me, and then she came down and she went to a dance over in Hilton, and some old man was trying to talk to her, and then he had a heart attack, right there in the Deke House, and he died. I don't know—" Abby paused for an instant as she wondered, Why am I going on like this to Benny, who'll probably never even meet Melanctha? And then she answered her own question: I'm telling Benny (Benny? Or is it Ben these days?) because he's so easy for me to talk to, he listens with his eyes.

And so she went on. "It's alarming in Melanctha, because of her mother, SallyJane. She had these terrible depressions and they gave her shock treatment and it killed her."

"Jesus." Ben's whole face was concentrated in distress as he listened.

"She was going to this terrible psychiatrist," Abby continued. "A real dumb Southern jerk. My mother couldn't stand him." She added musingly, "I could be a psychiatrist, couldn't I?"

"Sure you could."

"I think I'd like to work with kids." Then Abby asked him, "Do people still call you Benny now, or would you rather be Ben?"

"I guess Ben. But you call me whatever you want. After all, you're my oldest friend." And he grinned.

. . .

But it was as Ben that he was introduced to the Marcuses. To Dan and Sylvia, Joseph and Susan. And although she, Abby, was the point of contact, the mutual friend who made introductions all around, she had a sense of distance from her friends; she was able to observe, as though it all took place in slow motion—she found particularly interesting the response of the four Marcuses to Benny. To "Ben."

His good looks astonished them all. Abby even felt a certain suspicion cast in her direction: why hadn't she told them? (Though of course she couldn't have, not knowing what he looked like.) She also sensed, especially in the grown-ups, in Sylvia and Dan, a certain disappointment: they had expected a nice young Negro student; the facts, that he had played football and went to Harvard, had been just slightly amiss, or askew, but still nothing had led them to expect this tall dark prince who looked (Dan Marcus, the Hollywood magnate, must especially have thought) like a movie star.

Susan Marcus (knowing her more closely than the others, Abby could probably read her best) reacted visibly and strongly to such a handsome boy; her smile and her whole posture became flirtatious, at the same time that she looked at Abby as though to ask: Is this okay? Or is he really yours?

Only Joseph seemed a little reserved, his reactions withheld; he was waiting to see what this man was really like. What he had to say for himself.

It was soon announced by Dan Marcus that they were going to a restaurant near Union Square—a real authentic old labor place, all the old Italian Reds used to go there, Dan said. Tresca, all of them.

The restaurant, reached after a walk of fifteen minutes or so, was slightly seedy: a worn green carpet, large yellowed group photographs on the walls. The tablecloths, red-and-white checked, were stained. Abby thought that her mother, tidy Cynthia, would have walked right out, probably. ("Look, we don't have to eat here, besides there's no one around." Abby could hear her mother's pretty, slightly arrogant voice.) The place was only about half full, and what most struck Abby was the total lack of uniforms, such a contrast to the streets they had just walked through, where there had seemed uniforms everywhere, festive clutches of soldiers or sailors out on the town, officers or privates with their families or their dressed-up girlfriends, or with both.

As they seated themselves, Abby between Ben and Joseph, facing the older Marcuses and Susan, Abby remarked on that fact. "It's odd to see no uniforms in a restaurant these days."

Surprisingly, Joseph laughed at this, but in a somewhat angry, defiant way, and he spoke not to Abby but to his parents. "The old Reds are still isolationist, isn't that right? They think the pact is still on."

Pleased that she knew, more or less, what he was talking about, Abigail (tactlessly) asked, "You mean like Colonel McCormick and the Chicago *Tribune*?"

Dan Marcus opened his mouth as though to say a great deal, but Sylvia, his wife, in a firm way patted his arm and spoke first. "Now, darling." But she did not say it very nicely, Abby observed.

Removing his glasses, Joseph wiped at them in what Abby felt was a delaying tactic, postponing whatever he had to say. And when he spoke, this time addressing her, it was still without his glasses. "Not exactly *like,*" he began to explain, in a very kind and faintly amused voice. "The same conclusion, perhaps, but really from opposite points of view. The Midwest, and the Colonel, has to do with America Firsters, even Father Coughlin gets into the act, more or less. Why save Jews?—that's their reasoning, or part of it. Whereas some of the old Reds are still hung up on the Hitler-Stalin pact. They're a little confused, and behind."

Abby listened, genuinely and intensely interested, as much in contemporary history as in the particular political passions of this family, which were new to her. Her parents cared, Cynthia did and especially Harry, who was so pleased to be in the Navy; they liked Roosevelt, they thought he did a great job, and they hated Hitler, as everyone did. But in Sylvia and Dan Marcus, Abigail felt a passion that was both political and personal; the two were combined (or possibly confused, confounded). And Joseph, as he talked, explaining things to Abby, was being nice to her but was also hoping to seal off his parents, so to speak. To prevent an explosion.

She felt all that acutely—but as they faced each other, she and Joseph, sitting inches apart in the not large booth, she saw Joseph's eyes as though for the first time: a curious dark gray-brown, gold-flecked. They were the most intelligent eyes she had ever seen.

". . . a group in Cambridge," Dan Marcus was saying. "Very interesting. Anglo-Catholic Marxists. A Father Smythe is the head of it all—the head priest, I guess you'd say. They have interesting Sunday brunches, Ben. You might want to take a look. I'd be happy to write to the good Father."

"Oh, come on, Dan." Sylvia sounded inexplicably annoyed.

Ben murmured something polite about how nice that sounded.

"Of course I don't really know about your politics," Dan said; it was a gentle but insistent question.

"Unformed, I guess," Ben told him. "I like Roosevelt, and seems to me he's doing a good job with the war, and he got us out of the Depression. Or maybe the war did that. But beyond that I really don't know."

"Sounds like you're a lot more sophisticated politically than you think you are," Dan Marcus told Ben, with a large and very warm smile.

Mr. Marcus's sort of good looks did not appeal to her at all, Abby noticed. His features were all too regular, except for his oversized strong bright white teeth, and his eyes, which were brown and intelligent and small, a little close together—nothing like Joseph's eyes. He looked dishonest, Abby thought, and then she censored the thought: Mr. Marcus was probably really nice and kind and smart, he was just—just not a kind of man she had met before, and she, Abigail Baird, was much too critical. Judgmental. "So young to make such harsh judgments," her mother had said. "And such quick ones!" She was right, Abigail knew she was, and admitted as much; nevertheless, already she had observed in herself a tendency to return to whatever her first impression or judgment had been. She could still remember the first time she saw Benny, this tall skinny colored boy out on the playground at school. She thought he looked really nice, and smart, and she was right. Later she found out that his father was the janitor at the school, and a lot of kids wouldn't ask him to parties or anything, though he was friends with some of the boys he played games with. Ben could run faster than anyone, they all said. Abby began saying "Hi" when they saw each other around the school, or downtown, and then they began talking sometimes. And then they were friends.

She would like it if Susan and Ben became friends, Abby

thought. But would she? If they "fell in love" and Ben came down to see Susan at Swarthmore?

Returning her attention to Joseph Marcus, Abby noticed that his hands too were very different from his father's. Mr. Marcus's hands were stubby, reddish. Whereas Joseph's hands were long and thin and smooth. Strong-looking. It occurred to her that Joseph's hands looked sexy; odd, that was not a word she used a lot, and you don't think of hands as being sexy, she thought (but of course they are, *very* sexy—was her next more secret thought).

"Just what are you trying to recruit that handsome Negro boy for, Dan Marcus?"

An indistinct sound from Mr. Marcus, a protest of some sort.

"Because he's a Negro you think you'll get points with your L.A. comrades."

Another sound, louder but still indistinct.

"And Father Smythe, *shit!* This boy is not political, and he's certainly not interested in you. Are you so optimistic you can't even tell? Well, I can, and he's not."

"Oh, lay off, Syl. One episode." That came loudly and clearly through the wall to the guest room, where Abby lay, trying to sleep.

She was used to parental sounds at night, even sometimes to quarrels, but those were always succeeded by more familiar sounds of love. Making up. Making love. Abby had heard those noises all her life, and they had become soothing to her, reassuring. She waited now for such sounds to come from the Marcuses, but she heard nothing.

Disturbed by what she could not make any sense of, Abby lay there, wishing for sleep that seemingly would not come.

Who was this Father Smythe that Dan Marcus wanted Benny to go and meet—whereas Sylvia apparently did not. And what did she mean, saying Benny was not *interested* in Dan Marcus? The word, as used between the Marcuses, meant something else, something specific and very likely sinister.

Dan Marcus began to snore, hoarse, belligerent sounds. It had to be Dan, no woman could make so much noise.

Unable to sleep, Abigail, for whom that affliction was extremely rare, sent her inner vision back to Pinehill, to the woods around the town where she used to wander for hours, alone and perfectly happy. She saw with absolute vividness the gray November trees with their thin, faintly fluttering leaves, and the rich dark green heavy-boughed pines, and she smelled the pines and the fecund fall earth, the loamy dirt below the thick brown-needled carpet. She saw the clearing in the woods as she came to the desiccated cornfield, the rows of crumbling ruts and the tottering, tattered gray stalks. She began to cross the cornfield, heading not fast but very happily toward the creek, its ghostly border of peeling white poplars and leafless honeysuckle vines.

And then she fell asleep.

5

RUSS, James Russell Lowell Byrd, has often dreamed of his daughter's breasts. Long, soft, and white, floating upward in a foamy bathtub, or flopping down against her ribs as she stood up to dry herself. He *knew,* although (of course) it was not Melanctha's actual breasts that he had seen but SallyJane's, her mother's. Heavy-weapon breasts, concealed in pointed bras, aimed at him. Accusing breasts. And now his young wife Deirdre's breasts, stretched after pregnancy and all that nursing (nursing SallyJane, his daughter who would grow and soon have breasts of her own), now Deirdre has those breasts, like all the women in his life. Large and terrifying.

Would it help if he called them tits, as most men did? Would it make them smaller? He doubted it, but he could try.

Trying to shrug himself out from the dream, from the weight of the Melanctha-SallyJane-Deirdre breasts, he thought then with some tenderness and gratitude of Cynthia Baird, her sweet tender girlish pink breasts, delicate and vulnerable. Unthreatening. He should have married Cynthia, he thought, as though there were no Harry Baird and marriage were possible.

In the meantime, there he was, wide awake too early in this New York hotel room, with a big erection between his legs and dreams of his daughter, Melanctha, her breasts, weighing down his spirit, his whole mind.

He turned over onto his stomach, hiding his face in his pillow, his cock mashed down in the sheets. But finding no escape from his mind.

That night he was to take Esther Hightower out to dinner. Esther, also up here from Pinehill, doing her Jewish refugee work. Beautiful Esther, with her big high pointing breasts. Oh Jesus!

But when evening actually came, and he was seated with Esther—Esther across from him at a small sidewalk table at the Brevoort, on lower Fifth Avenue—he barely thought of her breasts; he only thought, and he said, that the dark red suit she wore was extremely becoming. "You're looking like a real stylish New York lady, Miss Esther. I don't see the Oklahoma in you one bit, nor the Pinehill either."

She answered in a serious way. "I feel very at home in New York. Really more than I ever did in Pinehill. Maybe it's because of all the Jews. In Pinehill, I'm the only Jew in town." She laughed to indicate the essential non-seriousness of that remark. "Although I guess a few of the students are Jewish. Very few," she added.

"That's changing now," Russ told her, in his own more "Northern" accent. "Over at the college they've hired three of these 'refugees,' one from Austria and two from Germany. The German ones are both Jewish, I believe."

"And the Austrian's a Nazi, probably."

"Now, Esther—"

"Well, the Austrians mostly were. They welcomed Hitler, the *Anschluss.* Except for the Jews, of course."

"The Austrian's a tennis coach, so he shouldn't do too much harm. One of the Germans is an economist, the other teaches German."

"I'll have to meet them when I come down to see Jimmy and the girls," Esther mused. "I've been studying German, hard. It's a real intensive course."

So many beautiful women passed by on the sidewalk, just separated from their table by a hedge. All ages and sizes and colors of lovely women, in their wartime short skirts and high heels, with the pointed toes. Hard for a man to imagine how they could walk; Russ could not, his imagination tripped at the very thought. But they did, some slowly and languorously, seeming to savor the unseasonably warm fall night, enjoying the men at their sides, the uniformed heroes back from or off to wherever, the glamorous ones. Other women, a few of them alone, or sometimes in groups of two or three, hurried past, but probably they too had some war-heightened rendezvous. They all looked so fresh, so beautiful, so remotely alluring. Admiring, and dimly lusting after them all, Russ felt infinitely old—a finished old poet, a finished man. A very old husband and father.

He watched as a shy-looking, very young, very thin girl walked by, her dark face wistful, he thought, as she scanned the terrace where he and Esther and other (rich, successful) older people sat and drank and talked, and perhaps made plans for love that might or might not work out. Don't envy us, he wanted to say to the girl. It is not what it looks like. But before he could further explain, in this imagined, partly paternal speech to the pretty girl, a young sailor rushed out of the restaurant to seize her arms, to bend and to kiss her, avidly, familiarly; they knew all about kissing, those two. And Russ now saw the girl's unshy, not wistful face as they broke off to laugh, still looking at each other, and then to leave the terrace, heading back into the restaurant.

"I could use another drink," Russ said; he felt that he had not said anything for a while—he was not being a good host, or "date," and so he added, "Sure you won't join me?"

"Actually I will have another lemonade." She laughed a little. "Jews don't drink, you know. Almost never." And then she told him a long, somewhat involved story about a waiter once who assumed that Jimmy, her husband, was trying to get her drunk—"I'd ordered something called a Horse's Neck, which I just thought meant no liquor, but apparently it's some kind of signal. Whatever it was I got was mostly gin. Jimmy drank it, he thought it was really swell."

"I'll have to remember that the next time I want to get a lady drunk," Russ told her, with his special small polite laugh, as he thought: That'll be the day, hell will burn first. I can't stand it when women drink, Jesus Lord. SallyJane, and now Deirdre, so often—

Reading his mind, it seemed, or maybe his expression, Esther frowned and reached forward to touch his hand, very lightly but kindly. As she said, "I'm sorry, Russ," she looked at him with her great depthless dark eyes that were full of pain.

Very suddenly then, Russ thought, or he knew, that he was truly, was absolutely in love with Esther Hightower, wife of Jimmy, the wildcat oilman, the writer, the ass. He loved her! and she would never, never in a month of Sundays, she would never love him! There would always be this beautiful distance between them, always. Beautiful! Enraptured by this perception, this marvelous insight, Russ beamed beatifically across the table at Esther.

Her telepathy seemingly turned off, Esther smiled back very pleasantly, and she told him, "I'm really glad you like it here. I do. Jimmy and I often come here when he's in town. They have the best vichyssoise—I can't get used to that name, can you?"

Not hearing much that she said, but able still to make the requisite sounds of polite response, Russ's poet-playwright's inventive, romantic mind raced ahead: he foresaw a lifetime of immense and extraordinary love for Esther ("My vegetable love will grow, / Vaster than empires, and more slow—"). Marvell? he thought so; in any case, old lines that he had always loved. And it was wonderful that she would never know—unless, miraculously, she could somehow read between the lines of some poem of his, some great new poem, for Esther, that he would start tomorrow, or maybe tonight.

But she would not love him. Not ever. She wasn't *like that* (he often thought in these phrases from his Baptist boyhood). He could not bear any more women who loved him, who "responded." Or who, in some cases, even with Cynthia, but even more so with that cat witch, that psychiatrist's wife, whose name he could never remember—in those cases, the women had started off the whole thing themselves. Initiated aggression—which Esther would never, never do; *she wasn't that kind.* Contemplating this long life, or perhaps a short one, of unrequited love, Russ felt a vast peacefulness. A wonderful release from so much anxiety and pain. From the terrible doom of sex. Forgetting for the moment that he was married, and to a young and frequently amorous wife, he thought: I'll never have to do all that again. Esther wouldn't even want me to.

"Well," he said, "maybe we should order?"

"We just did!" she cried out. "Russ, I don't think you were

even listening." And she laughed. "Well, you're getting the vichyssoise, and lobster salad. Whether you like it or not."

And Russ, the inland Southern boy, who secretly hated lobster and almost all seafood, told her, "Of course I heard. Sounds wonderful!"

As he thought, No more bad dreams. No more terrible hot breasts. Only dreams of Esther, who is lovely and regal. And unattainable.

Back at home, in Pinehill, Melanctha, like her father, had bad, obsessive dreams of her breasts. Over and over, in dreams, and then lying awake, she heard again that horrible voice on the phone: "Your tits—"

And there she was, that hanging heaviness on her chest, from which there was no escape.

And that old man, almost falling on top of her, then dying, at the Deke House.

She is not sure how she feels about being dead, herself. I am not suicidal. She has been forced to repeat this to the doctor who was summoned to see her, and, very coldly, also to Deirdre.

But, is she? She likes the word "suicidal." What she does not like is the idea of herself as a body, limp and dead. Exposed to anyone who wanted to see her. In the morgue or funeral parlor, wherever they took her, she would probably lie naked. All exposed. Dead.

In the meantime, she is so tired of her room, which is up at the top of the house, big windows on three sides, so that on very sunny days, like today, it gets very hot. Even now, in November.

If it wasn't important that everyone still believe that she

was sick, she could walk out into the woods. And then Melanctha remembered that no one was there today. All her brothers—even Graham—were off in school; Deirdre had taken the baby, SallyJane, somewhere for her birthday or something. Her father, Russ, was in New York, or maybe Hollywood by now, and Ursula was off. She *could* go out. She could step on dry leaves, and breathe the fall smells of earth and smoke and pines, and just air.

In a hurried way she pulled clothes on, her college dungarees and a big old gray sweatshirt that was one of her brothers'. (Deirdre: "Melanctha, you just swim in that old sweatshirt. I sure wish I'd had something like that when I was pregnant.") God, what a stupid bitch, and getting stupider, the more she drinks. Melanctha had not had a drink since Hilton, the Deke House.

Outside, in the woods, Melanctha breathed more easily, and with less anger. There was no one around, none of the people she feared and who so enraged her, both the easily named and the nameless.

The day was so bright; unused for a while to natural, real light, Melanctha was dazzled as her nostrils were assailed by many smells, and so strong, of rich fall rot, of wood smoke from some Negro cabins, much farther out in the woods, around by the creek. Almost happy, almost forgetting the body and the self that she could not bear, she walked along the dry leaf-crunching path, sure-footed over tough exposed roots and slippery needles, with almost nothing in her mind but November, and air. Just breathing.

But there is another person out in the woods. Someone walking very lightly and carefully. Someone else who does not want to meet anyone she knows; it must be a woman, with those delicate steps.

Mrs. Baird. Cynthia Baird, in a dark green coat, almost the color of pines. Surprisingly friendly.

"Melanctha! You are a nice surprise. I heard someone and I thought it must be—oh, several people I'm not dying to see." A complicitous smile, as Melanctha wondered who she meant that she didn't want to see. Deirdre, or maybe even Russ, Melanctha's father?

"It's nice to see you too," Melanctha answered politely.

"Shall we walk a little way? I just remembered this old path from when we lived out here, in the Hightowers' house. It goes from where you live almost out to where we do now."

"Oh? I've never walked exactly here."

Cynthia said, "Actually I don't think I've seen you since that awful night at the Deke House, in Hilton. That must have been terrible for you, Melanctha. Just awful. I started to write you a note but it was so bad—I didn't know—"

"It's okay. I'm a lot better now."

"Well, good. I was with a friend, Derek McFall, you know, the correspondent. And then later at the dance I just caught a glimpse of you." She added, without much of a pause, "I miss Harry a lot these days, and most of the time he can't call from London, and his letters take forever. I miss Abby too, but Swarthmore seems so much closer, and she'll be home for sure at Christmas."

"Oh, that's neat. I miss her too."

"I'll tell her I saw you." A big smile from Cynthia.

"She still likes Swarthmore?"

"Oh, yes. And she seems to spend more and more time in New York." And Cynthia began to talk about the Marcuses. At first Melanctha was puzzled, this stream of unself-conscious conversation from a woman she knew but really did not know at all—a grown-up, Abigail's mother. But then she thought,

It almost doesn't matter who I am, she needs someone to talk to. She's lonely—although "lonely" seemed an incredible word to use for a beautiful, stylish, *perfect* woman like Cynthia Baird.

"Dan Marcus is something in Hollywood, I think a producer, though I've never exactly understood what producers were. They're both Jewish, I guess, and they have these two children, Susan and Joseph. They seem to be Communists—the parents, I mean. I don't really know any Communists, do you? I guess Russ might, in Hollywood. You might ask him if he knows Dan Marcus. Anyway, they're very involved with Joint Anti-Fascists and Russian War Relief, things like that. All very worthy, I'm sure, though my Republican parents would not be enchanted to meet them, exactly. What I don't quite understand," said Cynthia, with a pretty, small frown, "is just what Abby finds so fascinating there. I wonder if I'm jealous! But almost all I hear about is the Marcuses, and weekends in New York. Good heavens, I've talked so much we're almost to my house. You'll come in for a cup of something hot, I hope?"

It was over fragrant English tea, in Cynthia's luxurious sun-warmed living room (bright silk cushions everywhere, and all the chairs were deep, enfolding) that Cynthia said, "I hope you won't mind if I say this, dear Melanctha, but now that you're feeling better, and you are! I can tell—I do think you should pay a little attention to your posture. I hope I don't sound like some gym teacher—" and she laughed, "but I used to have a good friend who slouched a lot, so it's something I know about. And maybe for the same reason. She had a really big chest, that she wanted to hide. Of course all of us flat-chested types really envied her. We thought, If only we had her problem! But she told me how it embarrassed her, a certain kind of attention she didn't like. She finally did start standing better, though, and that was a big improvement, honestly. I hope you don't mind my saying all this—please don't mind. Oh, Melanctha, I'm so *sorry*—"

For Melanctha had burst into tears, her whole body shaken with sobs, her throat choked, tears raining from her eyes. She had instantly covered her face with her hands, but the tears leaked through her fingers. So horribly embarrassing—embarrassment made her cry harder.

Cynthia now stood beside her; she patted and stroked Melanctha's shoulder, until as suddenly as the tears had begun, they stopped. "I'll go wash my face," said Melanctha.

In the pretty powder room, with its starched embroidered linen towels, jars of scented soaps and oils, as she splashed cold water on her face, Melanctha had a curious sense of feeling better, despite embarrassment, some shame. She had to admit it, she felt better now.

To Cynthia, in the living room, she said, "I'm sorry, really. I don't know—I've been sort of sick, I guess."

"Sit down and have more tea. *I'm* sorry. God, I'm so dumb sometimes. Harry tells me so. God, I say things that are really none of my business." She smiled, and laughed a little. "Please don't tell Abigail what a dumbbell her mother is."

Melanctha gulped at her tea, still curiously aware of an improvement in her spirits. "I'm really glad I came out for a walk," she said. And she forced herself to add, though shyly, "I'm glad I met you."

"Oh, I'm glad," Cynthia told her, and in a friendly way she laughed. "You'll have to come for tea again. I'll call you. And at Christmas, Abigail—we'll all get together."

As they regarded each other with affection and some curiosity, one of the things that Melanctha wondered was: Just what was going on, back a couple of years ago, between Cynthia and Russ? Impossible of course to ask that question, and so she asked the other pressing question in her mind: "What finally happened to your friend? The one with the big breasts and bad posture?"

"Oh." Cynthia seemed to hesitate, then to decide to speak. "Well, actually she had some plastic surgery on her breasts. Seemed crazy to all her underendowed friends, but I guess it worked out. She stood up better, and she was always pretty thin, so she looked more in proportion. And she married very well—at least twice that I know about." Cynthia finished with one of her small laughs, and Melanctha joined in.

And Cynthia added, "Of course it cost a lot, those doctors."

And Melanctha said, "I'll bet," very thoughtfully.

"I consider it for my face sometimes," Cynthia continued. "I mean, I know I look okay now, but how about when I'm fifty, or *sixty*? What I hope is that by that time I'll be less vain, more self-accepting. You might work along those lines yourself, Melanctha. Tell yourself every day that you are the way you are, and most women would give anything for a larger chest. And men love it—"

But Melanctha had stopped listening. It was almost as if she had left the room, though she still smiled in a polite, attentive way.

6

IN early January of 1945, in Pinehill, there was a stretch of sunny weather. Conversations in the A&P reverted to the warmth, the state of various gardens, local gossip. If anything, there was less talk than usual about the war. Not that wartime news had ever been a major topic—but in this lovely, extraordinary sunshine people generally felt less guilty about not discussing the war. Who wanted to hear about battles and deaths and home-front shortages—not this week!

"My rosebushes are just plum crazy," Dolly Bigelow told Cynthia Baird, in a shopping interlude. "They think it's spring. Just putting out buds all over the place, and the crape myrtle too, and the quince. I'm just mighty afraid they're in for a big surprise, the lot of them. Next thing we'll all be taking a dip in you-all's pool. Tell me, Cynthia darlin', how's old London treating your Harry? You don't get scared with the bombs and all over there? My goodness, there's Deirdre Byrd, still seems strange to call her by that name, don't you think? With her darling little SallyJane—now, talk about names that take some getting used to! She sure has put on a pound or two, hasn't she—of course I'm referring to Deirdre, not that darling baby. Billy says that her Graham—I guess I should say their Graham—anyway Graham is the worst little sissy in school. But you know how boys talk, not one grain of sense in a carload. But I surely hope he's not going to turn out like that—you know what I mean. His daddy Russ would kill him, or more likely kill himself. Speaking of children, you must be purely delighted to have your darling almost grown-up Abby visiting you for so long. And so nice that that young New York man of hers would visit too. Jacob? Jonathan? Joseph? Oh, I'm just getting so bad about names, especially those ones that are sort of, you know, unfamiliar. And to speak in a serious way for just one minute, that's one good thing this war has done, don't you think? It has surely changed around the way we all think about Jewish people. Why, some of those refugees over to the university are perfectly lovely, as I'm sure the parents of Abby's Jacob are lovely too."

"Joseph. And I've never met the Marcuses," said Cynthia when she could. And then she said, "Sorry, I've got to rush. I'm taking the afternoon train up to Washington, and I can't leave Abby and Joseph with nothing to eat."

"Oh, well—" Dolly's small bright eyes sparkled. "You're leaving those two young people in that house all by them*selves*? My, you certainly are—advanced."

Cynthia, used to Dolly, laughed. "Odessa's there in the apartment," she told Dolly. "And Horace. So they'll be fully chaperoned."

Dolly laughed too, with no humor at all. "Oh well then," she said to Cynthia. "That's all right then."

"Oh, I'm so glad you think so." Equally unconvinced—even to her it seemed somewhat careless—Cynthia smiled.

. . .

Odessa was indeed late. Late that same afternoon, after Cynthia's departure for Washington, Abigail, from her broad bedroom window, watched as tall Odessa with her curious swinging gait crossed the backyard, along the flagstone path to the garage and the apartment above that she shared with Horace. When he was around. "Some chicken and greens on the stove," Odessa had told Abby. "Be ready anytime you are, you just heat it up. Just a tad."

Abigail's room faced west, and now in the final brilliant burst of winter sunlight the white sheets on the tousled unmade bed were golden, as Joseph's bare back was gold, the smooth muscles sculptural. Abigail's sense of her own body was golden too; she was irradiated by an inner dazzle—as she wondered why no one had ever said (but who would have; maybe Cynthia?) or she had never read, not really, that actually making love was like—like *this.* Like a prolonged involvement of every nerve, every cell, an extreme of sensation. Like nothing possible in words.

She was smiling as she turned from the window to stroke the nice curve of Joseph's buttocks, slowly, admiringly.

Looking up, he smiled back before he said, "I'm sorry, I can't do it again, you've worn me down. I've heard about you younger women—" He smiled again.

"What I meant was," Abby told him, "why don't we sleep for a while?"

"You have the best ideas."

He turned so that his back pressed against her chest, her stomach; he reached around to her arms and clasped them around himself.

And with absolute pleasure Abby adjusted. And that is how they napped, for an hour or so.

Or rather, Joseph slept. Abby was thinking, in a somewhat confused way. Unsurprisingly, her thoughts had to do with sex.

She knew from studious reading on the subject—Abby had an energetic curiosity, what was actually a lively scientific mind—she knew that "orgasms" were what she had experienced before, while "necking heavily" with boys, in backseats, on sofas in darkened rooms. And boys did too; they "reached a climax" sometimes, making stains on their pants that embarrassed them a lot, poor things. She had always enjoyed, looked forward to that moment of release, that "climax," although in a way it was less pleasurable than all the intense and sometimes frantic kissing and touching that went on before. The "foreplay," which was always referred to in texts as being very important, especially to women, "crucial to their pleasure," but somehow, in some cases, said to be difficult.

However, none of those earlier experiences seemed to have any relevance at all to what happened with her and Joseph—happened for the first time in New York, when Sylvia and Dan, the parents, were away, and back at Swarthmore in his room, where she was not supposed to be—and now down here in Pinehill. Her previous experience, such as it was, and her reading did not get anywhere near it.

When she was older and went to med school, Abby thought, she would study this enormous and misunderstood difference in orgasms. Freud, she thought, had oversimplified. Clitoral versus vaginal, that was not the issue. Unless, and she smiled to herself, unless what she experienced with Joseph was both at once.

. . .

Gently caressing her, just enough to wake her up, Joseph was saying, "But now I can."

And so they did. Again.

The sex between her parents, Harry and Cynthia, thought Abby, must be really good too, which would explain almost everything: why they stayed together all these years, and why they made so many excuses to go off and take naps. During which there were always non-sleeping sounds. And as for Cynthia's occasional crushes on other men—a long time ago, Mr. Byrd, father of Abby's friend Melanctha, Russ; and now this Derek, the broadcaster—they were only that, big crushes. Cynthia was a romantic, her daughter recognized, and recognized too that she herself was not romantic; she was a realist, with a scientific bent.

Years ago, when Abby had first started kissing boys, she liked it so much that she thought she was a nymphomaniac, but with no idea of the meaning of the word. Probably, she now thought, "highly sexed" was more like it.

And most likely, she thought, the realistic plan would be for her to marry Joseph. To get all that over with, so to speak. She could go to Harvard Med (she was not yet worried about getting in) and Joseph to MIT, and they would live in Boston, somewhere in between. And after they both got degrees they might have a few children, or maybe not. They would both work hard and they would always make love, wonderfully.

She wondered what Joseph would think of her plan, but decided to postpone asking him for a while.

. . .

"My parents," Joseph told Abby as together they ate Odessa's good chicken fricassee and greens, "my parents are not entirely to be trusted."

"How do you mean?"

"Well, Communists are tricky. They change their minds. They change directions like a boat in some shifting wind. The wind of course being the Soviet Union. Mr. Stalin."

Abby laughed; her body's pure euphoria made even serious observations light and funny to her. "My mother's sort of unreliable too," she said. "But in a quite different way."

"Not so totally different, when you think about it," Joseph mused. "They're all romantics. Just in different areas. I mean, your mother's not exactly political."

Abby laughed again. "No, she thinks Roosevelt is very handsome, and she loves his voice." She added, "And I think you're very handsome."

Now Joseph laughed. "And I think you're very nuts. No, as a matter of fact you're not. Not nuts. But speaking of handsome, I'm a little worried about the way my parents are about Ben. They're too crazy about him. I mean, I can see he's a swell guy, but they're both—they're both sort of in love with him."

"You mean because he's so good-looking?"

"No, to them that's the icing on the cake. Because he's a Negro. That's catnip to Commies. Read Richard Wright. How they used him. And Paul Robeson. Whom Ben sort of looks like, don't you think?"

"You're afraid they'll scare him away from Susan?"

"Yes, and try to recruit him too." He looked across at her. "Anyone ever tell you you're a very smart girl?"

"Actually, Benny did. A long time ago. 'Smart for a girl,' I'm afraid is what he said."

"And you told him he was pretty smart for a boy?"

"How'd you know?"

"I know you, or I'm getting to. And I'm pretty smart too."

"For a boy."

Abby did not think: I am madly in love with Joseph, or even, Joseph and I have fallen in love. She supposed that it could be said that she loved Joseph, but it would not have been she who said it, not even to Joseph himself. For whatever reasons, rare at the time, she refused the non-wisdom of popular songs of the day. She did not think that love had walked right in, nor that it had to be you (Joseph Marcus). Her heart was not on fire, smoke did not get in her eyes. Unlike her mother, she was quite unmoved by all that.

Abby waited for Melanctha at their favorite drugstore table, the small round white table at the back, and as Melanctha walked in, her head up, not slouching so much, what Abby first thought was, Oh good, she looks much better.

When they were both interrupted. Dolly Bigelow, swooping down on them like a greedy sparrow. "*Well.* Such a treat to see the both of you two almost grown-up girls, and the both of you looking *so pretty.* And Abigail, your mama's off to Washington, I hear? You tell that Odessa she'd better come over to see me, now she's got some time on her hands. I *need* her, though a lot she cares, the uppity old thing." And Dolly now laughed, to indicate that she was not serious, and to say too that, really, she was; she really did think Odessa was uppity, *very.*

Before anyone could answer or even greet her, Dolly went

on: "And, Miss Melanctha, you are looking more up and perky every day. It must joy the heart of your old daddy, and that darling Deirdre. How are they doing these days? Haven't seen hide nor hair for a coon's age." And Dolly laughed again; she liked to pride herself on sounding more down home, more true country Southern than anyone. (Only Russ could outdo her at this game, but he did it in a kidding way.)

"Russ's in Hollywood, and Deirdre's fine," Melanctha told her.

And Abigail: "I'll tell Odessa."

But both girls smiled politely as they spoke.

Dolly looked from one to the other, with her bright, intelligent, small mean eyes. That day she was wearing a vivid green suit; normally acutely sensitive as to color—though less so than Odessa, on whom she had relied—she had chosen a green that was wrong; it gave her the look of a small unwelcome plant, quite possibly poisonous.

As though to the world at large, she next said, "Why am I just standing here, talking my fool head off when I've got a whole slew of errands to do, will you tell me that? Including getting all Archer's shirts fresh ironed and back to him at the Deke House." She turned her attention to Melanctha. "You-all must have had some kind of a time at Thanksgiving."

Melanctha stared up at her. Stricken. *Accused.*

Abby saved her friend. "I'll tell my mother to call you the minute she gets back, and Odessa too."

"Well, it was just really lovely to see the two of you—but now I've really got to get at it." And Dolly scurried off, not without a couple of backward smiles and waves.

. . .

"I'm not studying Miz Bigelow," said Odessa, with a lift of her head. "She get herself in some kind of trouble to do with the wrong clothes she bought, or even just napkins, and she expect me to get her out. I'm like her rescue woman, and then she blame me if'n it don't work out."

Surprised by this burst of confiding from Odessa, who was known to be proud ("uppity") and taciturn, Abby was also flattered; she thought, Odessa must think I'm okay, an all-right person she can trust. She's right, she can trust me, but I wonder how she knows that? My mother is trustworthy too, though not entirely, which is something else Odessa seems to know.

To Odessa, Abigail said, "I don't see any reason for you to call Mrs. Bigelow if you don't want to. You don't owe her a thing."

"That's it, but she think I do."

"You did all her decorating stuff for years, and then that store she had with my mother was mostly because of what you had in it. I think she can't get used to the fact that now you've got some money salted away, and you don't need her anymore."

"Most likely you be right." But Odessa's smile was uncertain; she too had trouble believing that she had money in her own name in the bank, and more to come in.

This money was from the store that Cynthia Baird and Dolly Bigelow had started about five years back, not long after the Bairds moved down to Pinehill from Connecticut. Cynthia had seen it as an outlet for napkins and such, handmade by various women in the surrounding countryside. Dolly saw it as a business, money of her own coming in. For a while it flourished, money did come in—though there had been trouble at the start about Odessa's part; Dolly thought the work should only come from white women, nice country people like certain cousins of hers and of her husband Willard's. Cynthia however insisted, and she won, and when the Bairds moved up to Georgetown, at the start of the war, they sold the store and Harry saw to it that Odessa kept getting paid, as a sort of founding junior partner. The trickle of money was pin money to Cynthia and to Dolly, but groceries to Odessa.

Against any logic but her own, however, Dolly still felt that Odessa owed her, owed her a little work here and there, advice and perhaps a little more work on certain domestic projects like sewing clothes or running up curtains. Odessa was known to have a superior and original eye for color.

Odessa resisted Dolly as best she could, and Cynthia tried to help.

All of which had led to some coolness in the Cynthia-Dolly friendship.

"You-all favor some of this Brunswick stew for your dinner? You and Mr. Joseph?"

"Sure, Odessa, sounds great."

"Well, you just heat it up when you've a mind to," Odessa instructed (so much for Odessa as chaperon) as Abby thought, How beautiful she is. She wondered how Odessa felt about sex, and for that matter about Horace. Of course she would never know, but her instinct, or imagination, or some other sense, informed her that Odessa and Horace had great sex when they were together, but that during his long absences, sometimes for a year or so, if someone else came along—well, Odessa could enjoy him too (as Horace most certainly would be enjoying other ladies along his way). All without a lot of drama of betrayal and hurt feelings, all that. But Abby knew too that this could easily be an idealized view of Odessa, a projection of her own feelings, or rather, her ideas about feelings, onto Odessa.

Odessa had changed very little in the five years that Abigail had known her. Tall and muscular, with broad shoulders and that curious walk, she remained unlined; her very dark, slightly slant eyes were lively and intelligent—they said a great deal more than Odessa actually spoke. It was in her eyes that one could sometimes read affection, or anger, impatience, or private pain.

How would it be introducing Odessa to Benny—to Ben? Abigail and Cynthia had discussed this, and Cynthia had said, "I think she'd be embarrassed." And maybe that was true. Cynthia did have an instinct, her daughter admitted, for "social" situations. However, in Abigail's imagined scene, Ben (probably with Susan, who seemed to have a bigger crush on him even than her parents did)—Ben would come down to visit, and there would be no more or no less of an interchange than with any other guest.

Odessa would not be a problem.

Dolly Bigelow would, as would most of the other people in Pinehill, whom Abby could list to herself, smiling with pure pleasure as she did so.

"And, Dolly, this is Abby's old friend, Ben Davis."

Well.

Waking the next day, close to Joseph's back, and aware that on that very afternoon, almost simultaneously, Cynthia would return from Washington and she, Abby, and Joseph would take the train up to Philadelphia, Abby felt a premonitory sense of loss, of deprivation. It was not wrenching, no pain or possible tears, just the thought, Why can't we go on like this? Why can't we sleep together every night?

His skin smelled—it smelled like Joseph's skin, no other words to describe it. And the bed smelled of both their skins, and their intimate moistures, of sweat and semen and whatever it is that women produce—odd that that word is not more generally known, Abby thought. She stretched, rubbing one bare foot against Joseph's nearer leg, so that he woke, and slowly turned to face her.

Smiling, he said, "Do you know that sometimes you snore? I mean, it's sort of cute, but you do. You make more noise than my roommate."

"Speaking of roommates," Abby began, but by then Joseph was kissing and touching her in a purposeful way. And so Abby for the moment did not finish what she had meant, or thought she meant, to say.

7

CALIFORNIA made Russ crazy—crazy, crazier, and then more crazy. He was not even sure that he was there any longer. This place was called Death Valley, California, or maybe Nevada. The Furnace Creek Inn. The furnace of death—in plain words, of hell. He smiled, and for one instant he saw himself as an actor, an old, experienced, and sated actor now playing the part of a poet, who witnessed with amusement the disintegration of his own mind. From poems to puns. Never mind that Shakespeare liked puns too. Never mind—now, never you mind: what did such phrases mean, closely examined?

They meant that he was in California, and that his mind was almost gone (but never mind).

Once before, or maybe several times before, he had been in California with his wife, at that time SallyJane, whom perversely he had renamed Brett, for all the good that did. And they had liked it in sunny California. Or at least he had, he was fairly sure of that—though it was hard to remember.

Outside the window now, steeply sloped gravel paths wound around and around, lined by waving palm trees that rattled their fronds at night like snakes, but that now in the false brilliant day barely trembled, barely stirred in the crazy January summer breeze. If it was January—Russ was no longer sure.

"In Los Alamos," the man seated across from Russ in the hotel lounge was saying, "about due east of here, maybe seven or eight hundred miles, as the Caddy flies."

"If I was to start off in the Caddy, I'd get all the way to home," Russ told him: it was Oscar, his agent; in a burst of intelligence he had just remembered Oscar. "I don't want to go to this Los Alamos. It may be east of here but not far enough east for me." He laughed, and heard his own bleak sound.

"Robert Oppenheimer," said Oscar. "Hell of a guy, from what I hear. A physicist."

"Why me?" Russ asked, in what he felt was a very reasonable way. "I don't know a thing about physicists." And he had just remembered that he did not have a Caddy out here—or for that matter, anywhere; in Pinehill he just had a nice old Chevy, bought after the Caddy died. He had flown out here from New York, after seeing Esther, and he would probably have to fly back, if they ever let him go. "Why me?" he repeated, feeling that he was backed by plain old common sense.

"To get you back on track," explained Oscar, using his own Hollywood version of common sense. "You called me, remember? Said you were tired of being a college playwright, little amateur college productions. You'd been sidetracked by Ursula's pig, you said—your very words. You'd like to get back in the money. And I can see why—all those kids, a lovely young wife. They don't come cheap, those assets."

"No, they don't," Russ agreed as he was thinking, Back on

track. I could take a train home. No New York. No Esther. No airplane. Russ had no memory of making any such phone call to Oscar, although the phrase "Ursula's pig" was vaguely familiar, and at the same time incomprehensible. And so he said, as though he knew what he was talking about, "Ursula's pig." Reminiscently.

"A great play," Oscar informed him. "But not right for out here. You knew that, remember? But this Oppenheimer thing, it's about the war and then again it's not. It's perfect. It's going to make someone really rich and famous, and I'd like that person to be you. I mean, you were doing great until that fucking pig."

The pig. Crossing Kansas, in his old Caddy, Russ had run over a pig. All his children—all of them, five? No matter. They were in the backseat, and his wife was up in front with him. Brett, SallyJane, Deirdre—*what wife?* Well, Brett, at that time, he'd named her himself, from SallyJane to Brett, but then she went back to SallyJane, and then he married Deirdre; it was beginning to come more clear.

When he thought of the pig, though, he recalled a horrible disgusting smell, dead-pig shit, and a great big woman, Ursula, who was very nice. Who was now, at times, his housekeeper. His wife's housekeeper. One of the people for whom he needed more money. And Deirdre, once his beautiful secret girlfriend and now one more fat wife, as SallyJane/Brett had been. Of course he remembered the pig, and Ursula, and later he wrote a play, raising pigs in Kansas, the Depression—a sort of *Grapes of Wrath,* with pigs for grapes, except that it was not a best-seller or a movie; nobody out there would touch it. Too fucking folksy, they all said, in one way or another. And so it went to little theatres, university playhouses, and won various prizes for Russ, and not much money. To Oscar he said, with his slowest, most Southern smile, "I reckon pigs are more in my line than physicists are. Come to think of it, I never even met a one of those guys."

Having left Death Valley, and Oscar, to whom he had said no, all that pig history returned to Russ's splotchy mind as his train east rattled and shook across mountains of sand, the desert with its obscene and terrifying shapes of cactus. Cross shapes, crucifixes. Or cocks, big giant spiky cocks. The phallic cross; he's never thought of that before, but very likely a great many people already had, and knew what they worshipped.

For all he knew, they were passing Los Alamos right now, the train with its load of soldiers and sailors, mothers and wives and girlfriends and children and luggage, all over the aisles, swaying across the fucking desert—where at least he had known not to go. Los Alamos. He shuddered against the worn green velour of the harshly upright seat, in which he had sat and not slept the night before. All around him babies had been crying, small children with their loud sleepless whines, and oblivious lovers, immodestly necking, repulsive in their need, their ugly greed for each other's grimy faces, their lumpy bodies.

Crossing Texas at night, endless black plains with here and there some sparse and scary vegetation, Russ took two long swallows of bourbon from his pocket flask and was visited by some half-remembered fragments of his last letter from

Melanctha. Partly to divert himself from the lunatic scene surrounding him, he tried to bring it into sense.

"My back hurts a lot, and my shoulders, the bra straps cut into them . . . the boys make fun . . . was my mother a Manic Depressive? Sometimes I think I am . . . I'm drinking your wine as I write this, in your study. It's French and sweet, very good. . . ."

Sleeplessness, and the actual, visible disorientation of alien land had made him even crazier, Russ knew, so that nothing in his mind hung together or made any sense. But he would go home and at least would check his will, to make sure there was money for her, Melanctha, and Deirdre, and the new SallyJane, his baby.

Sometimes, though, he had visions that had or seemed to have great clarity. Abstract visions, for the most part, of future history. Conflict, that was mostly what he saw. Large and small wars. Russians, Americans, white people and black ones. Whites against blacks, in cities, and blacks against blacks, in the cities and out in fields, everywhere.

He sat there, sick with sleeplessness, and terrified.

He could die.

He would die. Without some air. Without a drink.

Desperately, incoherently dying for either some fresh air or some more bourbon—or, dearest sweet Jesus, both! He lurched up from his seat, and slowly, slowly, stumbling over large and small sleeping and angrily wakeful bodies, he made his way toward the rear door of the car. Which, with hysterical effort, he was finally able to open. He stumbled then, and he would have fallen—maybe out, somehow between the cars, as he was meant to do, probably—but someone already standing there, a man, grabbed onto him, grabbed his arm and held him there, until Russ, with that help, could get up to his feet.

The other man was a Negro, but a sergeant in the Army, who said in a soothing way, "Just you take it easy, sir." A very polite, tall, extremely pale—Negro, but almost white.

Unable to speak, Russ tried to smile, but he found that difficult too; the circumstances, him and this Negro, this sergeant, out on this platform of a banging and rattling old train, in the Texas night—all that made him unsure what expression he should wear.

"You're not in too good shape," the Negro, the sergeant, observed.

"We still in California?" Russ asked the man, offering his flask.

"No-sir-ee. In Texas now. I'm heading home. Got my discharge papers, and a bunch of dollars, all set to buy some new civvy threads right in my hometown." The tall pale Negro went on about his discharge: how he got wounded in the leg while his platoon was out on maneuvers, in the California desert; he seemed to find this remarkably funny. "My accident war wound," he said, and laughed. "I got me a lot of money, all set to buy the new threads," he repeated. "Got a discharge and money just for getting a damn old limp." Extending his right hand, he added, "Name's Ed Faulkner, from Massachusetts," and he laughed again.

"Russ Byrd. James Russell Lowell Byrd, how's that for a moniker?" Odd that these should be the last words he ever spoke, Russ thought then.

For he was going to die. Russ suddenly knew that, and the knowledge made him smile. Oh, thank God. At last.

A few swallows of bourbon, could he possibly just be drunk, and not dying at all?

But Russ felt himself lurch, and then his hand unaccountably slid. He lost his footing and began to fall. The other man, the Negro, the sergeant, tried to grasp him but could not.

Like a huge fish, Russ slipped through Ed Faulkner's arms. To the floor, where he hit his head. Hard.

8

ALTHOUGH Russ had been a Baptist by birth and early upbringing—baptized with total immersion in a creek, Baptist Sunday school, all that—his funeral service was in the Pinehill Episcopal church. Actually, no one even related to Russ except his dead wife, SallyJane Caldwell, had been Episcopalian; his present wife, Deirdre, like all the Yateses, had been brought up Baptist too. But no one remarked on this somewhat anomalous fact, at least not publicly. The general unvoiced and very unlikely explanation for this alien ceremony, this foreign (sort of) final rite for Russ, would have been that as the most famous, most distinguished man in town (no doubt about that, despite Jimmy Hightower's best-seller, and besides Jimmy was from Oklahoma, not even really Southern)—as the most famous, brilliant, rich, and handsome man in town, old Russ deserved the best church, as to which there was no doubt at all.

"I am the resurrection and the life, saith the Lord: he that believeth in me, though he were dead, yet shall he live; and whosoever liveth and believeth in me, shall never die."

In the small and very old beautiful church—pre-War, pre–*Civil* War, that is—moted beams of light were filtered through ancient, grimy stained-glass windows, and now fell gently on the black-clothed shoulders of Russ's family, all lined up there on the front row of the church. Deirdre, veiled, and then Melanctha (whose hat looked borrowed, or maybe handed down? from SallyJane?), the four older boys—Lowell, Walker, Justin, and Avery. And Graham, who was almost as beautiful as Deirdre once was, much too beautiful for a boy, is what everyone said about Graham.

"Out of the deep I called unto thee, O Lord. Lord, hear my voice. O let thine ears consider well the voice of my complaint."

"Jesus said, 'Let not your heart be troubled; ye believe in God, believe also in me. In my Father's house are many mansions; if it were not so, I would have told you. I go to prepare a place for you.' "

The day outside was almost balmy, not quite warm. In the cemetery, conveniently around the corner from the church, brave quince blossoms trembled in the breeze. The mourners were grateful for their black winter coats, some of which showed a slight brown tarnish in the sun.

SALLYJANE MAKEPEACE CALDWELL BYRD, said Sally-Jane's big granite headstone, and right next to it the new one that said JAMES RUSSELL LOWELL BYRD.

"Between them they sure had a bunch of middle names," was whispered among the mourners more than once, along with the inevitable next question: Will they put Deirdre next to Russ? Has she even got a middle name? Come to think of it, it's hard to recall her maiden name; that is to say, her unmarried name. Yates. You remember Clarence? Emily Yates, her folks? Deirdre Byrd used to be a Yates.

"Man that is born of woman hath but a short time to live, and is full of misery. He cometh up, and is cut down, like a flower: he fleeth as it were a shadow, and never continueth in one stay.

"In the midst of life we are in death. . . ."

Over in another part of the cemetery, not quite out of sight, in the colored part, some Negroes were having a funeral too, a whole big clump of them standing around their coffin, which, unlike Russ's plain pine box, was draped with a great big bright American flag. Must've been some young man of theirs died in the war, who would have had as much right to a flag as anyone else—of course he would.

Perhaps out of respect, or deference, to the white service going on, the Negroes were very quiet; none of the loud singing or the shouting that people said went on at their own church. Though maybe not at funerals? No one knew. In any case, there they were, the colored, burying their own dead person, probably some young man the white people had always seen around, very likely, ever since he was a child, but they didn't know him. Lying there with the oversized, over-bright flag spread over his coffin box.

"Unto Almighty God we commend the soul of our brother departed, and we commit his body to the ground; earth to earth, ashes to ashes, dust to dust. . . ."

Some of the headstones were extremely old, in the white cemetery and in the colored too, old and broken, the dates and inscriptions hard to read, sometimes impossible. Although people seemed to enjoy just walking there. Dolly Bigelow had taken Cynthia Baird on a short cemetery tour not long after the Bairds had moved down to Pinehill. They had gone back many times, most recently just a week or so ago. "I declare, sometimes I feel like I know more folks in here than I do downtown," Dolly sighed as they passed the large cement stone that marked the grave of Clifton Lee, a man whom Dolly had certainly flirted with, and from the much discussed evidence of lipstick stains had kissed, a lot. But that was all that Dolly said that anywhere near referred to Clifton—and then she went on, "Those Hapgoods were always just the tackiest people. Would you look at that *pink granite*?" And a little later, in the Negro section, "Eliosa Caldwell. Why, he must've been a slave of some of SallyJane's people, you know the Caldwells were about the biggest landowners in the county before the War. Not this war of course, *the* War. My, don't our colored folk think up the most outlandish names in all get out? Eliosa! Beats even Odessa, now don't it?"

The trees too were old, some probably pre-War. A beautiful heavy dark stand of tall cedars perversely graced the Negro cemetery, but in the white part there were some lovely pines, though fairly new, and later in the spring, pretty soon now, the dogwood trees would bloom, all beautiful and white, like lace.

"O Lord Jesus Christ, who by His death didst take away the sting of death. . . ."

Jimmy Hightower stood somewhat apart from the crowd, near some pines; the boughs of the trees were thick and heavy and even the needles were longer and broader than those on younger pines. And maybe even after all this time in the South, Jimmy was allergic to pine? Some people were, and an allergy could come on a person at almost any age; poor Sally-Jane, a few friends remember, got allergic to poison oak not long before she died, poor creature, as if she didn't already have troubles enough. But there was old Jimmy, just sniffling away, like a man near dead of hay fever—but did anyone ever die of such a thing?

Russ must have meant to die, was one of the black and irrational thoughts that crowded against each other in Jimmy Hightower's mind. Another was: I hope everyone thinks I've got a cold, or some allergy, especially that chatterbox silly bitch Dolly Bigelow, who keeps looking over here. Easy to imagine just what she'd say, in her horrible high flat voice. Russ had never liked Dolly, Jimmy was sure of that—fairly sure, hard to know really just who Russ did or did not like. But no matter what anyone saw, or thought, or said, the truth was Jimmy couldn't stop crying; tears poured down and his nose ran like a child's. The thought of Russ dead, or almost worse, of Russ really wanting to die—all that was too much for him. The truth was, he had loved Russ Byrd—whatever anyone meant by that word, he had felt it for Russ. And now he did not see how he could go on living, much less writing, without old Russ to talk to. To check in with. Or even if they didn't see each other or even talk, just to know Russ was there, inhabiting the same time span, the same territory that Jimmy was.

"Russ wanted you to have this," Oscar, Russ's agent, had told Jimmy Hightower. Oscar was speaking of the Oppenheimer-physics story, which just prior to his death Russ had refused, certainly not mentioning this Hightower fellow as he did so, but what the hell? Hightower had written that big oil best-seller, and even though Hightower seemed reluctant, he, Oscar, had one of his strongest hunches that Hightower was just the guy to do it. Too bad about Russ, though; Oscar had genuinely liked him, although he had never understood Southerners.

And now Jimmy thought, Well, maybe I should do that physicists' thing, out in New Mexico. Continuing Russ's work, even work that he didn't want to do, though maybe he would have, eventually.

Jimmy thought, Russ, God damn it, why did you have to go and die on me?

Deirdre and Melanctha, as they had in the church, stood somewhat apart from each other. Deirdre's coat was long and a little too tight. Must have been an old one. Melanctha's was one of those chesterfields, with a black velvet collar—the ones so popular last year. Deirdre had on a hat with a heavy black veil; she could have got it out in Hollywood, like one of those women had worn to the funeral of Valentino, or maybe that Scott Fitzgerald that died awhile ago. But if Deirdre was crying no one could see a thing. Melanctha's hat was small, sort of perky on top of all that curly hair, Russ's hair—and if she cried no one saw her either.

Cynthia Baird, who, if anyone knew her history with Russ (and plenty of people did, a whole lot more than she thought)—Cynthia could have been expected to be thinking of Russ, at least, but she was not; she thought of Harry, over there in London with all those Nazi bombs coming down and God knows what horrible wartime dangers (not to mention the temptations of all those English girls with their ravishing clear bright skins). Cynthia superstitiously felt—though she knew it was crazy—that Russ's death was an omen, a warning that Harry could be next, and she thought: Harry's death would be the one unbearable thing for me. And she well knew that thought to be dangerous, and she knew too—of course, how could she not know these days?—that many women were bearing losses just as bad for them, husbands and sons and lovers. Parents, in bombing raids. Children, anywhere. Why should God not ask her to give up Harry, to whom she had not even been faithful? There had been Russ, and now Derek, who was not even in love with her, as he too often made clear. She tried to bargain with God: If You don't kill Harry, I'll be faithful to him. After the war.

But she noted that she was saying after the war, not now. Thus not ruling out Derek. Oh Jesus, she was hopeless, she knew she was—as she thought too that even if English girls had lovely skin their legs were often terrible, whereas she herself had very good skin, and her legs were exemplary. Gorgeous gams, Harry often said, to tease. And he said, I love your lazy legs.

"O Almighty God, the God of the spirits of all flesh, who by a voice of heaven didst proclaim, Blessed are the dead who die in the Lord. . . ."

After all that, and so ladened with their thoughts and memories of Russ, everyone needed a drink, and there were plenty of good things to eat and drink at Dolly and Willard Bigelow's house—they had kindly, insistently offered to do that honor, and so Deirdre, along with a reluctant Melanctha, had let them.

The furniture was all pushed back, as though for a dance, and the French doors that separated the living room from the dining were flung open, revealing a large and festive spread, almost covering all the white linen space.

"Well, I just thought to have all the things that Russ was most partial to, even if strictly speaking that does not make good sense. But isn't that what the Egyptians did, or somebody back then? Funeral meats? I wonder whatever those were, nothing to do with cannibals, I hope. Well, Willard would know—here I am married to what they call a classicist and I don't know the first thing about ancient days. And no, Cynthia, you can't help me one little bit, me and Odessa have got it all so organized you wouldn't believe. If she can just stop her sniffling. I declare, seems like she's more upset over Russ than there's the slightest cause for her to be. First we think we understand all about the colored, and then we turn around for a minute and we don't understand the first thing. And speaking of that, what on earth was Russ doing out on a railroad platform or whatever it was, out there *drinking* with a colored man, even if it was a sergeant in the Army? I just don't believe that, not for one blessed minute. Even if there is a war on, there's just got to have been something funny going on, by which I mean something bad, like that Nigra thought Russ had a lot of money on him."

Only Cynthia observed the quick look, the instant of pure hatred, that flashed across Odessa's face as Dolly went on about Russ and the "colored man." But Cynthia did see it, and she thought, *My God,* no wonder. Dolly forgets that

Odessa is there, or maybe forgets that she's "colored"? No, Dolly could never forget who was colored, although maybe in a way she does; Odessa is just Odessa, not a strong, complicated, and often troubled woman. A Negro woman.

And just why is Odessa so upset over Russ? Even as she wonders this, Cynthia has a stroke of insight: she thinks, Odessa is probably as superstitious as I am, and she thinks Russ's death is a bad sign for Horace, it's Horace she's crying about. She hasn't heard from him for a while, he's out in the Pacific.

When she looks back at Odessa, the hatred of course is gone; Odessa is passing around a tray of beaten biscuits spread with ham, Russ's favorite. When she dies, Cynthia for one split second wonders, will anyone remember that *her* favorite food was oyster stew, from the Oyster Bar in Grand Central Station? Well, Harry will. But so what, what will it matter?

Odessa had paused for a moment near the sideboard, Dolly's most valued "antique," of massive mahogany with walnut trim. "Pre-War." Still holding her big silver platter, Odessa stood there for a moment looking around, checking out who needed more food. Cynthia went over; she touched Odessa's arm in a friendly pat. She said, "Don't worry, Odessa. Things'll be better this year, I'm sure," and she smiled with as much conviction as she could pull together. Her warmth at least was real.

And Odessa smiled back, even as she murmured, "Yes'm."

Cynthia wished that Abigail had come down for the funeral, although she had urged her not to. "Wartime travel, you know," she had said to her daughter. "Someone might ask you, 'Is this trip necessary?' Like all those signs." But she did wish for Abigail and, more fleetingly, she wondered where in hell Derek was.

Curiously, Deirdre too had a fleeting thought of Derek; she thought, Now that I'm widowed, maybe Derek—? But what an evil thought, and with Russ just barely dead, and so terribly, killed by that colored man, probably. She began to cry again—even if Russ hadn't really loved her anymore. And then for him to go off and die in Texas, of all places. That was where the train was when he fell, or that man pushed him or whatever happened. And then they couldn't even get his body home. Or she let herself be talked out of bringing his body home: a lot of conversation with people in charge of transportation, all that, until it got to the point where she was just about told that it'd be unpatriotic for her to insist, Russ not being in the service or anything. So there was the coffin, empty, just weights in it, and Russ still back in Texas. Or the body of Russ was in Texas, decaying there: his immortal soul was up in Heaven, Deirdre had to believe that it was.

More or less accidentally, Melanctha and Graham were standing close to each other—so that everyone could see how much alike they looked. Russ's eyes, and his hair, right there on the both of them. The brother and sister. Never mind all those years when Deirdre first came back to town and pretended that Graham was her brother; he was Russ's son, no doubt in anyone's mind about that anymore. The two of them looked especially alike that afternoon, with their dazed deep eyes, which were Russ's eyes, dark blue, without tears.

Dolly Bigelow, who had drunk too much—as though to

prove her own too often expressed view that women shouldn't ought to drink—Dolly said, "It's just like Russ was right here with us, don't you-all feel it? Drunk as all get out and not really showing he was drunk, not showing anyone the first thing about how he really felt about anything. I'm going to miss Russ a whole lot, I just know that I am, but at the same time I'm not going to know who it is that I'm missing." And then, as unaccountably as a summer storm, tears overwhelmed Dolly—as though she could not stand the rest of her life without Russ Byrd.

Staring at weeping Dolly, Cynthia tried to keep what she felt from showing too apparently on her face, and then she turned away—but not before her eyes had caught the eyes of Odessa, and a look was exchanged between the two of them, between Cynthia and Odessa—a look that was the equivalent of a long conversation, a talk that very probably they would never have, but that would contain all or almost all of their thoughts about Dolly, and about Russ. About Horace, and Harry, and even Derek. Abby, and Nellie. About this beautiful and impossible place in which they both lived.

9

AFTER the death and funeral of Russ, instead of the longed-for arrival of spring, heavy, unrelenting rains set in, crippling and almost drowning the little town of Pinehill. Out in the country, the red clay roads were too slick for cars, and red streams rushed through the gullies of erosion in the fields. Rain and wind flapped the sides of the tarpaper shacks where people out there lived—without floors in their houses, most of them, so that in cold, rainy weather they walked on wet dirt, with cold bare feet. Odessa, who used to live out there, like that, with Horace and all her children, in dreams was still in that tiny house, where the wind whistled in through cracks. Now, waking in the middle of the night with a pressure on her bladder, she would almost reach for the tin pot under the bed—before further waking to remember that this is the Bairds' garage apartment, where she lives, and the bright clean white bathroom is right there, the door almost next to her bed, no need to reach for any pot. But these days she lives alone, no restless Horace thrashing and snorting beside her in the bed, and all the children off now with husbands and wives of their own—all except Nellie, not married and working now over to Raleigh. The tarpaper shack and the red clay roads were still more real to Odessa, though. Her feet were still cold, in spite of the rabbit-fur slippers that Mrs. Baird got for her. The Bairds and their house could vanish like a breath from her life. You can't count on whites to stay the same, and mean the same whenever they talk to you, Odessa knew that, although the Bairds and especially Mrs. Baird, Mrs. Cynthia, seemed much more reliable than most, probably on account of the Bairds' being Yankees and not used to the ways of white folks around these parts. But Mr. Harry could die in the war just as easy as Mr. Russ Byrd could, and *did,* and then where would they put Mrs. Odessa Jones, especially with Horace not around? Horace: she did not let herself think about what could happen and maybe already had to Horace, out there somewhere in the rain, in some rain or other.

"I declare, every colored person in this town has someway sent in word that she's laid up with what they all call 'misery in the laig.' " Dolly's voice for imitating Negro speech was, to Cynthia's Connecticut ear, more like a burlesque of her own Piedmont North Carolina dialect, or whatever it was.

"But the roads," Cynthia objected. "You really can't drive out there."

"Got nothing to do with roads," Dolly snapped. "You think every maid in town's got a car? It's even the ones that walk in here every day, it's like in the rain they all go on some sit-down strike, like the miners. Though with these darkies it's more like a lie-down strike."

Along the phone line, bad feeling between the two women surged high. Cynthia had reacted strongly (badly) to "darkies," not to mention the very idea of those poor women, and men too, being expected to walk into town on those horrible wet clay roads. And Dolly was having familiar thoughts and feelings about how Yankees, as smart as they all thought they were, did not know or understand the first G.D. thing about the colored down here, and the way things are supposed to go. After the war, Dolly thought, things would get back more to normal, the colored back to their normal places, working for folks and showing up like they were meant to do. She was about to explain some of this to Cynthia—or try to, Cynthia could be as stubborn as a mule, for all her Vassar College smarts—when, fortunately for everyone (maybe), the long-distance operator broke in.

"Mrs. Cynthia Baird? Is this Mrs. Baird, at 3871, in Pine-hill? I have an important call for you."

Cynthia's heart jolted, hard and cold, as she braced herself for the news. Somewhere within her a scream broke out: Harry!

As Dolly dithered, "Well, I'll get right off the line. Cynthia, you call me right back now, I'll want to know—"

"Dolly, will you please shut up?"

A loud sniff, and then a louder click, and then a male voice which was *not* the operator's spoke. "Cynthia? Good Christ, the trouble I've had getting through to you, you and your insane Southern lady friend. Listen, I'm in Hilton, and I really need to talk to you. I've got a car, and I'd like to start the drive over right now. I assume that's all right?"

Oh. Derek. Feeling faint, pounded and shaken by too many, too strong emotions, Cynthia said yes, of course—and later wondered what it was that he had asked.

An hour or so after that, an hour during which she drank some tea, and had some of Odessa's good chicken-vegetable soup, Cynthia still was shaken, though now by a new set of fears and anxieties: what was it that Derek needed to talk about so badly that he had an operator cut in, an emergency interruption? Could Derek possibly have some news of Harry, some source?

Rainwater dripped from his hat as Derek removed it, and from his trench coat, which he took back outside to shake off. He said, "Talk about cats and dogs. This is ferocious!" and he smiled and reached for Cynthia, to kiss.

The kiss was more affectionate than passionate, a little hurried. Not lingering—most clearly not a lingering kiss.

So that Cynthia wondered if he had not come, after all, to demand her hand. To forcefully claim her. Which she had seen as the only explanation that offered itself for his haste, his determination.

But right away he told her, "I want to talk to you about Russ. About James Russell Lowell Byrd. It's a very important interview. That you're part of, I mean. Do you think his wife would see me too, and maybe some of his kids? The daughter with the funny name? Maybe tonight, I thought. I don't have a hell of a lot of time."

He had put her through all that distress for questions about Russ? The panic over Harry—and the quite other panic to do with Derek himself? The skein of complicated emotions, both conflicting and intense, had left Cynthia weak and angry. Rather stiffly she asked Derek, "Shall I call Deirdre right now? Is that what you want me to do?"

He gave her a quick look, not acknowledging stiffness on her part, anything wrong. "If you don't mind," he said formally.

On the phone Deirdre said, "Derek McFall? Oh, I'd love to see him, really I would, you tell him that. It's been, let's see, over fifteen years? He was just in our school for that one year." Her voice trailed off, remembering, and then came back. "But today is a bad one for me and Melanctha too. This lawyer's coming over, 'long about five o'clock. So Derek would either have to get here real, real quick, or else make it some other day."

Receiving this message, which Cynthia delivered to him entire, Derek stood up. "Well, that doesn't give me a hell of a lot of choice, does it?" He grinned unconvincingly. "I'm sorry, angel. But I'll be back before you know it."

"You know where the house is?"

"You showed me once, remember? Out in the woods past the Hightower house?"

Did she show Derek that house? Cynthia did not remember such a drive with him, or any conversation about it. Though both must have occurred, to make him set off with such confidence, and so quickly.

What she really—intensely, wrenchingly wondered was: How much had she told Derek about her own connection with Russ? She and Derek tended to drink a fair amount; they did not get drunk, no lurchings about or falls or blackouts. (Cynthia had observed all that behavior in her previous life, in Connecticut, and to some extent in Georgetown, more recently.) But she and Derek drank enough so that the course of an evening, its threads and themes of conversation, sometimes became blurred the next day in Cynthia's mind, not to mention the details and nuances of repeated acts of love, which she would have liked to recall as vividly as possible.

Derek liked a good martini before dinner, and so did Cynthia, something she had discovered with him. And then along with dinner they drank what they called "Dago red," meaning cheap Italian Chianti, which was sold more or less in bulk, in large green bottles. Those dinners, usually cooked by Cynthia, less often taken in restaurants, were marvellous fun, the fun wine-fueled and fueled too by the anticipation of later pleasure, great pleasure in bed.

But what had she said in the course of those hours of heightened, delighted conversation? Drink made Cynthia voluble, she knew that, profligate with confidences, even confessions. Like a drunken Santa Claus, she bestowed bits of gossip plus some intimate glimpses of herself—all gifts. And what had she told Derek?

If Deirdre's lawyer was coming at five, Derek should be back at Cynthia's by five-fifteen or so, she thought, but then she further thought: Deirdre said "long about five," which can mean almost any time at all, in the long rainy, chilling evening.

The rain made a walk impractical for Cynthia—and Derek might always come while she was out. She turned on the radio but something was wrong, only static came across—or bombs; it had the sound of a bombardment. Outside everything dripped, the dark thick heavy leaves of the rhododendron, long pine needles, and the bare black branches of winter trees—as though spring had been frightened backward by the rain, retreating into invisibility.

Derek got back to Cynthia's house at five after seven. He said, "Christ, the lawyer just got there. And it seemed sort of rude to leave before he did."

Wanting to say, How about rude to me? Cynthia instead asked how it went. Did he get what he wanted to know from Deirdre and Melanctha?

Melanctha was not there, Derek told her, he did not know where Melanctha was. And yes, Deirdre had talked a lot, a surprising amount. "Generous" was how Derek described it.

She talked about her son, about Graham. Did Cynthia know that, that he was really her son, not her brother?

"Oh, we all figured that one out sometime back," despite herself Cynthia snapped. "He's the dead spit of Russ, as they say around here. Have you seen him?"

"No, but I never really met Russ either. Deirdre thinks I did, but I'm sure I'd remember." He smiled, not drunkenly but in a way that told Cynthia that he had had a few drinks with Deirdre—Deirdre the new widow—as they raked over her life with Russ.

One of Cynthia's reactions to this perception—shared drinks, a long happy time—was to think, Then why should I tell him a goddam thing? Who gives a damn about his lousy article? I for sure don't.

Derek said, "How about dinner? You feel like fixing a sandwich here, or would you rather go out?"

"Out would be better, I think."

The Pinehill Hotel, which catered to visiting parents and alumni, as well as unwary travellers, served stiffly formal dinners, overpriced and not very well cooked, in a too bright dining room. The only good thing there was the plenitude of fresh raw oysters, which were reliably great—if you liked raw oysters, which both Cynthia and Derek very much did.

The only other out-for-dinner possibility near Pinehill was a run-down barbecue roadhouse, about seven miles off, called The Pines. Much favored by students, it was known for serving beer to anyone at almost any hour—and for the hottest, possibly messiest barbecue for miles around. They chose The Pines, or rather, Derek did.

The drive out there seemed long, down the winding wet gray-white concrete highway, between high red clay embankments—now shining, wet, and slick—and past dark dim wet woods. And his choice of The Pines struck Cynthia as both perverse and slightly hostile; neither she nor Derek was a big fan of barbecue, and the students there tended to be rowdy, noisy. As they walked in, they were instantly assailed by smoke and strong smells of pork and tomato and spice.

"Not the greatest place for an interview," was Derek's comment.

Is that why they were there? Cynthia murmured, "Oh dear, I'm afraid not," in a helpless, innocent way which she knew to be unconvincing, and she looked up and smiled at him. They sat across from each other in a high-backed, hard-seated booth, where the streaky table smelled of beer and of catsup. Officially, The Pines served only beer, but if you knew what to say and paid enough you could get thick coffee mugs of rotgut bourbon, which is what they did.

What she was feeling as they sat there—in the cave of jukebox noise and student noise and the smells of everything, everyone there—Cynthia knew to be crazy, this blood-racing frenzy of jealousy and suspicion. For in a practical way (Cynthia prided herself on practicality), she wondered how much or indeed what at all could have gone on between Deirdre and Derek? (She was even alarmed by the alliteration of their names.) In Russ's house, as they waited for a lawyer who might have shown up at any minute—as well as, possibly, Melanctha? But crazy or not, Cynthia did feel that frenzy, that race of blood, and tightness in her chest.

At a table not far from theirs a group of students began to sing. "Violate me, in violet time, In the vilest way that you know! Rape me, ravage me, brutally savagely—"

Cynthia shuddered. "What a dreadful song, really."

Derek leaned forward. "You knew Russ pretty well?"

As though she had planned a speech, Cynthia told him,

"Actually hardly at all. Although"—and she laughed a little, a girlish, confessional laugh—"I had a sort of distant crush on him, and that's one of the reasons we moved to Pinehill in the first place. I'd read a lot of his poetry. Honestly, I even knew a lot of it by heart." She repeated the laugh. "But the times we met—well, I felt shy. I guess he was sort of shy too. Also, I guess people have told you, he drank quite a lot."

But: had someone told Derek otherwise, about her and Russ? Could someone have hinted anything of the sort? Could Russ—this was a horrid, unlikely, but possible speculation—could Russ have said anything to Deirdre, a marital confession? "Darling, it didn't mean anything, I just fell into it, and she's rather aggressive." Surely not, Russ didn't talk like that; still, Cynthia inwardly quailed and told herself that it would not have happened, given Russ's strict Southern notions of honor—*unless* two of those notions came into conflict, I-must-not-tell-anyone pitted against I-should-tell-my-wife-everything. The latter was most hard to imagine, though—Russ telling anyone everything.

Derek, sounding irritated, broke into her somewhat complicated stream of thoughts. "Of course he drank a lot. Russ was drunk when he died, remember? He couldn't hold his liquor, as they say down here."

Now the singing group was doing "The Ship Titanic": ". . . husbands and wives, little children lost their lives. It was sa-ad when that great ship went down."

Another horrible song. "What will happen to that Negro sergeant, do you think?" asked Cynthia.

Derek frowned. "The evidence against him is that he had a lot of money in his billfold. Close to a thousand. He said he'd cashed his discharge check in L.A., but still, it doesn't look good."

"Why not? 'Colored' sergeants aren't supposed to go around with a lot of money?"

Derek ignored her. "The bad part is, Russ's billfold was just about empty. Just a couple of single dollar bills."

"But that's just like Russ. He always went around with no money on him. It was sort of an affectation. Part of his pose, I'm just a poor country boy."

"I don't think they'd take that into account. Not in the current climate."

"But—but that's totally unfair. Russ wasn't in good shape. He could just have had a heart attack, like that man in the Deke House. No one said anything about Melanctha killing *him.*"

"No—"

"And Russ would never pick a fight, especially not with a Negro man he didn't even know. That just wasn't in him." Cynthia spoke more passionately than she had meant to.

Which Derek caught. "Come on, you said you hardly knew him."

She forced a giddy laugh. "My instincts are very quick and accurate." But then very seriously she asked him, "Can't you do anything?"

"To help this Negro sergeant I've never met?—when I never met Russ Byrd either, and can hardly attest to his good character? Christ, Cynthia, sometimes—"

In an unfriendly way, they stared at each other across the booth. Derek reached for his mug as Cynthia thought, feared, that he could get really drunk.

The barbecue sandwiches that they had both forgotten arrived. "Here y'are, folks," announced the grinning, small bald red-faced waiter—at whom Derek glared.

Derek said, "I never saw anything so repulsive in my life."

The waiter blinked, then recovered his grin. "Well, I always say it takes all kinds," he said before he scuttled away.

The waiter didn't make those sandwiches, was Cynthia's first thought; why take it out on him?

Her second was from ten to fifteen minutes back; she thought, Why *not* help a Negro sergeant you've never met, if he's being unjustly accused? You're a reporter, and you could help. Harry would, if he could, and I would, especially if I were a lawyer.

She took a dutiful bite of her sandwich, which was as bad as it looked. Chewing, trying to swallow, Cynthia imagined her own clean warm quiet kitchen, herself alone there, eating a couple of nice fresh scrambled eggs.

Looking across at Derek, she observed that he was doing everything in slow motion, trying for control, or at least to look controlled.

Too drunk to drive, she thought, and she experienced one long moment of panic before she got to her feet and said, "Come on, I'll drive us home." Tactfully adding, "You look tired."

"This is the worst sandwich," he muttered, but at the same time, surprisingly, he got up, reaching into his pocket, and handed her the keys—her keys, they had come in her car. "You're right," he told her. "Let's get out of here."

And they started back, not talking, as Cynthia concentrated on the drive in the dark and increasing rain. Among other things, she was thinking that Derek was probably unaware of her plan, which was to drop him off at the Pinehill Hotel.

Which is what she did—before going home to her scrambled eggs and relative peace, a peace somewhat troubled by persistent, anxious thoughts of Derek's hours with Deirdre—

and of the so far unknown Negro sergeant, unhappily with Russ when he died. And who was now being held in jail for questioning, in Texas. Her own raging sense of injustice kept Cynthia awake for hours, as she listened to rain on her roof—ordinarily a soothing, soporific sound, but tonight it sounded threatening, even accusatory: why didn't she go and help? And what on earth was she doing with Derek in the first place?

She was able to salvage some of her pride, at least, by replaying in her mind the small scene of her leaving Derek at the hotel. For she had done just that, left him there. She just reached for the door for him to get out. No thanks for the barbecue (certainly not). No gesture or good-night kiss (most certainly not). She left him there and she drove off into the rain, which seemed appropriate (in some B-movie way).

10

"HARRY!" Cynthia shouted into the telephone. Awakened at 3 a.m. by an operator who asked her name, then announced an overseas call, she had at first thought it must be some terrible, cruel joke—or, much worse, some terrible news of Harry. But then, though wavering and distorted, came Harry's voice.

"Baby, did I wake you? I got this chance to call you, so I didn't even calculate the time. What time is it there?"

"About three. But, Harry, this is marvelous, how are—?"

"Baby, I can't hear you either. You're okay?"

His voice came back and forth, in and out of focus, as though tossed on all those monstrous black Atlantic waves, then strung along wires and swaying tall poles all across the gigantic continent.

She shouted, "I'm fine! So is Abby, she loves it at Swarthmore, and I think she's in love with a nice boy, a physicist." And then, irrelevantly, "Russ died. Russ Byrd?"

"A physicist—isn't he too old for Abby? Not Oppenheimer?" She thought she heard him laugh.

"Oh no, he's about her age, just a little older."

"Russ had a heart attack?"

"I think so, but he was out on the platform of a train with

this Negro soldier—a sergeant, actually—so it's all going to be investigated. In Texas. Some people of course think that the sergeant knocked him down and robbed him. There'll be a trial, I'd even like to go—"

"Baby, darling Cynthia, I can't hear a word you're saying. Come back, I miss you!"

"*You* come back, I miss *you.*"

"Now I can't hear you at all, are you gone back to sleep? Christ, I wish I were there—"

"Harry, where are you?"

"We'd better hang up, I can't hear a fucking thing—"

Minutes later, as Cynthia curled up in her bed, alone, she thanked God that she was alone, no Derek at her side: Harry would somehow have felt that, felt some unfamiliar constraint, even guilt. But then she thought, It's not even God that I have to thank, it's myself; nevertheless, she retained a semi-superstitious gratitude—to fate. After all, she had tried to bargain with God, or whoever, about the safety of Harry, and so far it looked as though he, or *He,* would keep his side of the bargain.

The circumstances of Russ's death indeed were, as Cynthia had said to Harry, an awful mess. The fact of its taking place in a small town in East Texas was, as many observed, very unfortunate. In that particular town, there had already been a certain amount of "trouble"—trouble including a couple of razor fights and more than a couple of rock-throwing riots, all having to do with the occasional presence of Negro soldiers, many of whom were from the North, Detroit or someplace like that, and not used to Southern ways.

The local paper announced that in the "sudden death" of

the "promising" Southern poet, novelist, and playwright, James Russell Lowell Byrd, "foul play" was suspected, thus getting almost everything wrong, including the list of his children: nine, instead of the actual seven, and SallyJane Caldwell Byrd as the surviving wife, instead of Deirdre. The fact that the coroner had announced a heart attack was not mentioned.

As Dolly Bigelow put it, "However can they call a man of Russ Byrd's age promising? Promising what? More children? You reckon he had some more that we don't even know about, maybe out there in Hollywood? Like those novels that he was supposed to be the author of. You reckon they got him confused with Jimmy Hightower?" But Dolly too thought something was wrong. "Something suspicious, Russ just dying like that, out there with that colored soldier, and no money on him. And the colored soldier with a whole big wad on him, upwards of one hundred dollars, the way I heard it."

The "colored soldier" was actually Edward Faulkner, from Roxbury, Massachusetts, at twenty-eight one of the youngest Negro sergeants in the Army. And the dispute in Texas seemed to be, at first, about whether a civil or a military team should investigate—which was soon settled. Since he had been discharged, the Army could not try him.

All this came through to Pinehill in snippets, small paragraphs wedged in among the more important pieces of real news, about the war. News from Leningrad, from the Marshall and Solomon Islands, from the Ukraine and Crimea.

Since Deirdre was away, no one knew what she thought about anything.

. . .

Having wondered and worried about Melanctha, Cynthia at last decided simply to call her. If Melanctha didn't want to talk or to be seen, she could say so.

But what Melanctha said was, "Tea? I'd really like that. No, don't come for me. I can drive Russ's car."

"Russ." Had she ever called him Daddy, or Father? Cynthia couldn't remember. In any case, it was strange, very strange, to see what had been Russ's old dark green Chevy pull into her driveway, and to watch the brisk emergence of Melanctha, in a new blue coat.

"She sure do favor him," murmured Odessa, also watching, at Cynthia's side; they both stood near a window in the front of the house.

"The dead spit, as Dolly would say. Or almost," Cynthia murmured in return. And both women smiled, acknowledging mutual affection as well as the tacitly agreed on foolishness of Dolly.

Once inside the house, though, divested of her coat and sitting with the tea that Odessa almost immediately brought in, Melanctha looked less like Russ and more like an extremely pretty, almost beautiful girl—herself, pale and somewhat strained (her mouth especially showed strain, in its compression, tight corners); her eyes looked larger, a darker blue, and intense—hers were passionate eyes. Too intense, too passionate, Cynthia judged. That girl will have a lot of trouble; well, she already has. Melanctha's hair was pulled back smoothly (Cynthia approved of this), the thick curls (Russ's curls) all under control.

After some preliminary weather conversation—they agreed that the rain seemed ended, spring was almost there—Cynthia gently inquired, "Well, how're you doing, generally? You're feeling okay?"

"I'm really upset—" Melanctha flushed, and looked down. "I mean of course about Russ, but about that Negro, the sergeant. Those Texas people are saying all this terrible stuff, and there isn't anything anyone can do. Especially me, everyone says. Russ's lawyer—I guess he's my lawyer now—said for me to go down there or even call would be 'most unbecoming.' Can you imagine? Most unbecoming, when we're talking about a man who may be on trial for something he absolutely did not do."

The flush on her face was attractive, as was the animation with which Melanctha spoke. Still, her concentrated excitement made Cynthia uneasy—it seemed so clearly a cover for darker, deeper feelings, related to Russ.

"Actually," Melanctha confessed, "I did call one of the papers down there, and—you won't believe this—he said they didn't need any 'outside agitators.' God, what does he think I am, a Russian Communist?"

"Probably it'll all just die down, don't you think?"

"But, Cynthia, they could do something terrible to him, and it all seems like my fault, somehow."

"Melanctha, please, come on. Your fault? It's not even Russ's fault, really."

"Oh, I know." Suddenly all Melanctha's animation and the flush had gone, and she looked pale and sad and tired. "But in a larger sense, you know what I mean?"

Partly because she didn't know where to go with this conversation, Cynthia asked, "How's Deirdre?"

"She's gone to California, I don't know for how long." Melanctha's tone was that of someone talking about a rather distant acquaintance. But then in quite another voice she said, "I miss Abby, you know? There's all this stuff I could say to her."

"Why don't you call her? I do, all the time."

"God, I'm so dumb, I didn't even think—"

"I'll write down her number for you."

Getting up, going into the breakfast room for a notepad and pencil, Cynthia was thinking: Deirdre in California—could she be meeting Derek there? She had not heard from him since the day after she had let him off at the hotel, which was not unusual; he was not given to friendly staying-in-touch phone calls. But now she wondered, Could he be in California? And at the same time she chided herself: Deirdre's father's in California; it was Russ who went to California a lot, not Derek—and you, Cynthia, are nuts; come on, pull yourself together.

Handing the pencilled slip to Melanctha, she told her, "Abby seems to be out a lot of the time, though. Probably studying in the library, don't you think?" And she laughed, intending complicity.

Melanctha barely smiled before she said, very seriously, "I think this boy she knows sounds really nice. Joseph. His father's a big director, or producer, or something, and he sort of knew Russ, but I don't think they liked each other. Russ said he was a Communist." She hesitated. "I don't even know any Communists, do you? Unless, girls at Radcliffe I didn't know about, or at Harvard. I guess there were some."

"I'm not really sure I want to know Communists." Cynthia had not meant to sound so prudish, and she amended, "What I mean is, I know so little about Communism, really. Or for that matter about this boy, this Joseph."

"I'm going to call Abby tonight," Melanctha said. She had seemingly lost interest in Communists, or in Cynthia.

But Cynthia had a pleasant sense of having cheered her, at least a little.

. . .

In fact, the very next day Melanctha called, and in very high spirits. "I got Abby! She was right there, honestly, it sounded like the next room. I told her all about Russ and the Negro sergeant, and she said she'd talk to Joseph's parents, she's going to see them this weekend, and they're very interested in things like that, race relations and all. They have some committee."

"Have you heard from Deirdre?"

"Yes, she called last night, she sounds fine. Said she had some old friends out there, or something."

"Oh, well, that's nice."

"Old friends" did not necessarily mean Derek; in fact, why on earth should it mean him? Why does Cynthia even imagine that Derek is in California?

Derek and Deirdre spend an hour or so together, probably just talking, expecting her lawyer to arrive at any minute. Cynthia does not hear from Derek, and Melanctha says that Deirdre is in California. None of these known facts add up to anything positive, or even suggestive—except to Cynthia, who began to think that she was truly nuts.

Not being with Harry is not good for me, she thought—her most sensible conclusion for some time.

"They're really interested, the Marcuses," Melanctha told Cynthia. "I think they'll get involved, in some way." She was describing her most recent conversation with Abby, after Abby's weekend in New York with Joseph's family. Cynthia had talked to Abby too, and they had discussed the Marcuses, but had talked mostly about New York, how much Abby liked it there.

For some reason the notion of the Marcuses' involvement in the case—if there was to be a case—of Russ and the sergeant made Cynthia uneasy, and her attention wandered as Melanctha continued, intensely, about the Marcuses and the sergeant, Sergeant Edward Faulkner.

Outside the big living-room window, in a broad circle on the lawn, the daffodils were just coming into bloom, brave yellow flags on their tall green waving stalks. Cynthia, aided by Odessa, had planted them in the fall. "Don't matter 'bout too close together, Horace always say that," Odessa had advised, and she—she and Horace—had been right. In a few weeks there would be a foam of yellow there, the effect was of bounty, generosity. And then again next year, at this same time, more daffodils. And eventually Harry would be home to see them.

And Abigail, who said she was coming home soon and bringing Joseph—probably.

"Deirdre'll be back tomorrow, I think," said Melanctha, a few days later.

"Where in California has she been?"

"San Francisco, mostly. She says it's beautiful there."

As Derek used to say, "San Francisco is really beautiful." Inwardly quailing as she thought and remembered this, at the same time Cynthia managed to tell herself, to remember that Derek had also said that Venice was beautiful, and Paris, and Istanbul—and a town in Mexico with an impossible name: Oaxaca. Why should he be in San Francisco, with Deirdre, any more than in any of those places—or for that matter, in London, with Harry?

Some terrific lawyer, she said to herself *again,* as she tried to concentrate on Melanctha.

Melanctha, who was saying, ". . . that operation you told me about?"

Operation? Cynthia must have looked very blank, for Melanctha then explained, "You know, you had this friend, and she thought her breasts were too big?" (Those last words came out in an embarrassed rush.)

"Oh yes. Buffy Guggenheim, I think."

"Well, I thought about it a lot, and right now I could do it if I wanted to. You know, I got this money from Russ." She looked away, as much embarrassed by money as she was by her breasts, it seemed. "And I just don't think I will. Or anyway not now. I basically don't like the idea of it, you know what I mean? I'd rather give the money to someone. Maybe that Ed Faulkner. You understand?"

"Of course I do. I wouldn't like it either, I don't think. Even just getting your face done—and people look so terrible."

"I heard that Brenda Frazier had it done on her legs," surprisingly said Melanctha. "As a matter of fact it was Abby, she told me that."

"Well—really—"

"And I'm going back to Radcliffe next week," announced Melanctha, somewhat defiantly. "Abby and I plan to get together in New York sometime soon. I could even fly! I never have, it could be wonderful."

"I'm sure—" Cynthia had found all this darting about by Melanctha more than a little hard to follow, from Deirdre (and, in Cynthia's own mind, Derek) to the Marcuses, the

Negro sergeant, Russ, breast reduction surgery, Brenda Frazier's legs, and to flying to Radcliffe.

"Russ flew sometimes. He liked it, I think," said Melanctha. And she continued, as though to herself, "I think all those long cross-country trips in the big car depressed him. With my mother and all of us. I'm sure we acted up. I think the time he ran over the pig and it smelled so horrible—that's all I remember, the smell, and I do remember that Russ said, 'Pig shit'—what a shock! Anyway, I think that trip was the end of something for him. Maybe flying could help him think it all never happened."

"Maybe," Cynthia murmured in soft agreement, while to herself she added: Probably, Russ was so many different people, really, and flying up high he could forget the husband-father selves, and just be that. A high flyer.

11

HAVING always thought of sex as something that he would probably not be good at, Joseph Marcus was astounded at the bountiful, splendid success of doing it with lovely Abby Baird, who was in many ways the sort of girl with whom he had imagined himself a failure: a beautiful blond gentile from both Connecticut and the South. However, she was also smart, extremely smart, which did not concur with his failure-fantasy picture. But even the very first time, which she later confessed was her first time too, it was she who reached for his cock and thrust it so easily, slippingly inside herself. He came instantly, incredibly (Christ! No one had said it would be like that), but so did she, signalling her pleasure with a small high cry that he came to know, and to cherish.

They did it again several times that afternoon, sweatily, in the bright December sunlight that lay across his narrow dormitory bed—and afterwards almost every chance they got, sometimes in her room, sometimes on weekends at his parents' place in New York, where they were thoughtfully, tactfully put in adjoining rooms, what had been the maids' quarters up on the top floor. (His parents' knowing looks, just short of insinuation, were mildly annoying to Joseph, but what the hell, it was better than some sort of Republican puritanism, hypocrisy, he supposed, although sometimes he wondered.)

Logically—and Joseph was on the whole a very logical person—he might have been expected to conclude from his experiences with Abby that in a general way he was great at sex, "really a stud in the sack," as some guys he knew used to put it, and that he should try it out with lots more girls, more Episcopal blondes, and dark prim Jewish girls, and maybe a few wild Italian Catholics. But Joseph did not think this; in fact he reached an opposite conclusion, which was that sex with Abby was superior, why bother with anyone else? Besides, once that part of his life was settled, for good, all the rest of his attention and energy would be freed for work.

Joseph had spent a lot of his early years, especially summers, in various left-wing family resorts, and in those days no one worried much about what children were exposed to, in terms of conversations, theories, ideas. Thus Joseph and Susan, the young Marcus children, were always listening to long soul-searchings, analyses, and questionings as to marriages and love affairs, along with political speculation and theorizing (could rumors of the Moscow trials be true?). Joseph's picture of himself as a young child was of a skinny, tall, dark, bare-kneed boy, sitting at the back edge of a campfire circle, next to Susan, who slept, while the grown-ups, with their guitars, sang Spanish Civil War songs, songs from the Lincoln Brigade, and Spanish folk songs, often followed by heavy, mournful "Negro spirituals," an occasional Negro blues, late at night, in the cooling New England lakeside air.

Joseph's sexiest pre-Abby experiences had been at those camps, beside those lakes. He and a small succession of girls, not more than one a summer, would be out there on a blanket, or sometimes just sand, kissing and striving against each other. But Joseph's lust-driven fingers were always stopped by those quick-handed girls with their iron wrists. And the one time that he reasonably asked, "What's so much worse about touching than what we're already doing?" he was flatly rebuked for his logic by a buxom blond girl who after that refused even to kiss him anymore.

He was supposed to talk about love to these girls, Joseph knew that, but all that kind of talk bored him silly, as did the things the grown-ups talked about; both then and later in life emotional conversations struck him as the most total waste of energy. He thought that might explain his own choice of physics as a field of concentration—which was about as far as he got with introspection. His sister, Susan, reacted more or less oppositely: she enjoyed a lifelong preoccupation with the vagaries of her own and almost anyone else's mind; she was always happy to examine and question the motives and forces underlying and propelling anyone's love and/or work.

The second half of the twentieth century, Joseph believed—and they were almost at it—would contain remarkable, in fact stupendous developments in his chosen field. The release of atomic energy, just for starters. Its peacetime use. He imagined for himself a rather spare, dedicated life: a good lab to work in with similarly dedicated colleagues, and probably students; a book-lined, large-windowed apartment, full of music, especially Schubert and Brahms; outdoor weekends, mountain hiking and swimming—and all this he now envisioned himself doing with Abigail, plus all those nights of screwing. Infinite sex.

He only wished his parents would leave them alone. Sylvia and Dan Marcus were much too "happy about Abigail"; they even said so, often. It was as though they had feared that Joseph would never have a girlfriend, that he would die a virgin or turn out to be some kind of a queer. He had overheard his mother on the phone (she was not good at lowering her voice): "Joseph always has his nose in at least five books. Of course we're glad that he's so brilliant, we wouldn't know what to do with an all-American baseball kind of child. But I do wish he'd at least give the girls a chance. Carol Goldman has this adorable niece at Bennington who thinks Joseph is really cute. Well, that's not exactly the word I'd use for him, but still—"

What a bunch of bullshit.

He had not yet really heard his mother's phone pronouncements on the subject of him and Abby Baird, but he could all too easily imagine: "Well, it's the darlingest thing, and they think we don't know but they actually sleep together. And she's the nicest girl, and very progressive, actually, especially considering her background, originally from Connecticut and then for years in some little college town in the South that I never heard of. Pinehill? No, of course she's not Jewish, and I guess that could be a problem, but I understand that her best friend in Connecticut was this handsome Negro boy who's now at Harvard. His father was a janitor, so that shows something about Abby, don't you think? Well, now our Susie seems to have the biggest crush on him—" Appalling, Joseph thought, the predictability of his parents. Their views of almost any given issue. He almost forgot that he had not really overheard those words, just made them up.

Joseph's sense of predictability extended to and included his early view of his parents' Communism. They and their Party friends thought that anything Jewish, Russian, or having to do with Negroes was good, was *right,* "progressive." Most white Protestants, especially from New England or the South, were suspect—probably bad, reactionary, and (a word used too often) potentially Fascist. Thus, the Negro Army sergeant who had been out on the platform of the train, smoking and drinking with Russ—that Negro had been a good and decent man, and Russ, who somehow got himself dead, was bad.

Joseph could too easily imagine the Paul Robeson benefit concerts, Josh White, all the old reliable crew. He could not help a certain respect for singers, great performers like Marian Anderson, Louis Armstrong—who were never used in that way. Who retained more autonomy, more dignity—Joseph thought. He wondered how Abby saw all this; they would have to talk about it. Between all this sex and then trying to study, their conversation time had really been whittled down.

But: Edward Faulkner, the Negro sergeant from Roxbury, Mass. Joseph continued to have worrying thoughts about this unknown man.

Having a great crush on someone because he is both extremely handsome *and* a Negro is pretty stupid, Susan Marcus perfectly well knows. Besides, she barely knows Ben Davis, has only met him a couple of times. Thinking she is in love with Ben Davis is like something Sylvia, her mother, might have done—Sylvia as a young Communist girl at NYU, about a hundred years ago. Nevertheless, there it is, what she feels about Ben Davis can only be described as a sizeable crush. A couple of weeks ago, at the Downbeat, on Fifty-second Street, Susan heard Sarah Vaughn singing, "I've Got a Crush on You," and her heart had filled with images of Ben, although she was with a perfectly nice boy from Swarthmore, Herb Kaufman, who seemed to have at least a small crush on her: he kept asking her out, and taking her places, although she refused even to really kiss him. Herb grew up just a couple of blocks away, on East Twelfth Street, but they went to different schools: Susan along with Joseph to the Little Red Schoolhouse, whereas Herb went to Dalton, and then on to Andover. And his parents, both doctors, were not political—which these days meant reactionary, Susan's father, Dan, had explained. "Inaction is a form of action, in desperate times," he said. "A recent lesson from Nazi Germany, among others."

Susan was very pleased about her brother and Abigail Baird; she liked Abigail very much, and also this made Abigail unavailable to Ben, in that way. Abby had told her over and over that she and Ben were *friends,* never anything to do with boyfriend-girlfriend stuff, no doctor games when they were little children, even. So there was only Melanctha Byrd up at Radcliffe to worry about, and so far Ben and Melanctha had not even met, Abby said. Not that there weren't several hundred other terrific girls at Radcliffe.

Susan had not met Melanctha either. Abby talked about her, saying how much she liked her, but always sounding a little worried as she said this. Abby had a snapshot of Melanctha struck in her mirror: a pretty girl with dark curly hair, in a bathing suit, thin arms crossed over her chest, although she was smiling. "She's very self-conscious about her breasts," Abby had explained. "I think she has a real inferiority complex, and I can't see why. I mean she's pretty and very smart, and her father's famous and successful, I mean he was. I guess she was pretty upset about her father's death, but you know, parents die."

"I couldn't stand it if mine did," Susan said very quickly—

next thinking that in many ways her life would be simpler without Sylvia around. She had a very brief vision of herself at her mother's funeral, all in black, of course, and a new hat with a dotted veil, and she would cry a lot, and Ben would come, and he would take her in his arms.

She had had a dream one night about the death of the unknown Russell Byrd—well, her father knew him but not very well. In the dream it was Ben who was a sergeant in the Army, and accused of killing Mr. Byrd—and she, Susan Marcus, now a lawyer, tall and thin, in black—she, Susan, defended Ben.

Sylvia and Dan Marcus liked to hear their children's dreams; dream-recounting in as much detail as possible was an activity they both encouraged at breakfast. Susan had never enjoyed this much; her dreams were often embarrassing, and stupid. Dreams of flying, of swimming, of towers and steeples, all things that made her parents smile in a preening, knowing, "Freudian" way. No explanations necessary. Whereas Joseph's dreams were interesting, all of them, elaborate and fantastic, colorful—so marvelous in fact that at last everyone, including Susan, caught on to the fact that he made them up. "You don't want to be a physicist, you want to be a screenwriter," pronounced Dan Marcus, very annoyed. He didn't like to be teased, and he hated screenwriters—"a bunch of Southern drunks, most of them. No-good-niks. Except of course for a few of the comrades."

All too easily, Susan could hear the parental verdict on this dream. "So interesting, you conflate—or perhaps 'confuse' is the better word—two young and handsome Negro men, and turn the younger and more successful into a victim, and yourself into the avenging heroine. Hellman would die of envy, you should send it along to her."

It was partly to get away from her parents that Susan spent so much New York–weekend time alone in her room, listening to records or to the radio. Mooning around to music, as her mother put it. But Susan loved that music, all of it, big bands and small combos, the saxes and trombones, clarinets and drums—and especially the singers, and their songs. The words. The deep purple serenade in blue, the true love it had to be you. Frank Sinatra and Ella, Billie Holiday, Louis Armstrong, Trummy Young and Sarah; she loved them all, they all sang directly to her. She loved the Negro ones more, she felt. (Except for Frank when he sang "This Love of Mine.") When Billie sang, Susan *was* Billie. Billie singing her heart out to Benny Davis.

Even when Susan was home for weekends, sometimes with Joseph and Abby, sometimes not, her parents were out a lot. They had all their meetings, discussion groups, committees. Which was perfectly fine with Susan; after all the racket of a Swarthmore dorm, she liked the big apartment to herself. To play her records in. To moon around to music.

What made it even better was a recent discovery of Susan's, which was wine. There was always some in the icebox, some special stuff that her father liked with dessert, sometimes. Château d'Yquem. They drank tiny sips from tiny cut-glass glasses. They would have fits if they knew that Susan liked it too, in a larger glass. By herself. And she is the last person they would suspect, since she has always refused it at dinner. "I hate that sweet stuff." But just to be safe she puts some water in the bottle, a little, enough to keep the level up. And if they noticed anything they would never accuse the cook, not Anna, a Polish refugee to whom they all had to be extra nice, and understanding. Anna had a terrible time when Hitler came into Poland.

The wine made the music better and better for Susan, lying there, hearing it. She felt the music in her blood, in all her veins and nerves. As Ella sang, "Instead of making conversation, Make love to me, my darling—" Susan felt herself a beautiful grown woman, in a spotlight, singing to her lover, who was far out in the audience. Benny Davis.

One Sunday afternoon when no one was there, her parents at some benefit concert up in Woodstock and Anna off, Susan sipped through her usual small glass of wine, and found it even better than usual, and the music even better, a new record by Dinah Shore. "I'm through with love . . . For I must have you or no one, and so I'm through—"

She got herself another little glassful.

Drinking that one, listening to Trummy Young as he sang "Margie," with Jimmy Lunceford—"I'll tell the world I love you, Don't forget you're oh-oh promised to me—" Susan felt even better, more one with the music; the music and the beat were both inside and all over her.

When the phone rang, she considered not answering it; she did not need to hear that her parents would be a couple of hours late getting home; they were almost always held up at these Party things, one way or another. But if she didn't answer she would have to explain, to answer questions.

"Hello?"

"Hello." The man's voice paused uncertainly. "I wondered if Joseph's there. He and Abby Baird. This is Benjamin Davis, and I thought—"

"Ben!" Despite herself, despite knowledge that she shouldn't, Susan shouted his name. It was too much for her, his calling in the midst of all her music, her wild thoughts of him.

He said, "I just happened to be in your neighborhood, and Joseph said he might—"

"Oh, they could be here later on." As far as Susan knew, this was entirely untrue. "So come on over, I'd love to see you." *True.* She laughed. "I forgot to say, this is Susan."

He laughed too. "I thought you might be. Well, swell. I'll be right along."

In the next ten or so minutes, before the doorbell announced "Benjamin Davis," Sarah managed to wash out her wineglass and brush her teeth, comb her hair, and put on fresh powder and lipstick.

He was so tall! Susan, at the door, looked up at Ben's thick black eyebrows, his large strong nose and wide, heavy-lipped mouth. His very white teeth. If you don't kiss me I'll die, she thought and longed to say—but not quite yet.

Instead she said, a little breathless but still in control, "How about a beer?"

"Sounds good. Uh, you think Abby and Joseph will be along soon?"

"I think so. I was just listening to some music. Do you like Sarah Vaughn?"

"Yes, she's nice." He smiled. He was wearing a pale brown V-neck sweater, so beautiful with his dark brown skin, his beautiful smooth skin.

Giddily, Susan brought in two glasses and a large bottle on a tray, which she placed on the coffee table.

"Here, let me." Benjamin (Benny? Ben?) opened the bottle and held the tall glasses at a slant, the way you're supposed to do with beer, as he poured. He sipped, leaned back, and said to her, "This tastes good. Today is a warm one for March, isn't it?"

Susan's first gulp of beer hit her stomach heavily. An inner voice cautioned her to stop right then, maybe go out into the kitchen and spit it out, but another inner adviser told her that maybe if she drank a lot more, very soon, she would be all right. Hearing only the second voice, Susan swallowed as much as fast as she could. She did not feel all right.

Reaching forward with both hands to the table, she grasped its smooth cold edge. Wanting to say, I may die—she said instead, "If you don't kiss me, I may die," although at that moment kissing was the very last thing she wanted.

Ben stood up, bent toward her, and very lightly, very gently brushed his mouth across her forehead, and then he walked out of the room.

Susan thought she might die, such violence in her stomach, now rising to her head.

From somewhere she heard water running, and then Ben was back with a cold wet dishcloth, which he held against her forehead. As he said, "You must be allergic to beer, I never saw anyone—"

Not sure that she could make it to the bathroom, Susan nevertheless lurched to her feet and started in that direction.

She made it just in time to squat over the toilet bowl, praying for death, and for Ben just to go away—or, preferably, by some magic, not to have been there at all.

But he was still there, still standing but seeming to waver before her eyes as he said, or she thought he said, "I think you should go and lie down. Take a couple of aspirin on the way." He added, "Tell Joseph I came by, and hello to your folks—"

And then he was gone. Benjamin, who perhaps had not been there at all, leaving Susan alone and dying of love, or something. Truly and madly in love with beautiful Ben, and about to die.

Alone in her own bed.

12

THE day that President Roosevelt died, the twelfth of April, 1945, was an ugly day all around; Dolly Bigelow thought it was the ugliest spring day she'd ever seen. It was hot, too hot for that season, and the sky was yellow, darkish, like it was fixing to rain, but it never did, all morning. And all the new leaves that a couple of days ago had looked so pretty and fresh and green now looked real limp, and sick. Unnatural. Even the loveliest roses in her garden, the Queen Reginas, seemed to droop on their stems, and out in the woods, beyond the garage and the toolshed and the clotheslines, the dogwood, which was always so fresh and white, looked gray. Later, remembering that day, Dolly thought maybe she was exaggerating the awful look and feel of it, but no, it had been a terrible day all around. She was sure of that.

It was Odessa who told her about Mr. Roosevelt—well, wouldn't you know. Odessa, big as life, walking into the kitchen along about two in the afternoon, not ever a good time of day for anything in Dolly's experience, not unless you can take a good nap—but the very word "nap" made her think of something she would *not* think of (something with Russ, long ago). Anyway, two was the time Odessa was supposed to come, when she was due, but something about the way she always ambled in made it seem like she was late, or wanted to be late, or something. And there she was, just saying, "You hear the bad news on Mr. Roosevelt? Just come over the radio."

"No." But Dolly knew instantly just from Odessa's face what had happened, and her first thought was, I truly cannot stand this. I cannot live without Franklin Roosevelt. Him in charge. She reminded herself that very recently she had felt almost the same about Russ, who was definitely not in charge, and before that about Clifton Lee. And before that, well, her daddy. (Never Willard.) But Roosevelt was the whole country's daddy, with his beautiful voice and his beautiful eyes, and clothes—and that awful, ugly, pushy, unloving wife, that Eleanor, who gave him a lot more children than he wanted, probably, and not one of them one bit nice. Dolly loved Mr. Roosevelt more than anyone she knew had loved him, with a love that she kept mostly to herself, like Clifton (like Russ, whom she'd had to pretend to hate, a lot of the time). But in her very secret life it was she, Dolly Bigelow, married to Mr. Roosevelt, to Franklin—always with him and looking pretty for him and for photographs, riding along in his car wearing pretty hats, and staying at home to cook whatever he liked, not traipsing around on her own and giving out these loud Yankee opinions. Mr. Roosevelt himself was so elegant, such a gentleman; he didn't seem like a Yankee at all.

And Mr. Roosevelt's death would last forever. Of course any death would—but Dolly had this curious special sense of the permanence of Roosevelt, dead on April 12, 1945. Dead everywhere, that day and that death memorialized. Whereas with Russ—of course Franklin was just as dead as Russ was, but Russ's death did not seem as—*substantial.* That was the word that came to Dolly's mind, not making a lot of sense but she liked it, she knew what she meant by it.

Partly, she had an idea that Russ was still around here in some way.

"I think I'll go upstairs and just have a little lie-down," Dolly told Odessa, once Odessa had come in with her awful news: "He dead, down in Georgia. At the Warm Springs, someplace like that." Not wanting Odessa to see that she cried, Dolly hurried, almost running up the narrow stairs, the back stairs that led up from the kitchen.

As she and Russ had run, all those years ago, the both of them so drunk—after the first big party that Esther and Jimmy Hightower gave in their big new house, which was out there near SallyJane and Russ's house. It happened about a week after Willard's mother died, Dolly's awful mother-in-law, and that was where Willard was, up in Virginia still seeing to his mother's things. Old Mrs. Bigelow, dead at last, in Lynchburg. And SallyJane had stayed home with a headache that night. So there they were, Dolly Bigelow and Russell Byrd, both young, in their early thirties still, drinking too much the way everybody did back then—and just flirting up a storm.

The funny part was, and what ended up making that night just so amazing, she and Russ had never anywhere near flirted before, not just the least little bit. And so it was like the both of them were some brand-new person to the other, some strange new kid in school from somewhere else, sort of interesting and attractive.

There they both were, alone, not like married people, but

like kids. And they both got into the mood of this, this strange kid mood. Almost pretending they'd never seen each other before. And in a way that was true, although it might be more true to say they'd never looked. Certainly there were a whole bunch of things about Russ that Dolly had never noticed one bit, like how wide his shoulders were, and the tiny little lines at the corners of his eyes, and how small and dainty his earlobes were, not fat and hanging down like—well, like some people's earlobes. And who knows what he saw in her that night? She was wearing (she can see it clearly, just like yesterday) a new red silk dress, with one of those sweetheart necks that she had worried about a little, it seemed sort of low.

She and Russ giggled and whispered these silly questions to each other, like kids on a date—What's your favorite flavor of ice cream? Favorite flower? Best movie you ever saw?—as the party went on, and they drank and drank more bourbon, until everybody was going home, and then Russ said to her, another whisper, "How about I take you home, young lady?"

They didn't touch at all in the car. He just drove along, and when they got to her house she told him to park in the back, like everybody did, and when they got there she saw that the student child-help person had already gone home, like Dolly had told her to; the boys never, never woke up in the night. And so she and Russ went into the house by the kitchen, and in there they started up whispering again, like it was her parents asleep upstairs and she was this very young girl instead of a mother, with her own children asleep.

And then he started in to kissing her, then touching her breasts, reaching down into her dress, the both of them still like kids who'd never done such a thing before (although kids these days are up to the Lord knows what all).

They ran upstairs, first taking off their shoes, and they tiptoed into Dolly's (Dolly and Willard's, really) bedroom, and then Russ whispered, "I don't want to hurt you," just like she was some young virgin, and probably him too. But by this time Dolly was too excited for any more pretending, and she reached for him in a way that no young girl (no proper young girl) ever would. So that ever after that night, Dolly felt this terrible embarrassment (with Russ) and shame. And love, and hate.

And then all these other things happened to Russ, these other women. Like Deirdre. And the wife of that so-called psychiatrist, supposed to be treating SallyJane and killed her off with the shock treatment, finally. And Cynthia Baird. Cynthia thinks to this day that Dolly didn't know about their carrying-on, but of course she did. And God knows who all out in Hollywood. Or in New York. Even Esther Hightower, maybe.

Later, Dolly even started up all that flirting and finally going off for some kissing in cars with Clifton Lee; all that was just to make Russ jealous, which for one thing it simply did not do, he could not have cared one bit less if he even noticed—and for another she got sort of caught up and involved herself, she got to really liking poor old Clifton—and then he died. It was like her mama said to her, a long time back, "Honey, don't you ever try to make a man jealous, they only get jealous when they've a mind to, and it's liable to be when you don't even want them to notice. Besides, if you try it's going to backfire on you someway you won't like." Well, her mama didn't even know the half of it.

. . .

Lying there on her pretty pink ruffled bed, all chintz, with a matching skirt on the tables and curtains the same material, Dolly then thought that what she was doing was dangerous, really, lying there with all her bad thoughts, of Roosevelt and Russ and even poor Clifton; next thing she knew she'd be thinking about her daddy, dead now for fifteen years. She must not think about his terrible death—she had to get out someway, even if it was such a terrible day outside, and looked like a thunderstorm, and she was mortally afraid of storms.

In her little Ford car, though, letting it coast real slowly down the hill to save on gas (this terrible rationing!) as Dolly passed the poor little tacky tarpaper shacks where the poorest poor whites lived, she had this really bad thought about the war: she thought, without him things are not going to get any better at all, all the New Deal things that Mr. Roosevelt started will not go on, and we're not going to get along with those Russian Communists, like he tried to do, and the darkies will just go wild and kill everyone so they can take over the country.

She had got all the way down to Graham Creek before she had to start up the car again, but she left it real slow, and then stopped just before the bridge. The creek was high and brown and swirly. Somebody once said—it could have been Russ who said this, be just like him—that in a good canoe you could make it all the way down to Florida on this creek, but Dolly for one would not like to give it a try. On the other side was a dirty little sand beach, nothing like the fine white sand at Wrightsville Beach, or Nags Head, or out on Ocracoke

Island. And the poplars were a dirty white, their bark all peeling off, trailing down, like some bad skin ailment. Some little colored boys were usually out fishing there, but today Dolly didn't see a soul. Of course all colored folks are scared and superstitious over storms—though she should talk.

So peculiar for Russ and Deirdre to name that little boy, little Graham, the name of this dirty old creek, Graham Creek. Enough to make a child strange right from the start. But then Russ was strange as strange about names, always had been. I mean, thought Dolly vehemently, who on God's green earth that was in his right mind would name a baby for a colored girl in a book by that big fat Gertrude Stein? *Melanctha.* Lucky for Russ she wasn't fat and ugly too, but just strange, like her name, and those great big bosoms the size of watermelon, almost, passed down from SallyJane, her mama. Or for that matter, who would name a new little baby for an old dead wife? That poor little SallyJane, although so far she looked to be just a real normal happy little baby girl. But poor little thing now, to grow up without any daddy. No Russ.

Graham, that was one very odd little boy—or not so little now; he must be getting on to thirteen or fourteen, and real tall for his age. And just plain different from anybody else. You could say that Russ was different too, but different in a very different way. This boy was quiet, very—like Russ was quiet sometimes too, but then other times he'd talk up a storm, and laugh and make his jokes. But not one bit athletic, Graham wasn't, except for track; turned out he could run like a bird. A good-looking boy, you might say, and how could he not be, with Deirdre for his mama, and his daddy old handsome Russell Byrd?

Sometimes Dolly just clean forgot that Russ was dead.

For one thing, she was so used to his being around, and alive—and then his dying in Texas, on a train like he did, with that colored soldier; that made it all like some story, not something that happened to a person everyone knew. And maybe it wasn't true? maybe one day Russ would just walk back in and he'd say, Just what's all this I hear about me being dead?

Dolly began against her will to imagine Russ alive, but just as he walked into the room—into any empty room within her mind—the rain began, a terrible squall into which Russ had vanished. And there she was, alone in her car, down by Graham Creek, in the pounding, terrifying rain.

She had stopped the car right there on the cleared space before the bridge, which is probably where she would die that very day. She and Mr. Roosevelt dead the same day (at least now everyone would remember her death day). And maybe there was a Heaven, after all, and she would see Russ there, and Franklin. She put her head down on the steering wheel and sat there, hearing the distant thunder off in the hills, getting louder as it came toward her, and the rain now beating down against the windows of the car.

In Dolly's often told version of what happened next, it went like this:

"There was all this rain, heavy beating on the car, and along with that some other beating, like a person with a stick or some big fist. So I pulled all my nerves together and I opened my eyes and there at my window, right next to where I was sitting, just the glass between our two faces, was Russell Byrd. Not the old Russ we all knew but Russ dead and gone to Heaven and turned into some young angel." At this point Dolly always paused, her bright eyes brighter yet and opened wide. "I tell you I like to died, or at the very least fainted dead away."

It was of course neither Russ nor a transformed-angel-Russ, but Graham Byrd, son of Russ and Deirdre, once known as Deirdre's brother.

Recognizing him but still unable to speak in a rational way, Dolly opened the door a crack, and the boy, this Graham, said, "Oh, Miz Bigelow, I hope I didn't scare you none, I saw who you were and I wondered could you give me a ride home? I mean whenever you're heading back up that way?"

Dolly opened the door so that Graham could get in—of course she did, noticing that he considerably hurried, so as not to let in more rain. His face was all streaked, wet with rain, but then it came to Dolly that he was red around the eyes; the boy had been crying, he was not just wet from rain.

Her first thought was: This little old boy is still too old to cry, tall as he is—but then she softened some, and she thought, Grown men can cry too, sometimes. Willard did when his mama died. But who would have expected a boy to take on so about the President, about Mr. Roosevelt? She was taking for granted that that was what he was crying over. She asked him, as gently as if he was a whole lot younger than he was, "Graham, honey, you all right?" And she added, "I know it's terrible about Mr. Roosevelt, I feel real bad too. I feel awful."

Graham stared at her with those dark blue eyes of Russ's, and in a wondering way he asked her, "Mr. Roosevelt?"

It came to Dolly just then ("dumb old me" she used to add at this point) that Graham could have been crying about his daddy.

But what he said was, "No'm. I, I went for this walk with

Mr. Mountjoy, that's our, our Scout leader, and he—" Then Graham's whole face twisted up, and he shoved his fists (very dirty, Dolly noticed) against his eyes. Meaninglessly he told her, "He's gone now. Left me there."

This is something I don't want to hear about, I just know I don't, Dolly thought as she resolutely put the car in gear, backed up, and turned around. And started back up the hill.

The rain had stopped but the sky was still this ugly color, a greenish gray, like water that has got something poison growing in it. Heavy, scary-looking. Beside her on the front seat Graham sniffed. Dolly could feel him trying hard to stop.

Without quite knowing what she was saying, Dolly began to lecture. "Now, Graham," she began, "sometimes a grown-up will do something that a child will not understand, even a specially smart boy like you. I'm sure Mr. Mountjoy had his reason for going off and leaving you there like you say, but if I were in your place I wouldn't even try to understand. After all, he is the Scout leader, and he's got to know what he's about. I'm sure you'd best not even give it any more thought, and not mention it to anyone."

She went on for some time in that vein. When she looked over at Graham, he had stopped crying—of course he had; he looked serious, and much older than his years. And more like Russ.

"What you must always remember about this day"—and now Dolly herself began to sniffle—"is Mr. Roosevelt. This is the day that he died."

13

APRIL 13, the day after Roosevelt died, was one of the freshest and entirely loveliest days ever seen in Pinehill. Each tiny pale green leaf, the delicate petals of each pale pink or peach-colored rose, the white of the dogwood blossoms, barely trembling in the slightest new spring breeze—all perfect, and almost unnoticed, in the general aura of heavy trouble and confusion.

Cynthia woke early—early and appalled as she became all at once aware of several things, unrelated, but on the other hand—Oh God! she had dreamed of sex, of sex with Derek, and yes (Jesus!) she had actually come, and now she squirmed in humiliation at that memory. (Surely women weren't supposed to dream like that?) She realized too that she had been crying, and she remembered: Roosevelt. Dead.

Sitting up in bed, she shook her head and shoulders as though she could thus dispose of bad thoughts, but still more came. She thought of her father's death ten years ago, but so terrible, the months of pain, and even then the end of it, his actual dying had seemed sudden.

Then she thought of a recent article in the *Atlantic* or somewhere, by some refugee psychoanalyst, some follower of

Dr. Freud, who said that Roosevelt was a sort of "father figure" for the whole country—and, like her own father, strong and handsome, with a beautiful voice, and sexy, rumored to have a lady friend, or friends. As her father did, and Derek, probably.

Oh God, how trite I am, thought Cynthia. I am truly, utterly banal, I cannot stand myself (no wonder Derek is not in love with me). Roosevelt dies and I weep for my father, who was a mean old drunk, actually, and I have a big sex dream of Derek, who is also mean. I can't stand myself! she thought again.

Out in the early, still faint sunlight, beyond the white dotted-swiss ruffles of Cynthia's bedroom curtains, the new-bloomed flowers, mostly white, surrounded the barely lapping waters of the pool—from this distance, Cynthia's distance, like a wreath. A May Day wreath, although it was only April, April 13, which was a terrible day, so far.

Could Harry be dead?

No, he could not, Cynthia firmly told herself. Things do not happen in that symmetrical way, bad things do not come in threes, nor in twos for that matter. She added things up a little vaguely, not quite daring to count specific events.

Or maybe Derek was dead somewhere, wherever he was?

Appalled then, shocked and frightened by her own line of thought, Cynthia jumped briskly out of bed and headed into the bathroom where she turned on the water for her bath, adding an extra dollop of scented salts—although she knew that self-pity deserved no reward, or extravagant comfort.

Breakfast, however, was better. For one thing there was Odessa. And fresh orange juice and coffee and hot rolls.

"Oh, Odessa, I was afraid you'd be back at Miz Bigelow's again today."

"Oh, no'm." A pause. "Miz Bigelow, she's real upset. So upset over Mr. Roosevelt even if it seemed like she never held with him, with his ideas before, and the things she said about his wife. But she came home from this drive she took and she say how she had seen Mr. Byrd, Mr. Russell Byrd what's dead in Texas? And then she say of course not Mr. Byrd hisself but that little old boy, that Graham."

Odessa delivered herself of this—for her—longish monologue while passing through the swinging doors between the dining room and the kitchen, walking with her own unique highly personal mixture of haste and delay, which gave an odd rhythm to her speech.

"Dolly thought she saw *Russ*?"

Somewhat confused herself, still, from waking to such dreams, Cynthia did not grasp all this about Dolly.

"Yes'm. She thought was like in a dream, there she was out in the rain in that little old car. Thinking on Mr. Roosevelt, and there was Mr. Byrd, and him dead too."

"Odessa, I had the most terrible dreams last night."

Odessa's whole face seemed to grow wider, and to brighten. She and Cynthia had got into the habit of exchanging dreams, and usually she was sympathetic when bad ones were announced. But at that moment she said, "I had me this real good dream. Dreamed Mr. Harry come home." She added, more softly, "And then Horace too."

Cynthia stared, genuinely amazed. Much more than in her own dreams she believes in Odessa's dreams. Odessa's dreams are far less frequent and are flimsier than Cynthia's crazy dreams are, and Odessa's quite often come true. A week before Russell Byrd died (or got killed, or whatever, with that Negro soldier), Odessa had a terrible dream that Russ was in a fight, and she wouldn't even tell Cynthia how the end came out, not until there was the actual news of Russ, and then she covered her face with her hands, and she said, "I swear before the Lord, I never tell another dream." And she hadn't, not until today, until this good dream of Harry. And of Horace. So that now for several minutes at least, Cynthia was really happy, thinking of Harry, of Harry back at home with her—and the war all over and everything okay.

But then she thought that of course, after all, Odessa's dream might not come true for months and months, or even years—and even if it does mean that Harry is all right (and can all Odessa's dreams be so accurate, really?), Roosevelt would still be dead, and Russ (not that she cared about him so much anymore; still, it had been shocking: a body once as close as humanly possible to your body, now cold, and gone). And Derek was still off God-knows-where, very likely with Someone Else.

Go jump in the pool. That is what her father would have said, if he were around. So what if it's cold, still April? *It'll do you good, toughen you up.*

And her mother: There's nothing like really really cold water for the skin, it's better than any astringent. *Marvelous.* You won't need a face-lift.

Cynthia shivered, and gulped hot coffee, and she wickedly thought, Well, it's good they're not here.

And she wondered again if Harry's theory about concrete swimming pools was right, that keeping them full of water all winter prevented cracks. Maybe that was true in Connecticut, but not down here.

An hour or so later, acting on an impulse not unlike her father's "Go jump in the pool," Cynthia was in her car, and somewhat formally dressed, with a flowered straw hat and very clean white gloves, and driving, full of purpose, toward Hilton.

For in that hour she had been seized by an idea, or rather, she herself had seized on a plan that, instead of deflating, gets better and better as she thinks of it: she will go to the law school there, the law school at Hilton instead of Georgetown. No need at all to live in Washington after the war. And indeed, why didn't she think of that before?

Actually, Cynthia observes to herself, she has been overcome by the weather, the quintessentially lovely April day, more beautiful yet as it slowly and softly moves toward high noon, gently warming, with an infinitely subtle brightening of light. The needles on the pines that line the road are a vivid green, eroded red clay banks are moist and slick, and the creeks that she crosses, on narrow white concrete bridges, are a pale swollen sandy brown, swift, with their cargoes of flimsy trash, the winter detritus of dead leaves and broken-off twigs and branches. Cynthia opens the car window to the highest, slightest breeze, which just barely ruffles her hair as she thinks, Oh yes, I'll go to law school at Hilton, and Harry and I will stay on in Pinehill and be happy almost forever, after the war.

On the Hilton campus mimosa was everywhere in bloom, trees hung with pale red-edged powder puffs among the lacy green leaves. Cynthia, having parked near the old stadium and asked for directions—and noted how extraordinarily young the students all looked—headed along white hard-gravelled paths (among all those almost-children) toward the law school, a large prim brick building whose white steps she ascended, and walked down a wide dingy corridor until she reached a sign: "Law School Office."

Where she found, seated behind a desk, as though she belonged there—of all people, Abby's old friend, the daughter of Irene Lee and poor dead Clifton, little Betsy Lee. A perfect small blond girl, with tiny perfect freckles across her tiny, retroussé nose. And a too loud, flat-accented voice—as though, Cynthia later thought, she assumed that anyone old enough to be a friend of her mother's was probably deaf. Which Cynthia, who at forty-five usually felt more like twenty-five (which is closer to what she looked), was not, not deaf at all, and for that matter not a particular friend of Irene Lee's.

"This old friend of my daddy's got me this wonderful job," Betsy explained as Cynthia remembered hearing from someone—no doubt it was Dolly—that poor little Betsy had managed to flunk out of Sweet Briar.

Cynthia said, "How nice," and then she explained, "I guess I want to see someone about admissions. To the law school."

A simple enough statement, but Betsy looked as though Cynthia had made an outlandish proposition. But then some light seemed to dawn on her face—the wrong light, as things turned out. "Oh, you mean Abigail's changed her mind *again*? And here I thought she was all settled up at Swarthmore with her nice Jewish beau. From the nicest family, she said. Real interesting people, and smart, of course."

"No," Cynthia firmly interrupted. "As far as I know, Abby is still very happy at Swarthmore, and she is with Joseph a lot of the time, and she certainly doesn't want to go to law school. She's very determined to be a doctor. But I do, I want to go to law school. Here."

"But—" But you're much too old, grown-up ladies don't go to law school, or any other school, just a few girls in any graduate school. Betsy's face and her sudden staring silence said all that, in marked contrast to her noisy voice, and much louder in effect.

And so Cynthia further explained about Georgetown Law, her acceptance there and her decision to postpone—as, simultaneously, she thought, Why am I explaining anything at all to this dim baby girl? She hurried to finish. "So I think I'd like an appointment with the dean."

"Well, Dr. Montague's up to Nags Head, where they've got this lovely home. For Easter. He'll be back—oh, come next Tuesday."

"Then could I please make an appointment?"

Betsy's fixed smile persisted, as did her cast-in-concrete point of view; you could hardly call it an idea. She said, "But, Miz Baird, this year there's not but five young coeds in the whole law school, and Dr. Montague's said as how two of them anyway just might flunk out." (Clearly she liked this possibility.)

And you, you little moron, you just managed to flunk out of Sweet Briar, not an easy thing to do—Cynthia managed not to say. Instead she stood up and announced, "Well, week after next would be most convenient for me. Could you send me a note as to time?" She very much doubted that Betsy could, and decided to manage for herself on the telephone. She could easily pass herself off as an old friend of Dr. Montague's, from somewhere.

Driving back to Pinehill, on that ravishing April day, Cynthia thought of—she vividly remembered their first drive down to Pinehill from Connecticut, she and Harry with little Abigail in the backseat of their old (but terribly smart) wood-bodied Caddy. How young and hopeful they had been, and how broke! (They and the whole nation, all in their thirties then.) And how beautifully flowing the gentle land had looked.

And her mind had been full of memorized lines from Russ Byrd's poetry, Cynthia recalled, with a small sad private smile, adding: And my heart full of lust, for Russ.

Oh *shit,* she in a summarizing way added vaguely: no wonder things turn out as they do.

What she least wanted, Cynthia realized as she approached her own house, was to be in that house, right then. On a quick impulse she turned her car, and headed in a direction that led out of town. Toward The Pines, where she had not been since that fateful night with Derek—and which at this hour should be very quiet, very likely no students, quite possibly no one there at all.

As she drove she was still thinking with some irritation and amusement (less of that) about silly stupid Betsy Lee, and the whole business of the subtext: "Nice girls don't go to law school, and certainly nice grown-up ladies don't." Well, Cynthia announced to herself, in that case all the more reason. I'll go to law school in Hilton, and I'll be the best lady lawyer around (for surely that is what she would be called). I'll be the best around, the best lawyer, and maybe less of a lady.

At The Pines there were only a couple of cars in the parking lot, to which Cynthia paid scant attention, only noting the number. She walked in, observing the curious brightness of early-afternoon sunlight on the varnished, pine-finished tables and benches, and the walls of the narrow booths. Seeing no one around, she settled into a booth near the front, across from the cash register where, presumably, there would soon be a person in charge.

She lit a longed-for cigarette, and in an idle way she looked around at the gaudy neon-tubed jukebox, the big framed photos of giant football stars from Pinehill and from Hilton—from other days.

She noticed then, somewhat less idly, that there was a couple in one of the booths, down and across the room—who were, as the phrase went, all over each other. Necking. Students, in the spring, Cynthia surmised; rutting season. She noted then the man's blond hair, at the same time seeing the woman's long rich brown, and her broad fat shoulders, in a flowered dress.

It was Deirdre Byrd, and the man was Derek. Of course.

Frozen there, her blood chilled, Cynthia thought, I could get out of here before they'd know I saw them. However, just at that moment the owner of The Pines padded over to her, small and plump, in his dirty white apron, his foolish face expectant. "And what might be your pleasure today, young lady?"

Speechless, Cynthia stared at him—a character in the nightmare unfolding before her, her own nightmare, and one that was familiar to her: Deirdre and Derek McFall kissing, there in a booth in The Pines, in broad daylight. And then this minor actor offering her food.

Not wanting to hear the sound of her own voice in that room, Cynthia whispered, "Just a little tomato salad, please."

But she had forgotten to give it the local accent, toe-may-toe, and so the small fat man repeated it as she had said, "Oh, toe-mah-toe salad. Coming right up." Very loud.

Of course they had heard, Cynthia stared down at her

ashtray, the table, at her knees. As she began to hear what she had known would come next, the quick steps of Derek, approaching, as, behind him, Deirdre was heading into the ladies' room.

"Well," Derek said, "such a surprise—" His hand outstretched, his smile just faintly ironic. "I'm doing some more Russ Byrd interviews, and we nipped out for lunch."

"Oh really." Cynthia for an instant grasped his hand, and she smiled too, and her smile lied, as his had. Her smile told him (it must have) that she had seen them kissing, but also said (and this was the lie) that she didn't care.

It was all like a play that she herself might have written, or a dream she had dreamed. Her own nightmare.

Of course a minute later Deirdre was there beside Derek, freshly made up, in a tight pale pink sweater, with pearls. The two women remarked on how well the other was looking, how they really must get together.

It was an unbearable, understandable, quite horrible small exchange.

Cynthia cut into it, abruptly asking, "What's ever happened to that Negro soldier? The one with Russ on the train when he died?"

Derek answered. "Very interesting. He got clean and clear out of that little Texas jail, and no one's seen hide nor hair of him since. There's a rumor that he was let out by some of his own people, who didn't want to see him lynched. Oddly enough."

"Well, that makes sense, doesn't it?" Cynthia's voice was almost under control.

"Yes, it does." Derek stared at her, thinking, but of what? He said, "I've got to get the plane for D.C. at five. Come along, Miz Byrd, I'll drop you off."

And then they were gone, and Cynthia sat there, alone in the too warm, too bright room, unable to eat her small tomato salad. No matter how anyone pronounced it.

She was literally choked with anger, primarily at Derek, but then too at herself. How could she have wasted so much emotion on a man who almost denied the existence of emotion? Who prided himself on his own lack of feeling?

And then Cynthia was visited by an odd out-of-character thought, which was: I hope Deirdre gets him, finally. That would be just right for both of them, I think—I hope.

14

IN the large sprawling deep-country house that Russ had bought years back, when he and SallyJane Caldwell were recently wed (bought and added wings to, and an upstairs, and populated with children; then another wife, and a baby also named SallyJane), in that house Melanctha was rarely alone, but on a day in late April, home from Radcliffe for Easter vacation, she was truly all alone. Earlier, in a tentative way, she had walked through those rooms, as though reassuring herself that she was alone; she would not run into some stray brother, half-brother, half-sister, along a hall, or lurking in an upstairs bedroom. (Nor the ghost of a parent.) In a literal, practical way, she knew where everyone was, and that they would not be home, but still—she had an odd sense of another presence, and she wondered if maybe Graham was hiding somewhere in the house, for no reason except that he seemed to like to hide. He liked small mysteries—or large ones, probably.

Poor child, poor almost-young man. Melanctha felt a vague, uncomprehending pity for Graham. She had no idea what he was really like, nor, she suspected, did anyone else, least of all Graham himself.

The day outside threatened heat, intensity—so unlike the

clear cold chaste New England spring that Melanctha had left behind in Cambridge. Already on the pine boughs just outside her bedroom window (she had settled for the moment in that room), the pine needles in the sunlight were brilliantly green, too bright and sharp, strangely threatening, against a too bright blue sky. Fat white clouds lay heavily on the horizon. Nothing moved.

Melanctha's room, like the weather, was as unlike her Radcliffe college room as possible. Her Radcliffe room, in Whitman Hall, was a book-strewn mess, usually. Whereas this was a girlish fantasy—but it was Deirdre's fantasy, not Melanctha's: a four-poster bed with a starched and flounced white lace canopy, and the same lace on the curtains, and on the kidney-shaped dressing table. It was a room that in her waking hours Melanctha could not tolerate for long. (It was "done" by Deirdre and a local decorator, a "surprise" for Melanctha one summer while she was away at camp. Russ had told her she was "very spoiled" and ungrateful when she failed to respond as they thought she should.)

Melanctha had already left that room, then, and was halfway downstairs when a light knock sounded on the front door. Expecting no one—no one in her family would be home until about five, or later, and besides, none of them would knock—Melanctha hesitated, unaccountably afraid. Although it would only be some passing friend; strangers never came down that backwoods road in Pinehill in those days.

But opening the door she saw that it was indeed a stranger, and a Negro: a very tall, light-skinned (yellowish-brown) old-looking (tired, perhaps, or maybe sick) young man. His great brown eyes red-rimmed. In cheap-looking, newish clothes. Who looked scared.

Scared, but very determined. He asked, "You Miss Melanctha Byrd?"

"Yes—"

"Could I talk to you a minute?" His voice was a whisper.

"Sure, come on in." Melanctha's voice too, as she heard herself, was unfamiliar, strained. She sensed both his panic and his determination, and she wished somehow to reassure him. And to give him some food; he looked starved. But for the moment she saw no way to do either, to comfort or to feed, without making him feel like a beggar, which he so clearly was not. He was an intelligent proud man, scared out of his wits but continuing anyway on his own chosen course.

He followed her into the living room, but before she could tell him to sit down, as she was about to do, he began.

"I'm Ed Faulkner," he said, staring fixedly at her face.

For an instant the name meant nothing, and then, with a wrench, Melanctha thought, *Oh.*

He said, "I had to see you. To tell you—you know, your dad just fell down. Like a faint. Pass out. Maybe a stroke."

Feeling faint herself, Melanctha told him truthfully, "That's what I thought. You know, I never thought—"

He still stared, now silent, as Melanctha observed a very small but clear diminution of panic in him, and she wondered, Now could I offer him something to eat? Would that be all right? It was a social, or rather, a human situation for which she had absolutely no training, no experience. And instead of offering food she asked him, "But how did you—how did you get here?"

"I got family there. Family in Texas." As though that explained not being in jail.

He added, "Ne'r mind how," with the tiniest suggestion of a smile. And then he said, again very earnestly, "He just fell right down." He paused, and then said, "He was a real nice man. I could tell right off. We got along good." He added, "It was almost like he wanted to—"

"Well, he was mostly nice, I guess." Melanctha's own feelings about her father had never pulled themselves into a steady focus, and perhaps never would. She was affected, though, by this man's tone, which included piety, a proper mourning, and her own voice quavered (properly) as she added, "We all miss him."

"I have to go now." Ed Faulkner spoke softly, but most decisively, and he began to move toward the door in a curious sideways walk, as though he thought it rude to leave her there.

"Can't you have some lunch or something? Iced tea?" Melanctha was suddenly desperate. She even crazily wondered, was this man really Ed Faulkner?—the one who had been with her father when he died?

"Oh, no'm, I've got to get along—"

"Where're you heading?" She realized that she had spoken in an unfamiliar accent, and rhythm. Who was she—was she Russ, really?

"Well, up North. Up to Massachusetts, soon as I can. My folks are in Roxbury, outside of Boston."

"Oh, that's where I'm going too. In a couple of days, I'm going back up to Cambridge, that's where I go to school. What a coincidence, the both of us—"

"I reckon." He gave her a puzzled, unsmiling look. And then, almost out the door, he said, "Well, I do thank you—talking to me—listening—"

"Oh, I wish you could stay!"

For suddenly that was what she wished, more than anything. If he would stay, she felt that he could explain everything to her. If he would just stay and have something to eat. Or drink. Should she have offered him a beer? Or whiskey?

But he had opened the front door and was halfway out when he spoke, not just a mutter, not looking at her. "Well, ma'am, I thank you, I do. I wish you good luck—and your family—"

Melanctha watched him walk down the worn brick path, now lined with the bright yellow jonquils. He had a very slight limp: how come she hadn't noticed that before? And had she really observed exactly what he looked like? Could she describe him? The crazy idea came to her then that maybe "Ed Faulkner" was really Benny Davis, come down to check her out and disguised as another man. But that was crazy, she knew that instantly, and she thought, I'm not well, I am sort of crazy. Anybody mentions Russ and I lose track. Will I always be like this? I can't stand it!

And she wondered: *Did* Russ fall on purpose?

"Who was that colored man?" asked Graham, perhaps an hour later, as he came into the kitchen where Melanctha was making tea (tea, she drank gallons of tea, every day).

"What colored man?" She knew though, of course it would have been Ed Faulkner. But why would he have been still around here, after an hour?

"Just up the road a way. He was just sitting there, like he'd been taking a nap. In this funny brown suit."

Melanctha stared at Graham's dark blue eyes, so like their father's, Russ's deep blue eyes. So like hers too—except that on Graham everything was beautiful; he was lovely, as everyone had always said. And she was not, which of course no one said, although Melanctha could imagine, behind her back: "It's just the funniest thing, how that little old boy got all the good looks, and that Melanctha, who's the dead spit of her daddy too, well, I guess she just kind of missed out in the looks department. Maybe it's that Russ's kind of face was more cut out for a boy? Maybe, she'd've been a boy, Melanctha would've been a real good-looker too? Though all those others are not a lot to write home about—"

But now she wondered, Had that Ed Faulkner hoped or wanted to see *her* again? Had he fainted from hunger, since he wouldn't take any food? She asked Graham, "Did he look all right? I mean not sick or anything?"

"He looked sleepy." But Graham had lost whatever interest he may momentarily have had in this stray colored man. Which was typical of Graham, who had the attention span of a flea. Even Deirdre, his mother, said this of him.

"The clouds have changed color a lot," Graham now observed. "I think it might be a thunderstorm."

If there was a storm, what would happen to that man, a strange Negro with maybe no money? "I think I'll go out for a walk," Melanctha told Graham. "I'll try to make it back before the rain."

He was right about the clouds. What had been small and plump and white had swollen and turned black, heavy, menacing. Melanctha hurried along the road, staring out into the thin woods on either side, where she saw no one.

Passing Jimmy and Esther Hightower's big white "modern" house, she thought of how Russ had always disliked it; he had muttered, almost every day, "If'n that's what 'modern' is, let me go backwards, please. At least a century or so." She thought she saw Jimmy at the window, but didn't bother really to look, or to wave.

She heard and then saw a car coming pretty fast from the direction in which she was headed, from the highway. A gray convertible, top down, and in it Deirdre and that newspaperman she liked so much, that Derek. They slowed and waved, and Melanctha heard Deirdre call out, "You have a nice walk, honey."

What a dope: *honey.*

She continued to stare through the small trees and bushes that lined the road, though of course at the same time she thought that he wouldn't be there, he was either really hiding somewhere where she couldn't see him, where no one could, or else he was just gone. Got out to the highway and hitched a ride on some truck going north, or somewhere.

With a heavy reluctance she turned and headed home, very slowly now. It wouldn't even be all her own private house anymore; there would be Deirdre and that Derek McFall. However, after not many minutes Derek's car came toward her again, now that they had both changed directions. He slowed and gave her a wave and a big fake grin, then hurried on by, raising dust.

When she got home, Deirdre was nowhere around. Melanctha took some iced tea from the icebox and was sitting, sipping, in the kitchen when she heard Deirdre's voice from the front stairs.

"Melanctha, honey, is that you?"

Who the hell else would it be? Not saying that, of course not, Melanctha went around to the front of the house, and there was Deirdre, her fat all shrouded in a pink silk kimono, hair loose, standing at the top of the stairs.

"I've got this real sick headache," Deirdre called down, unnecessarily loud, in that quiet, emptily stretching house.

"Where'd Graham go?" Melanctha had suddenly remembered that Graham had been there before.

"Oh, he left this note, gone to the show with his scoutmaster, guess they went up the back road. But when you get hungry, you think you can get yourself something out of the icebox?"

"Oh sure."

Deirdre disappeared.

The storm began.

But its center seemed to be somewhere else, maybe over as far as Hilton, to the west. In Pinehill there was only a darker sky, and a steady silver rain. The thunder was distant, and the lightning pale.

Later, hunched over her potato salad and cold chicken, her glass of iced tea, Melanctha still thought, and thought and thought, about Ed Faulkner. How brave of him to come to see her. He cannot have known anything about her; for all he knew, she was some real Southern hysteric, some crazy woman who would call the sheriff right off, a strange Negro man at her *front door.* Whereas, actually Melanctha had never thought, had never imagined, that he did anything bad to Russ. But did she tell him that? She cannot remember! In fact she can hardly remember anything of their conversation, only his face, his yellowish skin and red-rimmed tired eyes, and his dusty shiny brown suit. And she had not given him anything to eat. Had she even asked? Had she treated him like she should have, like a guest?

Her mind was all clouded with guilt and confusion, there alone in the fresh-cleared April night, of which she was almost unaware. Upstairs, Deirdre had some music on her radio, which she did almost all the time these days, now that Russ was not around to stop her ("Deirdre, for the Lord's sake, turn that thing down!"), and some band, probably that jerk Glenn Miller, whom Deirdre *just loved,* was playing one of his Serenades, Sunset, Moonlight, some damn silly thing.

Melanctha sat there for a long time, feeling leaden, hopeless, without any real thoughts at all. Until she got up and rinsed her few dishes and went upstairs to bed.

A little later, she heard Graham come slowly upstairs—she knew his odd light hesitant walk—and go into his room, next door to hers. And later still she heard the awful, familiar sound of Graham crying. He sobbed loudly, though for a very short time, and sometimes Melanctha wondered, Did he want someone to go in to him? Was the crying a cry for help? But Deirdre never went to him; a long time ago Melanctha remembered Russ had told Deirdre not to. "You're already turning that boy into a little sissy," Russ had said, and even now, with Russ dead, Deirdre in that and in most things kept to what Russ had told her.

But Russ is dead, why should anyone do what he said anymore?

By the time, though, that Melanctha had got into her robe and slippers, and knocked very lightly on Graham's door, there was no sound, only a long interval before his sleep-weighted voice said, "Who's that?"

"It's me. You okay?"

"Of course. I was just asleep."

Rejected, but feeling that she had to accept what he said, Melanctha went back to her own bed—and found herself still plagued with thoughts of Ed Faulkner, the Negro soldier. The sergeant. Negroes were as badly treated in the Army as anywhere else, she had read; in fact just the same. And she had done nothing to help him.

Nothing, nothing.

But somehow she would help him, Melanctha determined—and soon. When the money came through from what Deirdre referred to as "the estate" (not "Russ's estate," *the* estate), she would give a lot of it to Edward Faulkner—somehow. (She would not spend it on any Hollywood kind of self-indulgence, like plastic surgery.)

First, though, she would have to go out to Roxbury to find him.

15

"I DON'T fall in love. Not ever. It's not my style," Derek said, intending sincerity, as he raised his head from Deirdre's delectable plump breast to meet the headlong gaze of her depthless, matchless, thoughtless blue eyes. But his words had a sort of mechanical echo as he spoke them, as though he were in a recording studio. And then he recalled, I said exactly those same words to Cynthia Baird a few weeks ago, and I hurt her, probably I've said them a lot; do I like to hurt women? Am I really queer? What a shit I am, basically.

But Deirdre, improbably, was laughing. A tremor that for one instant he had thought might be incipient sobs turned out to be the first of waves of laughter, deep rich belly laughs, that put tears into those lovely eyes. "You just say that to hear yourself saying it," she told him. "You think if you tell me that, you'll be safe, you won't fall. I've known just a bunch of guys like you."

"What do you mean, a bunch?" This was the first thing that Derek was able to ask. He was more or less in shock. "I thought Russ was the first man—the only man—" He found that he could not quite put this thought into words.

"Russ was the first man, you've got that right." She

stretched—like a lioness, Derek thought, with her great smooth muscles, her tawny skin. Her power. She said, "But then there was all that time in California with my folks, 'fore Russ let me and Graham come back here."

"Oh." Absorbing all that information, including the fact of her laughing, Derek was rattled with unfamiliar emotions, even as he said to himself, I am not an emotional man. And his member, which all afternoon had performed with such noble energy, such skill and zest and cunning, began limply to wilt.

They were in Derek's room in the Carolina Inn, exactly where he had been with Cynthia, and had made that same speech, but to what vastly different effect! Cynthia had worn that hurt-angry look with which Derek was familiar, on so many women. But not Deirdre: she thought he was funny.

He asked her, "You mean you weren't just a dutiful young mother out in California?" He had meant to say something hurtful, but nothing had come.

"Not hardly. My momma, she was the dutiful mother to the both of us, really. Me and Graham. So the idea of coming back here and pretending like Graham was my little brother seemed like the natural thing to do." She laughed again. "Seems like they were actually encouraging me to go out a lot, my folks were. I reckon they hoped some guy'd come along and take me off their hands. And they never did care a whole lot for Russ."

"I should think, with your looks, easy enough to find someone," Derek mumbled.

Another laugh. "Like I said, there was a bunch of them. And sooner or later I'd get this little speech about not falling in love. 'Not getting serious,' was usually how they said it.

Not knowing they were safe as safe, me being so young and stupid and so hung up on Russ it was all I could do to kiss them good night."

This time Derek managed a laugh. "But you forced yourself, just out of being polite?"

"Oh sure, and sometimes a plenty more."

Oh, thought Derek.

"Anyways," Deirdre continued, "just after the 'don't fall in love' speech came the 'why don't we get married' one. Are you going to ask me to marry you now, darling Derek?" And she gave her terrible laugh.

Wanting to say, *Certainly not,* Derek forbore, and forced a smile. And changed the subject. "Do you know this Jimmy Hightower very well?" he asked her.

Deirdre shifted her weight a little, rocking the somewhat rickety bed. "Round here we all know each other pretty well," she told him. "That Jimmy, though, he's a deep one. Only thing I know about him for sure is that he's plum crazy about that wife of his, that Esther. Dark sort of foreign-looking lady, must've been some looker in her younger days. Folks say that Jimmy had this sort of a crush on that Cynthia Baird for a while, but I don't believe it, such a cold, flat-chested talky lady. Russ liked her too for a while, they say, but I think that's not really likely. Russ didn't much like anyone, I sometimes think."

"But Jimmy Hightower?" Derek reminded her. "Russ liked him pretty well?"

"Oh, Jimmy. Well, you know he moved to Pinehill mostly to be around Russ. Same way that Cynthia, Miz Baird did, is what I heard. But what Jimmy wanted most of all in this world was to be a writer, and now he is one. Although Russ always said he was not a real writer and never would be.

Whatever a 'real writer' is." Finding this idea ridiculous, she laughed.

"Are you saying that Russ was a little hard on people who liked him?"

Not given to general ideas, Deirdre considered. "I guess you could put it that way," she concluded. "Most people made Russ kind of nervous, he was a real restless man. Like a horse. He got real tired of people. He was terrible tired of Jimmy, time his book was done."

"Russ was a big help, though?"

"I don't rightly know about that. For a big part of it I wasn't even here in town, and then when I was I mostly saw Russ just by himself." She shivered, rocking the bed again. "Long about then I got to feeling like some person Russ had got tired of, and by that time I was living in this big old house he'd bought me, with this little old boy that was his son. Our son, anyway not my brother."

Derek was thinking that, actually, he could perfectly well marry Deirdre. If he got her to take off some weight, she'd be beautiful again! Well, she still was, as far as her face was concerned. And for all her cheeky talk she was a patient woman, basically. A man's woman. All those kids would be off in school somewhere soon, except that sweet little SallyJane who was really no problem. And when he went all over the peacetime world, in his work, there would be lovely Deirdre, waiting like Penelope, in that nice big house all spread out in the nice old grove of trees.

Except for Melanctha; she was trouble and going to get worse, he'd bet on that. He thought of her difficult, troubled presence. Smart as hell, maybe as smart as Russ. And she was going to turn into just the kind of woman that gave him, Derek, the most trouble: sexy and hypersensitive, probably talky at all the wrong times, never knowing when to just shut up. Making a big deal of things that were not important, and not paying a lot of attention to the really major stuff, the headlines, the real news that was the core of Derek's world.

Deirdre giggled, and then she asked, "I ever tell you that SallyJane had've been a boy, we'd've named her Derek?"

Only about a dozen times, was the truth of it, but Derek contented himself with saying, "I think you mentioned it once or twice. Good thing she wasn't, probably."

His appointment with Jimmy Hightower was for early the next afternoon. It meant driving out that narrow white road into the woods that led eventually to Russ Byrd's place, now Deirdre's. Deirdre had told him that there was a back road between her house and the town. "Comes out real near that house what used to be mine, now belongs to those Bairds, that Cynthia and Harry." Deirdre had also said, "Russ and I used to meet on that little old road, when we were first getting to know each other, sort of accidentally-on-purpose." She said this with her laugh and her big-eyes significant look. The things women tell you that you really don't want to know.

Jimmy Hightower himself was out in front of his big white "modern" house (one wall was all bluish glass brick) as Derek drove up; he was mowing his lawn with a very large new-looking mower, its shiny sharp blade quite clean of grass. It actually looked too large and heavy for Jimmy to maneuver—as Jimmy himself almost immediately remarked.

"Goddam thing's really more than I can handle," he stated

(unnecessarily) as he wiped his hands on his pants (very new blue jeans) and shook the hand that Derek extended. "That'll teach me to try this gentleman-farmer routine. But you can't get good yard help around here these days." He grinned at this last, as though quoting others whom he found ridiculous. "Leastways, that's what they all say," he added. "Had this real good man—a colored, of course—named Horace, married to the famous Odessa, but he's off in the Navy somewhere. Hope he comes back all right."

By now they had reached the front door, bright white with its glass brick surround. With a small flourish, Jimmy opened the door for Derek, who was at least a head taller.

"The truth is," said Jimmy as they settled into adjoining cool leather club chairs in the living room, "anything's easier than writing. Which is how I come to do a bunch of house and garden chores that I'm not real good at. Ask Esther," and he smiled very fondly. "Russ used to say that a lot," he appended, now frowning. "Anything's easier than writing. So I honest-to-God can't imagine Russ and this Manhattan Project thing, this so-called musical. A musical about atomic physicists? Come on. None of us know what they're up to, up there, but you can bet your worn-out boots it's not songs and dances."

Derek leaned forward; after all, this was what he'd come to talk about. "You don't think he would have done it?"

Jimmy looked taken aback. "Well, since you put it like that, no, I don't. Funny, I hadn't thought in a yes-or-no way about it. But no, I think at some point Russ would just have said, I won't do this, I won't have any part of this crap. Although that's not a word he used."

"Why? Why would he have said no?"

"God, man, you really put it to a fellow. You know, I

hadn't really asked myself that question before you did. Well." His hands on his knees, Jimmy leaned back, considering. He half closed his eyes for an instant, and then came forward, quite suddenly and decisively. "Just because of that," he said. "Because it's crap. And not good honest horse manure, which I gather this new show about my native state is. *Oklahoma.* I could tell them a few things about that state. But I can't tell a soul a goddam thing about Manhattan or any project there. And neither could Russ've done it. And as of right this minute I'm not going to try."

"Why is the Manhattan Project so much crappier than Oklahoma?" Derek asked.

"Well, for Christ's sake, you probably know that even better than I do. You've heard the rumors. Last thing I heard, they were scouting New Mexico for a test site, for whatever it is they're making. A test site! Jesus, all I can think of is thousands of rabbits, dead. And I just don't see all that as a background for some love story. And with songs, for Christ's sake."

Derek laughed. He was finding this Jimmy Hightower very likeable, much more likeable, probably, than Russ Byrd had been.

"Shouldn't we have a drink on that?" asked Jimmy, getting to his feet. "We'll drink to what I'm not writing, and then I'll tell you all I can about Russ, I promise."

"I won't say no, since you put it like that." Derek realized that he'd been wanting a drink for hours, ever since that dumb scene with dumb Deirdre. As Jimmy hurried out of the room, in his mind Derek heard again Deirdre's laugh; he hated her laugh; could he really marry someone whose laugh he hated?

Returned with drinks, Jimmy settled his small neat body into the big chair, and began to talk, at last, about Russ.

"Well, as I knew the man," he began, "I find it hard to say any single thing about his character."

"It's not necessarily his character that concerns me," Derek told him—gently, not wanting to interrupt a possible train of thought.

"Hard to say anything at all," continued Jimmy—then going on to say quite a lot. "A very contradictory fellow, Russ was. Very moral, moralistic you might say, in that old Southern Baptist way, and by the way not much liking anybody knowing about that, the Baptist part, since the first time he got married he married up, so to speak. SallyJane, the one he renamed Brett, was an Episcopalian, of course she was, with her father the university president and all. On the other hand, Russ never saw the inside of any church that I know of." Jimmy straightened his body in his chair, as though to become more serious, more in focus. "The thing about Russ is—I mean was—he got tired of people. Don't think he could help it, poor fellow, just plumb tired and bored. Restless. I was boring him silly, time we got through with that book I was writing, but it was my first time out and I was a lot more worried about the book than I was about maybe boring Russ Byrd. Well, his lack of interest was a thing I could live with, pretty easy. After all, I've always got my beautiful Esther and two nice girls for my old ego. But the women in Russ's life, I think they took it considerable harder, his attention wandering off the way it did. Not necessarily to any specific person, just *off.* It was the worst for SallyJane—so crazy, his renaming that woman. Brett, she had no more resemblance to a Brett than I do." He laughed, and sipped at his drink.

"And speaking of names, what Southern man in his right mind would name his little girl Melanctha? A colored girl in a book by a Jewish lesbian woman, I mean I've got nothing against anybody in any of those groups, I truly don't. My Esther is Jewish, you know, and I think Melanctha is a lovely name, just the sound of it. But downright inconsiderate, for a child. The teasing she's had to take. And then to name the baby that he had with Deirdre, to name her SallyJane, that just strikes me wrong, entirely wrong."

Derek felt that this conversation had got out of hand somehow. Jimmy was going all over the place, was talking all around Russ instead of about him. Derek began to wonder if this drink was really Jimmy's first of the day; could he also have had a couple with lunch?

Scents of April, of fresh earth and new flowers, and juts of clear blue air were wafting into the room, on a breeze that fluttered some white lace curtains at the windows. A breeze that reminded Derek of—of what? Of some other April, now long past? How sentimental, how out of character, for him. But there he was, plagued by some nameless nostalgia, like a silly popular song. Could he be remembering the April when he lived down here, for that one year and went to the local high school (his father, a professor of botany, was at the college in Pinehill to do work on local plants), and he used to look at that impossibly beautiful girl, that Deirdre Yates?

When Jimmy spoke again, after what Derek then realized had been a considerable pause, he sounded entirely sober. "Matter of fact, and this is one big reason for not going on with this silly Manhattan Project story—I'm worried as hell about that project. It's got to be some explosive device, like a bomb. I read this story in one of the new science-fiction magazines, and those fellows had made a bomb to end all bombs, and of course once it was made they had to test it. And the next thing after a test is use, the way I see it. They'll explode the goddam thing. But where?—and who'll get hurt? That's the stuff I worry about, don't you?"

"Indeed," said Derek, thinking that if Jimmy was a big enough fool to believe what he read in science fiction, well—hopeless. "I have great faith in the judgment of Mr. Truman," he said, trying to concentrate—as his mind remained drenched with the April odors.

Not having thought in a clear way at all about what he would do on leaving Jimmy Hightower's, it still seemed logical to Derek to head from there out to Deirdre's house, down the hard white road between the towering full green pines. Arriving at Deirdre's sprawling mess of a house (Russ had clearly not had an orderly mind), he parked in the gravelled area that was bordered with a heavy burgeoning growth of privet. No cars around, but so far that meant nothing. On the front porch (which was more than a little rickety, he noted in passing, needing a new rail, and the steps could use a little work), he rang the bell. And then, since no one came, and he heard no sounds, he knocked, lifting the heavy brass and dropping it, several times.

At last the door slowly opened, and there before him, in blue jeans that were unbecomingly rolled to the calfs, her hair tied up in a scarf—there stood not Deirdre but Melanctha, Russ's crazy daughter, who according to Deirdre was nothing but trouble.

He said, "I'm Derek McFall, I'm a friend of your—of Deirdre's."

Christ, was she blushing? Why? She said, "I know, I think we met—in Hilton?"

Oh. Fucking dance, with Cynthia Baird. He said, "I'm writing a piece about your father, about Russ." He forced a smile.

"Yes," Melanctha said. "You were. Do you, uh, want to come in? Deirdre? I guess she'll be back . . ."

The living room, where Derek had of course been before, with Deirdre, looked even shabbier than usual. Derek somehow remembered that Ursula, the regular housekeeper, had gone up to Norfolk to see a sailor son on leave, or something. There were a few stray new-looking pieces of floral chintz (Deirdre's choice?) that jarred with the old, the worn Victorian antiques.

They talked about the weather, Melanctha and Derek, and agreed that April was one of the nicest months, and that this present April was especially beautiful.

"One April a long time ago it snowed," Melanctha related. "On Easter. Everyone was amazed, and they couldn't wear their new hats."

"It snowed a lot in April in Vermont," Derek told her. "It was great. Spring skiing!"

What had not been much of a conversation then languished.

It was hard not to stare at Melanctha's breasts, Derek found. They were so very large, large but somehow not sexy. Perhaps it was because it was clear that she herself did not like them, even found them shameful. She sat hunched forward, her arms clutched across her chest. Her expression was anxious.

And then quite suddenly she said, "Did you know that Hitler was dead?"

"What?" There had been certain rumors for weeks, Hitler locked into his bunker, and so the statement was not entirely preposterous; still, Derek had almost laughed.

"In his bunker. He shot himself. First he poisoned that woman, Eva Braun. I think it said he married her. Anyway, they're both dead."

"Christ, it's hard to believe." This was all that Derek could think of to say for the moment. He wasn't thinking of Hitler, really, or of Europe, the war. He was thinking of Deirdre, the bitch, who had gone off and left him at the mercy of this neurotic young girl.

Who now said to him, in a purposeful way, "Something I've wondered about, I hope you don't mind my asking?" She hesitated, as though he could answer before she asked the goddam questions.

He gave her a large false smile. "Ask away," he told her.

This girl had beautiful skin, he had to give her that: clear, of the palest peach, with a light, light flush of pink. Boys must long to reach and touch her cheeks, not to mention those massive but probably soft great breasts. Derek thought: Good Christ, I'm too young to be a dirty old man, aren't I? He smiled again, more falsely. "Something you wanted to know about Hitler? I'm not really an expert. Just a working journalist."

"Oh no, no." She barely smiled. "About that colored man, the one who was with my father on the train."

"Edward Faulkner, from Roxbury, Mass."

She stared at him. "Yes. But I mean, whatever happened to him?"

"He was in jail, in that little town in Texas where the train was. I can't remember its name. But it sounds like in that town the Negro population didn't like the whites much, and they were more numerous. By far. The Negroes were. And so they just spirited this Ed Faulkner right out of there."

"But then what happened to him? Doesn't anyone know?"

Derek frowned; he was not a man who liked to say that he didn't know. Instead he took another tack. "I wouldn't worry about him not getting caught and punished eventually if I were you. Even if they're not entirely sure what, if anything, he did. They're bound to catch up with him. Lucky he'd been discharged, though, so it's not an Army case."

To Derek's astonishment, this crazy girl's eyes filled with tears; she looked terrified and not at all relieved in the way that he had expected to relieve her. To further reassure her he continued, in a gently authoritative voice, "He'd never come up here, I think you can be certain of that. That's something you must not worry about."

Melanctha's face contorted, her eyes began to overflow, and she seemed to choke, to find speech impossible. Then whirling back from him she tore into the depths of the house, and he heard her feet pounding up the stairs.

Leaving him standing there by himself, like a fool, in the April sunlight.

16

THE summer that everything happened, 1945, in Europe and Japan, Abigail spent in Pinehill with her mother. Thus, the two women sometimes celebrated and sometimes reeled from international events, but in truth both paid more attention to certain private concerns, connected to the very important men in both their lives: Harry Baird and Joseph Marcus, Ed Faulkner and Benny Davis, and Derek McFall. In more or less that order.

So much went on, in fact, that almost no one noticed the weather, which was remarkably fine, though very little time was spent in talk about it. Lovely soft days followed one another, broken by an occasional and very gentle afternoon of rain, just enough to keep all the flowers beautifully blooming. In the town there were ravishing roses everywhere, climbing on arbors and fences, or else low-lying, in bountiful bushes, in every variety of color and fragrance. White or lavender wisteria grew and thrived and blossomed all over town—and out in the woods, for the most part unseen, the loveliest dogwood flowered, amid secret gigantic rhododendron clusters, near the sweet-smelling caves of honeysuckle vines.

Cynthia had not heard from Harry for—it cannot have been more than a couple of weeks, but it seemed forever. And how she missed those jaunty, funny, often sexy letters—how she missed Harry, she now thought. Terrible song lines ran through her mind: "I'll never smile again, Until I smile at you—" in Frank Sinatra's heartbroken sentimental sexy voice. Or even, "This love of mine—"

She thought that Harry could have been killed, so easily, in a raid. And not "identified" yet. Or (and she had to admit that this seemed almost worse) he was off somewhere with some English girl, or not a "girl" but a bona-fide lady, maybe; Harry had always been something of a snob, she reminded herself. Or maybe just someone very young, who thought of him as a glamorous foreign hero.

She began to go through his letters, as though there might be a clue—although he would not be likely to mention a woman who had caught his fancy. Whom he fancied: was that what the English said?

"Raid . . . shelter . . . rations . . . proper tea . . . the ancient spires . . . raid . . . noise . . . scared shitless . . . I miss you! . . . our boys . . . I can't tell you . . . off to the country for the weekend . . . Devon, beautiful country . . . how are you, really? We must talk . . . direct hit . . ."

Bits and pieces of Harry. Cynthia thought that phrase, and then she thought, Oh God, suppose that was literally true? Suppose she was sent a box, bits and pieces of Harry?

Was she going crazy? These were ghastly, impossible, unthinkable thoughts, and yet she continued to think them.

In a magazine that she found in the beauty parlor, Cynthia read a story about a war-widowed woman, coincidentally a green-eyed blonde, who found comfort and happiness at last, at the end of the story, which seemed long—with a much younger man, a student who had been too young for the war. In law school, Cynthia wondered, how old would most of the other students be? And then she chastised herself: how could she? Although of course she *could,* and in the horrible, hideous event that Harry should be killed, after proper mourning she *should* pull herself together, see that she was still attractive, and look toward other men. Certainly not Derek, and probably her fellow law students would indeed be too young, but someone would be around, probably.

In another issue of the same magazine, in the same beauty parlor (Cynthia was a once-a-week regular), she read an article about husbands coming home. Women must not necessarily expect things to be all perfect all at once, she was cautioned; various readjustments were highly possible—were liable to occur. Wives must be understanding, non-demanding, calm and patient, and loving. It was even possible, the article then seemed to whisper, that problems of a sexual nature could arise. And although this was not funny, certainly not, Cynthia felt an inward smile at all this—maybe a smug smile, as she thought of Harry, of the easy and reliable happiness of their sexual life.

But: on still another day, Cynthia checked more carefully on the dates of the letters, and she clearly saw that she had not had a letter from Harry in twenty-four days, exactly. Which was not "a couple of weeks," it was more like three. This was ominous, any way you looked at it.

Abigail, who had said she was coming down in early June, called to say that she and Joseph had been offered a cabin on a lake in Maine—Sebago Lake, just north of Portland—and would Cynthia mind very much if she came in a couple of weeks? Oh, and would it be all right if Joseph came down too, for a week or so?

Neither of these plans was entirely "all right" with Cynthia; in fact, she experienced an acute pang of disappointment at the news that she would not, after all, have Abby to herself for the time that she had envisioned, and the pang was more painful since she felt it to be inadmissible, *wrong:* she had no right to be a demanding, possessive, and thus guilt-engendering mother.

And so she told Abigail that that was okay, fine; she would look forward to seeing Abby—*and* Joseph—in a couple of weeks. Enjoy Maine.

And in the meantime she kept busy gardening, doing extra cleaning and polishing in the house. She told Odessa to go up to Greensboro and stay for a while with her sister; Odessa loved this sister, and the bus trip was only a couple of hours.

Squatting in the pansy bed, trying to make sure which small green sprouts were weeds, and not the sweet William, before she pulled them, Cynthia thought that the worst mothers—and, come to think of it, the worst wives too—are the "hurt" ones. She was not sure how she had come by this piece of wisdom; she had never been accusing in that way with Harry or with Abigail—well, neither of them had ever really hurt her. So far.

Perhaps this knowledge came with some current intimation from them both: why did Abby want to go off to Maine with Joseph and then to bring him home when she came? Well, she thought she could answer both of those questions. But why hadn't she heard from Harry?

She did not know.

She missed Odessa a lot; Cynthia recognized this fact with a little surprise, but then she thought, Of course I miss Odessa. It was not that they talked a great deal in an intimate way, which they did not, but Cynthia was used to the warm human presence of Odessa, to the small sounds she made as she moved about the house, or the garden (Odessa made an almost humming sound, very soft, with no particular tune), and the clean, fresh, slightly sweet smell of Odessa. And actually she did depend on Odessa for certain crucial advice, relating usually to what to wear, what color with what. "Do you think, Odessa, with this dark green skirt, the pink silk shirt would be good?" "Well, you could do that, ma'am, but seems to me like that navy-blue silk shirt be better, but I don't know." She did know, though; the navy and green were elegant together. Odessa was a genius at color, Cynthia thought. She wished she could somehow tell Odessa not to call her "ma'am," but that seemed not the thing to do. She worried that Odessa wasn't doing any more sewing these days, what with wartime fabric shortages. Well, after the war. But what would she wear for Harry when he came home? Which most of the time she was quite sure that he would, maybe someday soon.

She was actually out in the pansy bed again when the phone rang and she ran in, out of breath, to hear Harry say, "Baby, guess where I am? Well, almost next door. I just flew in to D.C. and there's an Army transport plane going down to Durham—Camp Buttner, I guess—in half an hour. Can you meet me at four-twenty-three?" He laughed. "Give or take a few minutes."

After two years' absence, she is supposed to meet him in a couple of hours? Cynthia gasped, "But, Harry, I can hardly—"

"Christ, Cynthia. Pull yourself together. I'm tired." He added, "I want to see you," almost angrily.

At least I'm clean; that was one of Cynthia's ludicrous thoughts as she drove toward Durham, and tried not to think of what she had left undone. Well, the bed like herself was clean, she had just had time to change the sheets; she had meant but forgotten to take a steak from the freezer; had not had time to do her nails or iron a nightgown; she had fortunately bought salad things and a cake from the curb market yesterday.

It was probably about midnight when Harry said, his voice a little too loud in the dark, silent room, "I'm sorry, I guess I'm a little out of practice."

"Oh, so'm I!" Cynthia fervently lied. "But the great thing is, you're home! We have all this time."

Lowering his voice, Harry muttered, "I guess I'm tired."

"Oh, darling, of course you are. There, just go to sleep. Harry—darling."

The next day Harry spent mostly in his study, and Cynthia stayed in the garden, working on weeds and improving her tan, and trying to recall and to adjust to various magazine prescriptions: patience, kindness and affection, understanding. Those were the words that she remembered, and surely she could—? But, a small inner voice insisted, what about her own purely sensual feelings, her disappointed arousal? There was, she supposed, an obvious answer to that one, but she had never done that before, that "forbidden solitary vice," as she thought the sex books from her girlhood termed it. It seemed an odd time to start.

In any case, why should just one night be so worrying? They would have hundreds—thousands, even—of nights to make up for lost time. (But why was that thought so discouraging?)

The next night was not much better.

Nor was the next. It could be said that Harry was able to perform, but Cynthia was not, and even under these special circumstances she did not want to lie, to fake it.

Of course all over town there were welcoming parties: Harry was home—and the war in Europe was over.

"Harry Baird, if you're not a sight for sore eyes! You're just the handsomest *thing!* now isn't he, Cynthia? And you're looking mighty pretty yourself, Miss Cynthia—sure does perk up a lady when her lord and master comes home to roost, now doesn't it though? Harry, we want to hear every single *thing* about your time in London. With all those bombs, weren't you scared, not one little bit? And isn't Cynthia looking just as pretty as a picture? You-all must be celebrating up a storm. No, no one would blame you if you left this party real early, you must want to get home to your bed. Well, pardon me for saying it. I just meant they must need some sleep."

That was how, to Cynthia, every person at every party sounded, full of warmth and enthusiasm, prurience and sexual innuendo. And then she and Harry would go home from the parties, half-drunk, and pass out on the bed—to which, everyone thought, they had so much looked forward.

In early July, Abigail arrived, with Joseph Marcus, whom Harry had not met before and whom, Cynthia's instincts informed her, Harry would not especially take to. Harry would be nice, kind and polite and very "interested" in anything Joseph might say, but Joseph was not really Harry's cup of tea. A young physicist, with Jewish-Communist parents, not to mention the lover of Harry's very young and only daughter? All that asked a lot of Harry, a nice but basically very conventional man, with a lot on his mind these days. Cynthia herself did like Joseph, more and more; there was something wonderfully exotic about his eyes, an almost slant, and an interesting yellow-brown color. Also, perhaps more rationally, she thought that Joseph was both extremely intelligent and extremely sexy.

Harry and Joseph argued about the bomb that had been tested in Alamogordo, New Mexico.

"It'll scare the Japs into total surrender," said Harry, with military authority. "Christ, they're not going to risk that kind of destruction. Truman said—and Churchill—"

"I wish I were sure of that." Joseph's voice was both tentative and worried. "It doesn't seem in character for them to fear anything, to act on fear. Not from what we've seen of them. And then a lot of our fellows, the scientists in New Mexico I mean, are so hung up on this thing, what they call 'the Gadget'—Lord, as though it were harmless. I just can't believe they're not going to want to use it."

Both men, their two faces so very unlike, now wore very similar expressions, intense frowns of sincerity. Cynthia thought, Men! Harry is really saying, My generation is very reliable; I am a reliable, thoughtful serious person (which he was). And Joseph was saying, I don't know, this is all brand-new; I don't trust anybody around this "Gadget," this horrifying bomb.

Harry said, "I know Truman wouldn't use it unless it was

absolutely the only way we could win this war. Save our men's lives."

"But costing how many Japanese lives?" asked Joseph. "You have to count them too."

Unable to bring herself simply to put Abby and Joseph in the same room (what would her mother have said, and for that matter what would Odessa think?), Cynthia had put Joseph in the guest room, which was just across the hall from Abby's room. Convenient and discreet enough, except that in that old house the floorboards creaked, and thus Joseph's nightly trek across the hall was loudly broadcast, though by morning no one paid much attention to his return.

Cynthia only minded because of the situation, continuing, between herself and Harry. She was envious (God! envious of her daughter), and envy made her cross. Everything made her cross.

"Mother, don't you feel well?" Solicitous Abby, with the dewy flush of sensual happiness all over her face, and in her voice, and in the springy, confident way she walked.

"Yes—no, I'm fine," Cynthia told her daughter, and then she burst into tears.

They were sitting on the edge of the pool, their bare feet dangling in the water, both wearing shorts and halters. As she covered her eyes with her hands, pushing back tears, Cynthia thought: This is a hell of a place to cry, and what a time. To Abby she said, "Darling, I'm sorry, I just don't feel so great. I think it's the heat."

"Oh, I'm sorry." Quickly, Abby reached to pat her mother's shoulder, and she said, "It is hot. Do you think it's hard on you, having Daddy suddenly come home?"

Very startled—they did not go in for habitual frankness, and how, and what, could Abby know? Cynthia hedged. "Maybe. You know, you read these articles about readjustment." She tried to laugh, and did pretty well. "Maybe that's what we're doing. Readjusting."

Or maybe, she thought, I'm having an early menopause? Very early? And she recalled various horror stories of her mother's about that (supposedly) inevitably terrible time for women.

It was indeed extremely hot. The weather had changed from balmy and caressive to heavily oppressive, like a love affair gone bad. That was Cynthia's thought as, later that night, she and Harry lay carefully apart. Well, it was too hot for touching, it really was.

Not so, though, for Abby and Joseph, whose sensual fervor seemed, if anything, increased by the heat, and perhaps a little by the illicit fact of doing it in Abigail's parents' house. They even discovered a couple of new positions for themselves, new ways of doing things.

But in an interim of quiet, as they lay there in Abby's drenched and hot white bed, their bodies slick and for the moment exhausted, Abby told Joseph that she was worried about her parents. "They don't sort of sneak off for what they call naps anymore," she whispered. "You'd think that now especially they would, I mean with my father just home."

"Maybe that makes it harder for them. What we're reading about—'readjustment.' "

"That's sort of what my mother said. Well, God! I hope they get over it."

"My parents have never 'sneaked off for naps' and they're

still married. People get over stuff. You're supposed to know that. You're the doctor."

"Not exactly. Yet."

"I'm not even sure I want to be a physicist anymore."

"You're worried about stuff out in New Mexico?"

"I sure am."

17

AFTER the bombs that Joseph had predicted were actually dropped, on August 6 (Hiroshima) and August 9 (Nagasaki), and after a shared initial reaction of horror—although no one at the time had any idea of the range and intensity of destruction—arguments around the Baird household increased.

Harry felt, and he said, that Truman had no choice; he had given the Japanese an ultimatum, joined in by Stalin, Russia. If he had not used the bomb, God knows how many more American soldiers would have died. Probably more than the 80,000 known as instantly dead in Hiroshima, the 40,000 in Nagasaki. At least that many American soldiers: 120,000?

"Nevertheless," Joseph said with passion, "we cannot think of human life in terms of those numbers—any numbers. The bomb should never *never* have been used. Morally, entirely wrong."

"Besides," added Abby, who agreed with Joseph, "there may be long-term effects we don't even know about. We're just beginning to think about radiation. Doctors are. We just don't know what happened."

Cynthia too agreed in a general way with Joseph, although she did not quite say so. She felt that things between her and Harry were already touchy, possibly incendiary. She observed, though, with a certain objective (or nearly objective) interest, that it was the two supposedly scientific minds in the group, Joseph and Abigail, who on mostly moral grounds objected to this ultimate use of "science," whereas Harry, the reluctant military man, argued for it. Quite often she inwardly sighed over everything; it was all too much for her, she felt.

And then, days after the bombs, the war was over: the Japanese surrendered and everyone celebrated, and they all forgot about how much it had cost.

To Cynthia, Harry seemed frenziedly happy. Of course she too was glad that the war was over, but Harry was manic, hyperexcited. He brought out champagne for the four of them, Cynthia, himself, Abigail, and Joseph, in the stifling August heat. It was still hot at night; they sat around the pool, as though the water might make them cool, and toasted the end of the war.

Heat increased the smell of chlorine, and of privet—and of all their bodies; all four of those people had bathed or showered at least once that day, but still some scent of warm flesh and talcum powder lingered, plus light perfume from Cynthia, and Harry's new English aftershave (Cynthia imagined a present from some sad deserted English lady friend).

Exuberant Harry declared, "You see? It worked! Mr. Truman, the other Harry, that is"—he laughed—"old Harry did the right thing. If he hadn't dropped those bombs, we'd still be at it until God knows when."

No one had the heart or the energy to disagree, assuming they wanted to.

. . .

Cynthia had read a little about a mental illness, Manic Depression, which was characterized, she thought, by wildly erratic mood swings such as Harry had seemed to exhibit since he got home, and she wondered, Could that be what was wrong? Had Harry come down with, succumbed to (however you put it, the notion was ominous) this disease of the mind? Did it run in his family, possibly? This seemed hardly the moment to ask as she looked over at his still basically boyish, Irish-charm face, and heard his old warm, seductive laugh—and smelled (again) the new English aftershave, a light lavender.

This Manic Depression was usually treated with electric shock, Cynthia had read—what an entirely horrible idea! Also, that was what had killed poor SallyJane Byrd, the first wife of Russ, mother of Melanctha and those boys. When she went down to that terrible doctor with the awful sexy wife, whom everyone still talked about.

Oh, poor Harry! she thought.

On the other hand, it could be just an ordinary Nervous Breakdown, not Manic Depression. Friends of her father's had those breakdowns a long time ago. But Cynthia did not remember what anyone did to cure them, anything recommended; she seemed to recall that people went to Florida, Palm Beach or someplace like that, and took long walks.

Now Harry was pouring more champagne—from the bottle in the silver ice bucket that he had brought out (silly, in this weather; the ice all melted right away, no matter what you did).

Fireflies, tiny and bright, came darting out of the black

around the edges of flowers, in and out of dark bushes. Fascinated, Joseph explained, "We don't have them in New York."

"Children down here catch them and put them in jars and keep them in their rooms at night," Abby told him, and she reminded her mother, "Graham and I used to do that, remember? I showed him how."

But it was Harry who answered, "I sure do! And they were all dead in the morning, usually, and you were upset. It's hard now to remember you and Graham being such friends, isn't it? What a sissy he's turned out to be, I guess no wonder."

Abby frowned. "I don't think—"

But Harry went right on, "Joseph, drink up! We've barely touched this bottle—can't let it go to waste."

"I'm afraid I'm not much of a drinker, and I do have to get up early tomorrow. The train—"

All around them, invisible in the heavy night, tree frogs croaked their full-throated sounds, and somewhere off in the distance a lone hound bayed.

Cynthia was thinking that she had also read about men who came home from the war with afflicting ailments they did not want to talk about, but which were not necessarily "social diseases." (If the disease was "social," you would have to talk about it right away, wouldn't you?) Maybe ulcers, or hemorrhoids, something embarrassing. Maybe some little infection in the penis itself, noncommunicable but incapacitating? How little we know about these things, thought Cynthia as in her mind she heard, inappropriately, the song "Oh, I hope in my heart that it's so, in spite of how little we know."

"Well?" said Joseph to Abby as he stood up.

She stood too. "Okay!" and she kissed her parents good

night, and started back to the house with Joseph—a little too eagerly, Cynthia thought; couldn't they even pretend to observe proprieties? And then she thought, But what am I talking about? Who am I to talk?

Almost before they were out of earshot, though, just as the screen door to the house slammed shut, Harry began to talk, in a fast, compulsive way; it sounded rehearsed. Except that it also sounded as though he was starting in the middle.

". . . so trite," he said. "When I stand back from it, I can hardly believe this is me. But maybe the other stuff was trite too. Being faithful to you, the way I planned. But then in Devon there was this girl, she's Scottish, funnily enough she's a Lady, actually. Lady Veracity McCullough."

He paused just long enough for Cynthia to say, in a furious low voice, "I can't think why you're telling me this."

"Cynthia, darling, I don't blame you for being angry—"

"Oh, *good.* I mean it, why do I have to hear this?"

"Because I'm serious," he said. "Veracity and I—oh, darling—"

"Veracity. Oh Jesus."

"Cynthia, darling, come on—"

"Will you please stop calling me 'darling'?"

There were more tree frogs, throatily protesting, and another hound, with a deeper, more dismal voice. And always everywhere, the fireflies, and the jarring smells of chlorine, and privet, and wine.

Sounding for the first time quite angry, Harry told her, "Besides, I don't necessarily want to live down here. You've made all these plans, and gardens and swimming pool. And now your career law school in Hilton. Where do I come in?"

"Oh, Harry—"

"I like it in Washington, I've never really liked this dumpy town."

". . . well, I wish you'd said—"

"You weren't looking! You've been so fucking busy down here, you never looked at me—"

"Harry—"

"Well, I'm sorry, but—"

"I suppose Veracity looks at you all the time—"

"You're being cheap—"

"I know, I should have said *Lady* Veracity— Harry, we've got to stop this."

In disbelief, in the heavy hot dark, they stared at each other. Each remembering everything at once. Their life.

On a single impulse, they reached toward each other, and Harry pulled her to her feet. In a frantic embrace, they kissed, and kissed—until in the midst of kissing Cynthia fatally thought: *Lady* Veracity?

Standing back from him, she said, "Harry, please just go and sleep in the study. You've made me very tired." She patted him on the shoulder.

"Cynthia—darling, I understand how you must feel."

"You do not. I'm going up to bed."

Joseph asked, "Do you think we should get married?"

Abby gave it some thought. "I guess. Eventually."

"Or we could just live in sin forever."

She thought again. "That makes a big deal of it too, though, don't you think? Living in sin forever is as assertive as getting married."

Joseph laughed. "You're right, of course you're right."

After a small pause he said, "I think you're so smart, and so beautiful, you're so sexy and you always make me laugh. And I never say that stuff, does that bother you?"

"No, really not."

"And you don't mind that I don't talk about love?"

"No." She added, "It's not the kind of conversation we have."

"Well, for the record," he said, "I do love you. Assuming that we know what one means by the word."

She laughed. "For the record, me too."

To her own great surprise, as soon as she got into bed, alone, Cynthia began to cry. Almost worse, popular songs throbbed through her mind, their silly words thronged. The one I love belongs to somebody else—songs of love, but not for me—memories of you—dreams—blue—*you.*

And then she slept for a while.

Waking an hour or so later and acutely aware of all that champagne, she got up and went into her bathroom, for a very quick cool shower. Somewhat relieved, having also taken aspirin, she came back to bed in a rather different mood. Lady Veracity indeed, she thought. Why did I even have to listen to that stuff? And I didn't tell him a thing. I could have gone on about Derek—Derek McFall, or for that matter Russ Byrd. Even if they don't have English titles. How dare Harry? How cheap of him, how trite: American Naval Officer and His Lady. It's the dumbest story I ever heard—and I wish it were someone else's.

Her next sleep was sound and deep, and lasted until she heard Abby and Joseph, doors opening and closing, a suitcase banging down the stairs. She got up and put on a robe—not, by design, her prettiest, just a clean practical summer robe.

Harry emerged from his study, looking red-eyed, reproachful, in a travel-worn robe. And so it was together that they went out to say goodbye to Joseph, whom Abby was to drive to Durham, to his train.

Abby said, "I think I'll stop off and see Melanctha on the way home. She's back to Radcliffe soon. You know, their funny wartime schedule."

Joseph thanked them, and said he hoped he would see them in New York, or somewhere—maybe they would come up to Swarthmore? He'd had a wonderful time, he said (with possibly the smallest blush?).

Smiling to herself at their visible happiness with each other, their sheer young healthy well-being, as she thought, Oh good, I'm not envious of my daughter, Cynthia went into the kitchen, intending to make coffee, but Harry right behind her said that he wanted to make breakfast. "Just sit down," he told her. "I'll do it."

Not saying, Oh how nice, an English breakfast, but tactfully sitting down and not helping, Cynthia watched some very busy small birds on the grass outside. So wholly intent on their tiny projects, they were, as they hopped here and there on the yellowing grass, bright-eyed and observant.

Seated at last, with breakfast toast and coffee on the table between them, across from each other, Harry began—as Cynthia had almost, somehow, known that he would. "I think I was crazy last night, I must have been. I can't drink anymore—the champagne. Veracity—today the whole thing feels totally unreal. I mean I did have a sort of a fling, well, you must have too? I hope you did, I guess."

This last was clearly invitational, but Cynthia declined, and only looked at him as though unsure what he meant.

"Well," he managed to continue, "I'm really sorry for what I put you through. You must have thought I was crazy, not to mention—"

"As a matter of fact, I do think you may be having a sort of breakdown. Probably. I don't know much about this stuff." She had not at all known what she was going to say, but Cynthia continued firmly, "I think what you said about Pinehill and us is true, though. I love it here, and you don't. You love living in Washington."

"Oh, I'm not so sure about that."

"I'm pretty sure. Seeing you there, I saw you'd found your element. And what I think is, you should go back up there. If you think you need an excuse, there's always the Navy, some unfinished business." She caught herself: Why am I planning his life for him, even inventing his excuses? But she went right on. "And I think you should find some sort of psychiatrist up there. You could ask Dr. MacMillan."

"Jesus, Cynthia, I could find my own doctor. Assuming I need one."

Standing up, and managing a smile, Cynthia told him, "I really think I have a headache. I guess I'm not a very good drinker anymore either. I'm going up to lie down."

Back in bed, before she mercifully fell asleep again, Cynthia's first thought was, Will things get any better for us, after the war? And then she thought, Shit, it's already after the war.

Part Two

18

YOU could tell Deirdre almost anything and she would believe you—or so Melanctha thought. Later it occurred to her that maybe Deirdre believed what she chose, and that it had been convenient for her to believe Melanctha when she had said, "I guess I'll be heading up to Cambridge next week. Early registration." Deirdre, not having been to college herself, would not know that after you've been a freshman you do not have to register again. Or maybe she was as anxious to have Melanctha out of the house as Melanctha was to be gone? To be back in Cambridge, in the familiar dormitory, Whitman Hall, but alone. No one else would be back yet. Just a few of the maids around, maids who liked to open all the windows wide, to air out the rooms before the girls came back with their dirty habits, their cigarettes and their coming in at night with beer or worse on their breath.

Melanctha, who did not smoke and certainly did not go out drinking beer or anything else, to a great extent shared their attitude. Alone in the now smokeless smoking room, she savored the air, which even then in early September was brilliantly blue, electric. Which spoke of fall, in intensely New England accents.

She was supposed to be studying, in fact reading two

novels for a course in American literature, Faulkner's *The Sound and the Fury* and *Absalom, Absalom!* These were assigned not by the professor—an elegant Henry James scholar, who was worried by Faulkner, made nervous by his "Negroes"—but by the section man, a young poet.

Not really wanting to work, Melanctha leaned back with the books on her lap, in the lumpily padded maple sofa, beside the opened window, and remembered her father, Russ, the poet, saying (incorrectly, as almost always), "Ten years from now no one will give a thought to Henry James, who as Mr. Faulkner once said was a very nice old lady, and everyone will have recognized Mr. Faulkner as the giant-above-us-all genius that he is. Or was, if he's drunk himself into the grave by then."

Melanctha opened one of the books—it was *The Sound and the Fury,* Russ's favorite, and she began to flip through pages (she had read the book several times before), and there were all the old familiar words: bright, brave, honor, truth, death—and Caddy, and caddie. All those old words to which Melanctha responded as to the sound of a bugle, a call to tears, even as she thought: This is a bunch of shit, of brilliant junk, I hate it, I hated Russ—and she remembered without even looking at it the end of the other book, the end of *Absalom, Absalom!* where Shreve, the Canadian, asks the Southern Quentin, "Why do you hate the South?" and Quentin answers, "I don't, I don't. I don't hate it!" She thought, I hate William Faulkner. Probably his ancestors owned slaves who were the ancestors of Ed Faulkner, whom I must find. And for the first time she acknowledged to herself that that was her true reason for coming back to Cambridge so early, alone.

. . .

The house in Roxbury that Melanctha picked, almost at random, as belonging to Ed Faulkner's family, was large and gray-shingled and shabby, and far enough from the street and the sidewalk to seem vague in its outlines, indistinct. Certain parts of it—a tiny unattached house (cabin, cottage) in the rear and a rotting, half-fallen shed—would seem to have been added more recently than the building of the house itself, and maybe on the cheap. However, despite all the disrepair, the decay, the sheer size of the main house, its sprawl across its high, commanding hill, made it clear that this had once been a grand house.

"The colored have taken all of it over, all of what used to be the grandest neighborhoods, and they've just let it go to rot, the way they do." In that manner, Hattie, one of the Irish maids at Whitman Hall, had described Roxbury to Melanctha, who had asked for directions. And Hattie went on, "But you being from down South, you must know how they do?"

"No, it's very different. They live mostly out in the country, they don't move much, and certainly not into fancy neighborhoods." She had tried to explain, even as she had thought, I don't know what I'm talking about. The Negroes may all move North after the war, which is now. "Up here it may be all they can afford," she said vaguely, at that moment hating both Hattie and Mayor James Michael Curley, who presided over Boston—charmingly, dishonestly. Mayor Curley, Melanctha was sure, would agree with what Hattie had said: "You let the colored into decent places and they wreck them as quick as they can." And Melanctha would argue back, and she would be right, but they would win the argument.

A familiar sense of total frustration and outrage almost choked her.

. . .

In the Boston telephone directory under Faulkner, in Roxbury, there were fifty-seven names. The impossibility of getting in touch with such a number of people was relieving, and actually Melanctha could not imagine the necessary conversations: "Ed Faulkner? *Who*? Why? Which one? How come you looking for him?" (That last being the crucial and impossible question, since she didn't know herself.)

On the map Roxbury was just across the river from Cambridge. Very easy on the subway, although she was a little uncertain about the names of the stops along the way—and she did not want to ask one of the maids, especially not Hattie.

Which is how she ended up in Brookline, on her first try, instead of in Roxbury. On Longwood Avenue, in front of Harvard Medical School.

The crisp and bracing air of earlier that morning had evaporated into midday heat. Fall leaves hung limply from their trees, and a steamy odor of tar rose from recent patches of street repair. A hot breeze from the coast, the Atlantic, smelled of salt and dead fish. A foreign, alien land; only the tar was familiar. What on earth was she doing there? What was this quest for Ed Faulkner? Should she ever find him, what on earth could she say or do with him? His coming to see her in Pinehill had really been enough, and more.

Students from the med school hurried past her, men in Army khakis or Navy blues mostly, a few civilians. No visible women. And Melanctha felt herself to be invisible; she who had no reason to be there, actually. Dazed, she stumbled over to a bench and sat down.

A very large Negro woman in decorous black sat near her, with a younger, much smaller woman, also in black: her daughter? Were both of them maids somewhere? Could they know Ed Faulkner? At that preposterous thought, Melanctha covered her mouth and forced a cough, as though she had spoken those words aloud and the women could have heard.

Or had she possibly come out here, so stupidly unconscious, because she hoped to see Abby's friend, the mythically handsome (supposedly) Ben Davis? Who, she then remembered, is not even in med school; he turned it down and switched to some other line of study. Besides, if she were in fact looking for Ben Davis, how would she know him, or for that matter, how could he know her? Especially as she sat there on that bench, her hair too curly and long, her breasts too large (she was as usual hunched over to hide them). Kind Abby, her friend, would not have said any of those things describing her, Melanctha. But Abby could not possibly be out here, on Longwood Avenue, in front of Harvard Medical School, looking for Benny Davis, who did not even go to med school.

Melanctha felt that in some inner and crucial way she was seriously off track, maybe truly crazy, which she could *not be;* she could not be crazy, could not be like her mother, crazy SallyJane. She could not have gone mad in this heavy sultry unnatural displaced heat, which seemed to Melanctha to have risen up from the South.

With the utmost care and deliberation she got up from the bench and walked toward a sign that read Bus Stop, and then listed directions to Park Street, the all-change stop in Boston, which she wanted. And that was where, with the most extreme care as to both choosing and getting off and on cars, she at last arrived and found the easier-to-manage subway to Cambridge: Kendall, Central, Harvard Square.

She got off at the Square, and walked back through the Cambridge Common, past the Commander Hotel, to Whitman Hall, where at last upstairs in her room she fell across her bed in total exhaustion, forgetting dinner, forgetting everything—almost.

The next morning, she got up, rested and *okay,* and she walked to the Square for breakfast at St. Clair's. And then she took the subway to Park Street, changed to a trolley, and proceeded to Roxbury with no trouble. And she found, after walking around for a while, the tumbling-down gray house that she thought must belong to the family of Ed Faulkner—for no reason at all except the strength of her own instinct.

Recent hot weather, including this day's heavy, turgid heat, had yellowed and almost flattened the overgrown grasses that surrounded the broken cement path leading up to the broad and (very likely) once grand front door. The house and its scraggly yard were raised up, separated from the sidewalk by a grayish sagging concrete wall, at which Melanctha now stood, gazing up at those blank wide windows, that door—when something amazing happened: the door cracked and then swung wide open—and out came Odessa! Great tall Odessa from Pinehill. Who used to work for awful Dolly Bigelow, and then for Cynthia Baird, and now sort of lives at Cynthia's in a garage apartment. But now here she was in Roxbury, next to Cambridge, Mass. Odessa in a puffy yellow dress with a ruffled white apron, and her hair piled up in some kind of a yellow turban, so that she looked even taller, more majestic.

But of course it was not Odessa, who would never wear yellow (she always favored dark clothes, maybe because she was so big), or ruffles on an apron, or a turban, for heaven's sake. It was just a tall scowling woman of about Odessa's size, and of her color—and whatever was wrong with her, with

Melanctha? What kind of Southern-bigot-racist was she, thinking all Negroes looked alike?

Laboriously, tired and defeated, Melanctha made her way by trolley car and subway back to Cambridge. Back to the dorm and to the empty smoking room, where she did not feel like reading. Especially not *Melanctha,* which the section man thought was Gertrude Stein's masterpiece and which she was supposed to be reading along with Faulkner.

She heard the phone ring down at the switchboard, which was one floor below where she was, and she half expected someone to answer; then remembered that no one would, there was no one else there. She smiled to think that no one, *no one* could find her there.

But someone did answer the phone, and the next thing Melanctha heard was her own name, "Melanctha Byrd! Miss Byrd!" in the harsh angry Irish voice of Hattie, who seemed to be the only maid around. "Melanctha, line one!"

Goddam it, she thought. It had to be Deirdre, just checking on her. Damn it, damn Deirdre. And no way to pretend she was not there: Hattie had seen her come upstairs.

But it was a man's voice that said, "Hello? Is this Melanctha?" And in just that first instant she thought, A colored man? He sounds colored. And then, Bigot, Southern pig—she lambasted herself.

But she answered, "Yes?"

"This is, uh, Benny Davis? Abigail's friend. Uh, Abby told me you'd come back to school early, and I thought—"

. . .

His face was powerful, the skin bright black and smooth and mysterious, especially in the candlelit booth where they sat, in the Oxford Grill. His eyebrows were also thick and heavy, and his brow commanding. His lashes were thick (almost too thick, for a man?) his nose long and broad, and his mouth—his mouth was—you could only call it *sexy,* long and curvy, a beautiful (too beautiful) mouth.

Earlier, as they had walked in, Melanctha had had a terrified sense of being stared at, as though at any minute someone might loudly, horribly cry out: Who's that nigger with that young white bitch, or is she maybe part nigger, with that kinky hair?

But that voice was a Southern voice, rural, redneck (no one in Pinehill said "nigger")—and she was now in Cambridge, Mass., where people stared because Benny was so conspicuously handsome, and probably a lot of them knew who he was: Benny Davis, last year's football star, now 4-F because of a football injury, a torn ligament that made him limp a little—who had turned down early admission to Harvard Med, just saying he didn't want to be a doctor anymore.

Now, halfway through the second Scotch, which she had not much wanted although it tasted better and better, Melanctha was saying, ". . . and I didn't really know what I'd do about this Ed Faulkner if I found him, you know?"

He said, Benny Davis said, "I do know. Those imperative impulses that you don't quite understand." His voice was deep and gentle—beautiful.

"Imperative," Melanctha echoed, in a pleased whisper, mostly to herself. She felt that he had understood whatever she meant but had been unable to say. She was a little dizzy, and blinked to stay awake.

And Benny then said, "And now I'm going to order us up some French fries. They're really good here, and I'm hungry, and you'll have to help me out. You get one whale of a lot."

French fries! How could he have known? Melanctha loved French fries above all else, just great crispy French fries with catsup; she could eat French fries forever, at any time, even times like now when she didn't really feel like eating—although she knew that she should eat something, she had not got around to lunch. If she didn't eat she'd be drunk; she might be drunk anyway.

"Do you know Abby's friend Joseph Marcus, and his sister, uh, Susan?" Ben was asking, quite out of the blue, it seemed to Melanctha.

"Not really, I mean we haven't met, but of course I've heard so much. You know," she told him, "French fries are my truly favorite thing. I love them." She had meant it, but how incredibly silly she sounded, how girl-undergraduate, and worse, how Southern. Her very accent must sound terrible to him although she did still catch certain Southern turns in his speech.

"Really nice, the whole family, I think," Ben told her, sounding not entirely as though he meant it, something perfunctory in his voice.

"You met them all?" Feeling better at the very prospect of French fries, Melanctha was curious.

"Uh, yes, I did. A couple of times. Together and sort of separately." He looked away, around the room, as though conceivably the Marcuses might all be there—at separate tables, maybe. And then he said, with a laugh but sounding as though he absolutely meant it, "I think Joseph is almost good enough for Abigail."

"Oh good, I'm glad you think so. She really likes him."

They were still talking about how great Abigail was when the French fries came, and at even the first few bites Melanctha felt better, so much so that she said, "You may have saved my life. I was feeling a little rocky."

"I thought maybe you did."

"Maybe you should have been a doctor, after all."

"Maybe so. I just wish I knew what I was—was going to do, I mean."

"But you could be anything!" Good Lord, was she drunk, after all?

Wryly, "I'm afraid that's true," he said. And then he asked, "How would you look with your hair cut really short? You've thought about that?"

She could feel an uncomfortable, unreasonable blush. "Not lately, I mean I've been really busy. Trying to decide stuff." As she thought, I'll get it cut tomorrow. I'll call the Ritz, they're supposed to be best—she remembered that Rosalyn, the most beautiful (and richest) girl in Whitman Hall, had said that.

Ben said, "In a way, you remind me a little bit of Susan Marcus."

Melanctha forced a laugh. "She has long kinky hair?"

"Oh, come on, not at all." He mused. "Don't know what it is."

Melanctha immediately thought, All white girls are alike? She drinks too much? One more nice-girl incipient alcoholic . . . I wonder if her parents drink a lot too; it seems to run in families, I think.

"Her parents are kind of, uh, odd," Ben told her, exactly as though she had asked the question aloud.

"Odd how?" God, so are mine! she wanted to say.

"Well, they talk a lot about the Party, I guess they mean Communists, and they say a lot about Russia that sounds sort of, uh, sentimental. I mean I admire that army too, they've been incredible, but I don't know, with the Marcuses it's more like worship."

"Oh." The oddity of the Marcuses, then, was entirely unlike that of her own parents, nothing to do with drinking, or sex, or depression, nothing like that. Following her own rather than Ben's train of thought she told him, "My stepbrother's coming up to Harvard next year. He's really my half-brother, I mean, my father was his father too, but no one was supposed to know that, and then after my mother died my father married his mother, that's Deirdre. His name is Graham. He and Abby used to be really friends—in fact, he was the first one of us she met."

"I sort of remember, something about the pretty little boy with a beautiful mom. Is he still a pretty little boy?"

"Well, not exactly."

Feeling better, Melanctha became more aware of her surroundings. Immediately before her there was the giant glass bottle onto which many colors of candle wax had dripped, like a painter's palette, she thought. Not having seen this done before, she assumed it to be accidental.

And she had never sat in a booth in a public place, or for that matter, in any place with a Negro man. She knew that she should not think of it that way, but still she could not resist the thought of Dolly Bigelow, for example, or Irene Lee, any of those women from home, from Pinehill, walking in. Would they screech, and try to get her out of there, or just plain faint dead away? No, neither of those; she knew exactly what they would do, which would be to pretend she was simply not there, and certainly that Ben Davis was not there—and then they would go home and talk about it for the rest of their lives, if not longer. "You-all won't believe this, but up in this sort of restaurant in Cambridge, near Harvard College, we saw that Melanctha Byrd, we'd know her anywhere with that hair, and those—that *chest*—"

"You have the nicest smile," Ben Davis told her.

"Oh, I was thinking"—she grinned—"I was thinking of getting my hair cut really short."

A little later, she was able to ask him what she had been wondering all night, off and on: "How come you have sort of a Southern accent, growing up in Connecticut?"

"Both parents," he told her. "Up from Alabama in the twenties, round the time I was born."

After another pause, Melanctha said (again), "These fries were terrific. Just what I needed."

"Sure you don't want anything a little more substantial, like a hamburger? A nice steak?"

"Oh no, thanks, I really don't." Melanctha had spoken more vehemently than she meant to, but the very mention of those foods had made her stomach roil and churn again. She was not all right.

Observant, and very kind, Ben Davis said, "I think we'll take a cab. I don't feel like all that walk either, my goddam leg."

After walking up to the Square, they quickly got a cab, and the drive from there to Whitman Hall was brief. However, in the course of that drive Melanctha had time for two observations: one, that she felt much better, she was really okay now; and two, that she liked this Ben Davis very much. In a curious way, he felt to her like a very old friend, someone she could perfectly trust, who was warm and kind, with no bad surprises.

19

Lady Veracity
Has an infinite capacity
For inventive mendacity
Despite her opacity
—stupid tenacity—
—her pushy audacity—
—well-known rapacity—

THUS Cynthia somewhat bitterly amused herself; it could go on and on, she saw—such a fortunate name, from her point of view. At the same time, she invented for herself an actual Lady V., whom she saw as tall and skinny, like a crane, with a great long pointed "aristocratic" nose, skimpy hair, and no breasts. Although at the same time a more reasonable interior voice informed her that under no circumstances even for a moment would Harry pay the least attention to anyone who looked like that. He liked medium-sized green-eyed blondes, with nice teeth and pretty breasts. Like her. Cynthia's eyes teared for an instant at this recognition, but in the next minute she was angry again as she thought, Was it possible that Harry thought the two of them looked alike, she and this mythical Lady V.?

That fall, after what Cynthia thought of as the summer of Harry's disclosure, they were still at what seemed a standstill, Harry still saying that he had never truly cared for the Lady V.—"Vera," as he now referred to her. She remained Lady V. for Cynthia.

"Christ, I barely fucked her!" Harry once in desperation cried out.

"How on earth did you manage that?" was Cynthia's irony-laden response. "I must say, it suggests some interesting gymnastics. 'Barely fucked.' My, my."

By now it was late November, in and around Pinehill a smoky, dry month. Outside of town the gray dirt crumbled in abandoned cornfields, beneath the broken stalks and scarcely distinguishable furrows. The honeysuckle vines that edged the creek were bare and heavy and tough, and the creek was low, dingy brown, and sluggish, its cargo of dead leaves, twigs, and trash slow-moving. The sky was an enormous sweep of gray, cloudless and unchanging until the very gradual darkening of twilight, which came much earlier each day. It seemed. Blue clouds of smoke rose from the country cabins where Negroes and very poor white people lived; the air smelled of that smoke, or dryness, thin dry leaves and dry earth.

In Connecticut, such a sky, with all that looming heavy gray, would have surely meant snow, but down here not so, Cynthia had finally learned. Down here it almost never snowed, maybe a few times every year or so, and the gray sky only meant that this was November.

It was easy to lose track of how quickly the dark came in these shortening days. One afternoon, Cynthia, having taken a favorite road that wound through pine woods just beyond the southern edge of town, watched the night fall quite suddenly; the sky was almost as dark as the heavy pine woods on either side of the pale dim road.

She knew where she was; she did not think she was lost. However, along with the advent of darkness, all the air around her in an instant seemed suffused with a thick, sweet, and pungent odor, and at the same time she began to be aware of voices, not far off. A cluster of voices, some calling orders. Male voices. Negro? White? She was not sure. It did not occur to her to be frightened; rather, she was curious: what on earth was that smell, and what were those men doing?

She walked on toward what she recalled as a large cleared space, what had been an old cornfield. Before she saw anything ahead, she gradually became aware of heat, and then she saw it: a very large bonfire, there in the center of the field. A bonfire with a giant black pot suspended over it. And above the pot was a sort of box; whatever was in the box dripped into the pot, and attached to this primitive contraption was a very long shaft, a wooden pole, at the outer end of which was a heavily plodding mule, who slowly trod a large circle around the fire.

They were grinding sorghum, and Cynthia now remembered that Russ had once described exactly this process to her, including the dark and the smell, the mystery! Which is how, though basically unmechanical, Cynthia had instantly come to comprehend what she saw. One of the men occasionally prodded the mule with a switch, and another man, wearing what looked to be a heavy mask, stirred at the pot with some huge crude spoon, then yielded both mask and spoon to another man. Probably no one could stand the heat or that smell up close for very long.

The scene had a ritualized quality, a pageant of November. She remembered that Russ had explained to her about sorghum, and described it thus. Like the scene of a play. Of one of his plays.

And so Cynthia walked on home and thought of Russ. She was filled with thoughts of Russ as well as of that vision, the bonfire in the center of the dark; and the men, some were black, some white, she had slowly realized; and the mule, plodding with infinite deliberation in its circle, treading the husks of the sorghum into dust. And the smell. She had never smelled anything so sweet and so bitter, together. So powerful.

She was still in a state of confused and strong emotions an hour or so later. She had even made herself a drink, something she did not usually do alone. When the doorbell rang, her heart jumped violently, as she crazily thought, Russ! And then, Derek?

It was Melanctha Byrd, who stood there on the front steps, her thin face strangely lit by the glare of the porch light.

"Melanctha! How nice. Come on in. I'm really glad to see you."

Finding as she said this that she meant it, Cynthia stepped back, gesturing for Melanctha to come inside.

But Melanctha hesitated. "I was just sort of driving by," she said. "And I saw your lights, and I thought—"

"You thought we hadn't seen each other for a while, and that's right. I'm so glad—but don't just stand there, come in."

Saying all this, even taking Melanctha's arm, Cynthia silently thought, God! Southern people are impossible! All tied up in their own impossible knots of infinite politeness, traditional behavior.

"Melanctha, let me get you a drink," she said.

"Oh! well—okay, that would be very nice."

Melanctha still stood there tightly as Cynthia asked, "How about a glass of sherry? That's what I'm having. It's California but pretty good. Melanctha, please sit down."

"Yes'm, I do like sherry. My mother—" She seemed to decide not to finish this sentence, but she did sit down, and by the time Cynthia came back with the sherry and glasses on a small silver tray, she was almost composed.

However, when she began to speak she was breathless still; Cynthia heard an undercurrent of hysteria in her voice.

"This amazing thing," she told Cynthia. "You know Ed Faulkner, that colored sergeant who was on the train with Russ when he died? And later he came to see me here, that really strange visit, that I told you?"

"Yes, of course I remember."

"Well, the strangest thing of all. I got this letter from him and he's in New York. Well, that's not so strange by itself but he's staying with the Marcuses. You know, Abby's friends?"

"Of course I know. But good Lord, how on earth?"

"I don't honestly understand it myself. They found him in Roxbury someway. Some cousin of his? It's all got to do with them being Communists—the Marcuses, I mean. That's how they found him in Roxbury."

"Good Lord."

"You know I went to Roxbury myself, looking for him, but of course I didn't have a clue." And then, in an entirely different nice-Southern-girl voice, she commented, "This sherry's really nice."

The strange story, which no one ever got quite the straight of, began in Johnsville, the town in East Texas that the train went through, going from Los Angeles east. The town where Ed Faulkner had relatives, and where, quite senselessly, Russ Byrd had died.

Johnsville was just a flat crossroads town, with some one-story clapboard houses, several stores, and two churches, Baptist and Presbyterian. One of the stores was a bookstore, and here the strange part starts: it was run by an elderly, tall, skinny (nearsighted, gap-toothed) Marxist scholar, also an avowed Communist, who called himself Leon Trotsky McDermott and made a great point of renting, not buying, his store. Of owning essentially nothing. He would have preferred to be called Leon but was locally known as Mac—Mac the Red. He and his wife, a woman from working-class radical Jewish parents in New York, had formed a Marxist study group, so far consisting of themselves and a much younger couple, the Mansens, from Ely, Minnesota. The McDermotts, Leon (Mac) and Anna, referred to this group as their Cell, and indeed they had written to and contributed in not very large amounts to Party Headquarters in New York; there was a signed letter from Earl Browder himself to prove it.

At the time of Russ Byrd's accidental death in their town, this group, in a state of panicky excitement, was sure that Ed Faulkner was going to be lynched: the Klan or some local citizens' vigilante-posse would steal him from the jail. And when he was actually stolen out of jail, they could not believe that it was his kinfolks, some nice local Negroes whom they knew, who had taken him out: easy enough, a Faulkner cousin was the jail caretaker, Ed was by no means the first escapee. And even after Ed Faulkner had been tried *in absentia* and found innocent (Russ had died of a heart attack), the Cell still felt that Ed needed protection, and they wrote again to Party Headquarters in New York, to Earl Browder. Ed Faulkner would surely be hounded down in secret by the FBI; he surely needed to be saved. Leon—Mac—felt that the Party would know what he meant by that, that Ed Faulkner was a good candidate for recruitment; the Party was always interested in new Negroes, even among the non-famous, and—who knows?—the case against Mr. Faulkner could always be reopened by some of Russ Byrd's angry Southern people (right-wing-bigoted, even possibly Klan—never mind that Russ was not known to have any such connections). And Ed's address in Roxbury, which was easily obtained from his cousin the handy janitor, was sent along with the significant details of his personal history.

The involvement of the Marcuses in all this came about in a coincidental but very simple way. Susan Marcus, an eager member of the Young Communist League, known as Ypsils, did occasional part-time volunteer work at Party Headquarters, down on Union Square and not too far from where her parents lived, in the Village. And it was Susan Marcus to whom this large and somewhat confused sheaf of papers was handed. And Susan, a careless speed-reader, leafed through and stopped at the name Russ Byrd. She had heard of him because of Abby Baird, her brother's girlfriend. And so she wrote to Ed Faulkner, in Roxbury, mentioning the connection with Melanctha, and asked if he didn't want to come down and stay with her family in New York. They had plenty of room and they'd be happy to have him. And in case he was looking for a job, her father just might be helpful there too. She indicated that they all, including Melanctha, felt bad about what had happened to him, his just chancing to be there when Russ fell down and died in Texas.

Ed took them up on this invitation. He thought maybe he'd stand a better chance of finding a job in New York—or he might decide after all to try to go to college, on the new GI Bill. He wrote to Melanctha, feeling that she was somehow responsible for the coming of the Marcuses into his life. The Marcuses, he wrote her, were about the nicest folks he had ever met. They were so good and kind to him, all of them, like parents. Like brother and sister.

"Anyway," Melanctha wound up her story, and taking a gulp of sherry, "there he is living at the Marcuses. I guess Susan's taking this term off, working in her father's office along with the work in politics that she does. I sort of guess Ed will work there too." And they'll start kissing and being in love and all that, maybe even get married, Melanctha further thought, and of course did not say. But it wounded her, this idea—not so much from jealousy; she had not liked Ed Faulkner all that much, it was surely okay with her if he found a girlfriend. She was wounded, rather, by her own perception of being left out, always, permanently. People seemed to pair off in a natural way, but not her. She could not imagine the partner she was meant to have. Her doomed sense was that such a person did not exist.

"If only it would snow," Cynthia said abruptly, out of what had become a silence. "I still don't understand the weather down here. It looks like snow but then it never does."

"One year it snowed," Melanctha told her. "It was terrific. My father pulled us up and down the road on our sleds, and my mother made snow ice cream."

"Snow's fun," Cynthia agreed, hearing and not at all liking the wistfulness in her own voice. But she had just been visited by a thought or a feeling not unlike Melanctha's; she thought,

Everyone just now seems to have someone else. Harry and this crazy thing about this Lady Veracity. Derek and Deirdre.

To Melanctha she said, as lightly as she could, "I suppose Deirdre's off somewhere with that Derek McFall." As she spoke, she realized how much she had wanted to say—to ask this.

"Oh no, they broke up. Or I think they did. I'm maybe wrong," said Melanctha unhelpfully.

"The thing is, I don't really like November down here. But I guess it really could snow. Let's have some more sherry, shall we?"

"Oh sure. Thanks."

The two women smiled uncertainly at each other as Melanctha held out her glass.

And simultaneously, separately, they wondered what to say next.

20

THE Marcuses are so nice to Ed Faulkner that he is confused. Mrs. Marcus especially, who wants him to call her "Sylvia," or "Syl." "That's what most of my friends call me." And she keeps asking him what he likes best to eat; she can cook anything he likes, she says: Is steak his favorite? Pork chops? Does he usually have grits for breakfast? Cornbread? Ham and eggs? She acts like she wants to be his maid, for Lord's sake, or some waitress at a counter. He somehow does not dare to tell her that his true favorite thing is lobster; his daddy used to buy it down at the wharves, in Boston. "And lunch?" she asks. "Lamb chops? Is there any special salad you really like?" Yeah. Lobster salad.

Does she possibly want him to fuck her? It doesn't seem like that could be it at her age; she's got to be a lot past forty, a white lady with a husband right there. Still, Ed has heard of such—although he surely hopes that's not what she wants. In the meantime he just answers her the best way he can. "No'm—I mean no, Sylvia—no, *Syl*—I like both steak and pork chops pretty good." And, "Yes'm—yes, Syl, corn bread is good. I have to say, I'm not real fond of grits. I guess I had a little too much of that in the Army."

The truth was he'd never had grits at all before he went into the Army. His mom, who was born in Harlem and right proud of it, could not abide the sight or smell of that "down-home stuff," as she called it, and his daddy came along with her, as far as food went. Being there in Roxbury right next to Boston, they liked to eat Chinese, or Italian, for a treat. Ed's daddy did deliveries for a big liquor store, the North Station Liquor Mart, and he made good money, what with the tips and all. So sometimes for a real treat there'd be that lobster. And maybe some shrimp and clams.

Mr. Marcus—of course he asked to be called Dan—wanted mostly to talk. At first this was bothersome, all the things he brought up, and questions he asked: How did Ed feel about serving in a segregated army? Did he really think Truman would do anything about it? Was it strange for him, being down South after growing up in Massachusetts? How were the schools in Roxbury, did he think? Had his parents gone to school up there too? Had he played a lot of basketball in school? (Because of his height, six feet four, Ed was used to being asked about basketball; the truth was, he never had played. He was clumsy on his feet; the only sport he ever did well at was track, and even in that he never set any records.)

What Ed soon learned was that Mr. Marcus, "Dan," liked to answer his own questions. He liked to make little speeches about his own opinions, so that all Ed had to do was smile as though he agreed, as though he even knew what Mr. Marcus was talking about.

"Of course it's really a class issue, isn't it, as much as race. The Negro people in the South and a lot of Northern places too are held down to slave wages. I'm not sure the FERC has made all that much difference, are you? And I just don't know about Mr. Philip Randolph. Seems to me like he's what you might call a capitalist tool. Or even what you would call a Tom, don't you think?"

"I reckon."

Ed noticed that when Dan Marcus talked like this, his voice, his accent tended to get sort of Southern, really more like somebody on a stage talking Southern. Or talking Negro, maybe.

What Ed could never explain to Dan Marcus—not that he even wanted to try: Dan would have been much too interested—was his own trouble with all those down-South Negroes. Those supposed-to-be brothers of his, same color, although he was lots lighter than most. Same nappy hair and big mouths. But half the time he could not understand a word they were saying. And they thought he was some kind of a snob, a Tom, for talking like a Yankee. Talking white.

"Were you sorry not to go overseas?" asked Mr. Marcus. "I reckon you were. Missing Paris. You know, unless it's changed a lot there's really no color line there. In fact I've heard that a lot of Negro GI's—and in England—and I'm sure Italians—"

On and on he went, smiling, enjoying his own speeches, agreeing with his own opinions and probably imagining that Ed did too.

Susan Marcus wanted to flirt with Ed, but she didn't know quite what kind of flirting to use, and she tried out different ways. She was all the time mostly after getting his attention.

She was a pretty enough girl, Susan was, in her blond Jewish way, with her straight-down hair that was curled (too curled) at the ends, and her chunky frame—built like a fireplug, that girl was, or as they used to say, a brick shithouse.

One of the attention-get things that she did was wear tight sweaters. Too tight for her small boobs; she was not any Ann Sheridan, or Lana Turner either.

She wore a lot of bright colors too. Had somebody told her that that was what Negroes liked, loud pink? ("Nigger pink" he had heard about down South.) And a terrible pea-green sweater that she had. Ed really liked to see girls in black dresses, even black sweaters, and pearls. Black really set off a girl's looks, he thought, no matter what was her color.

Another thing that Susan tried, along with the bright colors, was serious conversation. She told him a lot about her work down at "Party Headquarters."

"People say all these bad things about the Party," she told him. "All this terrible anti-Communism. It's a lot like anti-Semitism or being anti-Negro. But we get in some amazing reports. There was this group down in North Carolina, at the university there—in Chapel Hill?—and they started up this credit union, for Negro people down there. The first one ever, so Negroes could borrow money, like anyone else. Honestly, those Southern people are hard to *believe,* don't you think?"

"I got some pretty nice family down there."

"Oh—*well.*" He'd caught her that time. No way she could say, "Well, all Negro people are nice." Although she may have really thought that, that's how ignorant she was.

And so, partly to tease her, he said, "But you're right. Some of those down-home niggers I met in the Army, bad stuff."

"Oh, I hate that word!" He could tell that she really did hate it, she shuddered all over.

But he couldn't resist more teasing. "Nigger? Down South they use it all the time, every color of folks." He smiled at her, being nice. "But you don't like it, you don't use it, okay?" She took him seriously—she was really a serious girl. No chick. "Oh, I won't," she said. And then, "But I guess it's sort of like certain words my father uses, words about Jews. And some jokes he tells. Awful jokes, about Jews. But he says it's okay for him since he is one. I don't quite get it, do you?"

"I don't know. I guess not."

And then in a flirty way she told him about guys she dated at Swarthmore College. "There was this football player," she said. "A classic. Big and stupid and conservative! Gee! The worst kind of a bigot, a Fascist, really he was. I just went out with him a couple of times. A football player, honestly!"

"Those guys aren't all so bad," Ed told her. "A couple of them in our high school, just plain regular guys. And smart."

This was not strictly true. The football guys at Roxbury High were boneheads, and besides they were white. Ed didn't even know them, to speak to. But it was fun to tease Susan, she got so confused, so easily.

But, "Oh well," she said. "Talk about smart. We knew this guy who played on the team at Harvard. And very smart, he was going to go to med school but then he decided he didn't want to be a doctor. And he was—a Negro." She added recklessly, "He's extremely good-looking."

And I'll bet you really went after him, Ed did not say.

She went on about this Harvard football player, this Negro. "He's a friend of my brother's girl, Abby Baird. And she's a big friend of that Melanctha Byrd, the one you know." She had said more than she meant to say, he could tell.

And he was no help. "You mean the one whose father I did not kill on the train?"

She looked so miserable that he felt a little sorry for her as she murmured, "Yes."

He said, "That Melanctha's a real nice girl. I reckon your brother's girlfriend, that Abby, is too?"

"Oh yes, Abby's terrific. Even my mother likes her. And my father forgives her for not being Jewish."

Ed thought, White people are as crazy as niggers.

The one of the family that he liked by far the best was Joseph. When he was with Joseph, the two of them just talked, like regular people. Joseph was not the whole time thinking, I'm talking to a Negro. Like the rest of them did.

Joseph talked mostly about his plans. After MIT, what kind of work he wanted to get into. "There's some very exciting projects going on these days in physics," he told Ed. "But I'm sort of worried about government connections with them. You know, the new HUAC. The House Un-American Activities Committee. Hell, they start poking around and interfering, and they could decide my parents are un-American."

Ed laughed. "You mean on account of being Jewish?"

"Jewish Communists. Already that sounds un-American. I mean, if they start investigating physicists who want to work on the Manhattan Project, for example, they might conclude that I don't come from a very reliable American family. I'm not saying that this is going to happen, but it could. I know a lot of people who're worried."

Ed didn't understand a lot of this; it was stuff he had never heard of, mostly, and he didn't like this sense of being "ignorant" (like people said niggers were), and he had at that moment a new and startling idea. He said, "You know, I've been thinking, now that my Army discharge is all cleared, all okay, maybe with this GI Bill I could go to some school out west, like Wisconsin. I hear Madison's really neat."

"I've heard that too. But why not try for the top? Try Harvard, or Swarthmore's very good. You'd like it there. I did."

"Harvard! Jesus, I'll be real lucky to get in at Madison." This was not entirely true. Ed had a high B+ average in high school, considered not bad at all in that tough, competitive school.

"Actually I think my mother wants to get out of the Party," Joseph next said, in a worried way.

"You don't want her to?"

"Oh no, actually I think she's quite right. I mean, the Moscow trials and all that, not to mention the pact—and Finland. Well, I just think she's right," he said, seeming at that moment to understand that Ed probably did not realize what he was talking about. "I just don't like my parents arguing," he explained. "No matter who's right."

"My mom's the one always right," Ed told him. "Especially when she's not."

Ed had in fact heard the Marcuses arguing. His room was right next to theirs, and so he heard:

"—but the Party—"

"—Richard Wright—"

"—the KGB, you can't deny—"

"—exploitation—"

"—collectivism—"

"—the trials—"

"—at Harvard, Father Smythe—"

A bunch of half-heard, mostly unfamiliar names and phrases, mixed up with the familiar ones that he heard when his own parents argued—he guessed, when anyone did.

"—you always—"

"—you don't understand—"

"—I can't—"

"—you never—"

"When you go out to Madison, I'll come to see you, okay?" Susan had to shout above the noise of the band, a trio really, but loud, a bass and a sax and a trumpet, plus a guy that sang—looked like part Indian. They were perched on small chairs at a tiny table with another couple they had never seen before; the waiter just put them there with no questions, no apology. At a cellar joint on Fifty-second Street where Susan had handed out a couple of tens just to get them in—all her idea: his birthday, her party, she said.

He teased her. "Not your folks' famous Party, I hope."

For a minute she didn't get it, and her blue eyes got wide, inviting pain—and then in another instant she had caught on, and with a small ironic smile she said, "Nothing like that, I hope."

Or that is what he thought she said. You couldn't hear in this place, especially with that guy up there singing, along with the band, the trio. Now singing "Margie."

"You are my in-spir-a-tion, Margie,
I'll tell the world I love you—"

He had a good beat, this singer. As they say, a great sense of rhythm. But he did, he broke up the words into beats. And he had a good big friendly smile, all white teeth. The folks loved him, white and black too, and they clapped along. Especially Susan, her whole body was caught up in that beat; she listened, and nodded and swayed.

In the Army, Ed had heard a story about some white chick who could actually come, listening to Louis Armstrong. Well, he liked Louis too, who didn't? But really—

Ed thought about later, how they'd be kissing in the taxi going home, getting all worked up, and then more kissing in the downstairs living room, on the big wide velvet sofa where he always worried: were they making stains? But, tonight: would he get it inside her? (She has told him she isn't a virgin, so there isn't blood to worry about—he hoped.) And would she really be doing it with him, coming for him? Or would it really be the singer guy she was fucking, fucking a darker Negro?

As for him, he'd be doing it with Lena Horne, a really beautiful woman. Not any fat little old white girl.

21

"WHEN we first moved down here, I used to go on long bike rides, or else I'd just walk as far as I could," said Abby. "And one day I came right down here, to the creek, and I was standing on the sand, I guess actually sitting down on a log, I'd decided to take my shoes off and wade, and this extremely pretty little boy came along and told me not to, he said the creek was too dirty for wading, and then his mother came up—I mean his sister, she said she was his sister. And it was Deirdre and Graham. We talked, and I asked them to come home with me for a Coke or something—that was when we first got here and we lived in that sort of penthouse at the Pinehill Hotel. But that's how we all met, how my parents met Deirdre, and they really liked her. I remember I was sort of jealous, I wanted her to stay my friend, not theirs. I thought she was closer to my age than to Cynthia's and Harry's. Graham was just this very small boy, but so pretty."

Melanctha, to whom Abby has just said all this, sighed deeply as she said, "He still is pretty. I worry a lot about Graham." With a small wry laugh, she added, "When I'm not worrying about me."

Abby agreed with her. "Yes, he is worrying."

"I mean, at Harvard, some older boy who, you know, liked

boys could assume that Graham was like that too . . . 'queer.' And Graham's such an innocent, I think. I mean, he seems a lot smarter and more knowing than he is. He's always been like that."

Abby nodded, agreeing again.

This conversation took place on an oddly bright day in December; it almost looked like spring, it was almost warm. The two young women, both home for Christmas vacation, had said this to each other earlier on the phone, and had decided simultaneously on a walk in the woods.

All the paths in their repertoire of woods walks would take them, in one way or another, down to the creek. They had chosen the way that led through some small deciduous trees, now leafless and gray, then down a fairly steep pine-wooded hill, to a narrow and mostly overgrown white road (no one was sure where ultimately it went). Across an abandoned cornfield in which there were still some falling and fallen gray desiccated stalks.

After the cornfield came the border of the creek, from early spring through summer and into fall a rich thick green, poplar leaves and honeysuckle vines, announcing the creek. Now in December, after a long dry fall, despite the deceptive weather the poplars were bare and peeling, white sentinel ghosts. And the vines were withered, brittle underfoot. The creek, so rich and rushing, so full in rainy spring, was now a thin brown stream, a muddy bed of rocks and rotting branches, winter leaves.

In other seasons, a small gray sandy beach edged the water. Much wider now, its sand was darker, coarser—where Melanctha and Abigail stood, considering and talking.

Melanctha continued the topic of Graham at Harvard.

"He's entering in March," she said. "Some special early entrance program that they started during the war. I think it's a bad idea, he's so young. Just sixteen. Dumb Deirdre just wants him out of the house, I think."

"She's still seeing that reporter, that Derek whatever?"

"Derek McFall. I don't think so, I'm not sure."

"I think my mother sort of likes him too, or at least she used to," said Abby.

"They're splitting up, your parents?"

"I don't know, I honestly don't. My father—Harry's coming down for Christmas, but I think that's mostly so he can get to know Joseph a bit better. Before we do anything official." Abby laughed, although in fact she found her parents' situation quite depressing. All those jokes from Cynthia about "Lady Veracity"—she'd now found a couple of dozen rhymes for that name, and the joke was getting a little stale. Also, Joseph was worried about his own parents not getting on, big political fights all the time. He was looking forward to getting away, spending time with Abby in Pinehill, but Abby was not sure that things would be better down here.

Melanctha asked, "You're getting married soon?"

"Oh God, I doubt it." Abby laughed again, less convincingly. "Marriage might spoil everything, the way I see it. I mean, why bother?"

"Well, if you wanted to have children—"

"We don't, we don't believe in it. There're too many people already."

Despite the unusual bright day, the warmth, both women felt a certain lowering of their spirits as they talked. Good friends for years, each had imagined that a few hours with the other would be cheering, instead of which the smiles that they exchanged contained sadness, and a certain wry acceptance of the fact that friends are only so much help to each other.

She dreaded Christmas; that is what Melanctha was mostly thinking. All her brothers would be home from their schools, and Graham, getting ready for Harvard, talking about Harvard, and her baby half sister, SallyJane (God, how could they name her that?). Silly Deirdre trying to act like she was everyone's mother. And big Ursula back out from Kansas again, being a sort of ambiguous housekeeper-servant-houseguest. (Russ many years ago in Kansas had run over a pig—Melanctha could still remember the smell, and Russ and then all the boys yelling "Pig shit"—a pig that belonged to Ursula; then when SallyJane was sick, Ursula had come to stay, and stay, although Deirdre couldn't stand her, Melanctha knew, and probably Ursula hated Deirdre too.) In any case, for every reason, Melanctha hated the coming of Christmas.

As did Abby—what with her parents, and Joseph's worries over his own family.

They were staring up the creek to where it bent, and a clump of pussy willows leaned out over the slow brown diminishing water—both silently staring, as though some help might come up from out of the water.

Which, astonishingly, it did.

Something dark brown, small and bobbing along, but not a piece of wood, an energetic little head emerged—not a bird or a rabbit.

Melanctha softly cried out, "It's a puppy!" and she splashed out to where on a small shoal it had just managed unsteadily to stand—the puppy, trembling with cold and trying to shake off water, something it did not quite yet know how to do. Reaching the little dog, Melanctha grabbed it up, cradling him inside her coat, peering down. The puppy raised his head and gave one light lick to her chin. An investigation, possibly—what was this new strong dry source of warmth?—but Melanctha took it for love.

She breathed, "Oh, he's so lovely!" She added, "How could anyone—?"

"He could have just wandered off and fallen into the creek," Abby told her. "Will Deirdre let you keep him, do you think? My mother—"

"She'll have to, it's not just her house. Shall we go on back?"

And they began the slow trudging walk back home, across the cornfield and up the pine-wooded hill to the smaller, lighter woods, to the road.

"Your sweater's really wet," Abby observed. "But he's so cute."

"Oh, I don't care!" Melanctha grinned, and patted her dog, nestling him more securely beneath her muddied camel-hair coat.

They agreed to call each other soon, and to get together during what they both termed "these goddam holidays." "I'll come and see your puppy," Abby promised, wistfully adding, "My mother loves dogs, in case Deirdre doesn't."

"Oh, to hell with Deirdre."

The little dog turned out to be very pretty indeed. Melanctha, brooking no objections from anyone, bathed him in the kitchen sink, and dried him off with several towels—so that everyone could admire the wavy, silky dark brown hair, and enormous brown-black eyes. "His name is River," she said.

"Why River? Why not Creek?" irritatingly asked Graham.

"I suppose you mean Graham Creek."

"Well, that's where you found him."

"Be like naming you Pinehill Hospital."

"I wasn't born there, I was born in California—" As if they all didn't know where Graham was born, and to whom. To Deirdre, and to Russ.

"You children!" Deirdre called out from the dining room, where she had been arguing with Ursula over menus, and cooking: what was good for the children. "You-all are supposed to be grown up!"

So are you, you dumb slut, Melanctha muttered under her breath, just out of the hearing of Graham. The other boys, as usual, were off somewhere, and SallyJane slept.

The beautiful puppy, River, could be said to have got Melanctha through that holiday. Melanctha bathed him in her own tub, and then surprised Deirdre by cleaning out the tub, cleaning up the whole bathroom. And River surprised them all by being even handsomer, wavier, and silkier than before.

"Too thin, though," tall, gaunt Ursula observed. "That little dog needs some flesh on those little bones." And for once Melanctha agreed with Ursula. "He sure does," and Ursula set about making a special mush that they used to feed dogs in Kansas.

Otherwise, taken to the vet, Dr. Marx, River was pronounced an exceptionally healthy dog, about four months old, probably. "Don't exactly know what breed," said Dr. Marx when questioned. "Part Lab, part collie, maybe part setter, I'd guess."

River was friendly and playful but showed no real interest in anyone but Melanctha, at the sound of whose voice or footsteps he raced forward with small yelps and licks of love. At night he slept on Melanctha's bed, cuddling his small body next to her back, or if she lay on her side in the bend of her knees.

Abby, while acknowledging to herself Melanctha's greater need for a dog, generally for love and companionship (after all, she had Joseph, there for Christmas), still could not resist the thought that they could have somehow shared the puppy. Joint custody, she wryly thought. After all, they had come upon him together, and just because Melanctha was the one to go out and pick him up, did that mean—? But even as she inwardly voiced this query, its sheer childish selfishness came loudly through, and she erased it from her mind.

However, Abby had to admit that she could have used some help, from somewhere.

Harry had come down for the week of Christmas, and at night he and Cynthia went out to a lot of local parties: the Bigelows', Mrs. Lee's, the Hightowers'. During the day, they nursed hangovers and exchanged bad jokes at each other's expense. Abby thought if she heard one more Veracity joke she would leave home, for good.

Cynthia had fixed up the guest room for Joseph, everything pretty and fresh and clean, flowers in a silver pitcher on the dresser. But as things turned out that room was where Harry slept; Joseph stayed with Abby, in her room.

About which Abby and Cynthia had a whispered conversation in the kitchen, the first morning Joseph was there (one among many whispered conversations, in the course of that holiday):

Cynthia: "Abby, I really can't let you just—"

Abby: "Oh please, would you rather we tiptoed around, lied about where we sleep? We live together—"

"I know, but—"

"Besides, last night Harry was in the guest room—"

Cynthia had no answers; everything that Abby said was true.

The trouble, for Abby, was that she and Joseph spent most of their awake time in bed talking. His parents were separating but not exactly saying so, Joseph told her. His father was moving out to L.A., "at least for a while, he says," his mother was staying in New York. "The apartment's rent controlled, you can't believe how cheap. I think around two hundred."

"That wouldn't be so cheap around here."

"Yes, but New York—a block off Fifth?"

His sister Susan was trying to transfer to Wisconsin. "She's got this bee in her bonnet about Madison. I don't know, she must have met some guy who goes there. I know her, that's how she functions."

"It's a good school—"

"I know, but I just don't think that's it. Susan's a long way from being academic." He sighed. "Anyway, it's creepy at home, she may just want to get out of it all. I wouldn't blame her."

"Creepy how?"

"We're being spied on. I know that sounds melodramatic, but we are. Crazy stuff, like the mail comes and a lot of it's been opened. Some of your letters, by the way."

"God, how embarrassing."

"I know, and the maid says somebody went through the garbage can. Talk about embarrassing."

"Jesus."

"Yeah. My father thinks the FBI's investigating him, and Mother thinks the Party's after her."

Neither of them at that moment added what they both knew to be true, which was that an FBI investigation of either (or both) of the Marcuses did not bode well for Joseph in terms of future jobs in physics.

All terrible, and nothing to be done.

But why are we even having this conversation? Abby wondered. Why are we talking so much? She was thinking of a recently discovered sexual pleasure for which they had no name, or words, but which was intensely exciting to them both.

At just that moment, Joseph moved closer to her ear, and he whispered, "We're wasting time—"

"Shall I—?"

He murmured something, some assent, and Abby began to move slowly down his body, licking lightly at all that smooth stretch of skin.

In Cynthia's room a couple of doors beyond, she and Harry were less happily engaged, in what threatened to be an endless conversation. It had begun with some of the old familiar phrases: "—you always," "—you never—"

There was then what seemed to Cynthia a protracted interval in which they were making speeches to each other, each striving to sound in the right, to sound generous and wise. And honest, terribly honest, as though they had discovered honesty (a much overrated virtue, Cynthia thought).

" 'In love' is hardly the point anymore," said Harry. "We *know* each other, you and I. I've known you longer than anyone. I think you're beautiful even early in the morning. Or usually you are. And you're sexy. I just seem to have this problem—"

"Well, maybe it's my problem," Cynthia assured him. "Maybe it's me. Or maybe we just shouldn't expect sex to last." She was really thinking, though, that she had never been so tired, and that the burden of what he did not say was exhausting. She did not, could not say: And what about Veracity? Are you up to snuff with her? Do you mean that sometimes I look awful in the morning early? Well, as for that, you look pretty awful yourself, with that half-gray stubble and those bleary eyes. But I feel mostly friendly toward you; sometimes I actually hope that Lady V. is nice—nice to you, I mean. Marrying a Lady might be just the thing for you. Maybe we're meant to be friends?

She said none of that, but those and similar thoughts kept her awake for a long unaccustomed hour.

River did various bad puppy things around the Byrd house, none of them original; he barked at the mailman and chased the paperboy, who came on a bike; he dug up some recently planted (by Ursula) bulbs and scattered them around the lawn. He peed under one of the boys' beds, and worst of all he made a smelly mess on Deirdre's puffy boudoir rug, so that it had to be thrown out.

Melanctha defended all these terrible acts; to her they were mostly funny. She thought River had a great sense of humor, and she said defensively, "The bulbs may come up all around the lawn, and that'll be beautiful, I think. Those boys' rooms are such a mess, I don't see how anyone ever even smelled dog piss." And, "That leftover meat loaf Ursula fed him wasn't good for him. I don't think dogs like meat loaf." (Besides, a "boudoir rug," what could be tackier? She heard her mother's voice in this unspoken judgment.)

The clearest fact about River, aside from his increasing beauty and energy as he visibly changed from a puppy to a young dog, was his total love for and loyalty to Melanctha, feelings that were more than reciprocated. There were really no words for Melanctha's emotions concerning River. Love, gratitude, affection, admiration, adoration—all of those came close but did not quite say it. River warmed and brightened the very center of Melanctha's heart; she had no idea how she had lived before they met. She thought, If anyone ever hurt River, I would probably kill him.

Sometimes she worried about the future of River, along with her own. She had heard from someone, maybe her father, that in Paris it was fine to bring dogs into restaurants. She and River could go and live in Paris?

On the other hand, River seemed to like it very much where they were; he liked the house, liked running up and down stairs with his big growing feet, nails clicking on bare floors. And especially he liked the woods that surrounded the house where he and Melanctha went for walks every day. Sometimes he ran ahead of her, but never for long and never completely out of sight.

Melanctha stuck to those woods around her house. For every reason, she did not take him down to the creek.

Maybe, she sometimes thought, she should take a little apartment in town and get some sort of part-time job at the college, and take a course or two, and still have afternoons free for River?

In not too many years, as she saw it, everyone but her would have moved out of that house. Deirdre would marry that Derek, or someone or other, and she would have to take little SallyJane along. And the boys, including Graham, would all be at college and then off to jobs somewhere.

And then there would just be River and her at home, the house and the woods left all to them.

Although sometime they might take a very small trip to Paris.

22

IN Cambridge, that heady March with its wild swooping winds of spring, Graham fell in love with almost everyone he saw in Harvard Yard. So many incredibly handsome young men, many of them ravishing in their uniforms or in their Harvard civilian uniform of tweed and gray flannel. Lucky for him, he thought, that a New England tradition of reserve prevailed; if anyone had smiled in a friendly way, he would have come unglued. He thought of the words of one of his mother's favorite songs, "He'll look at me and smile, I'll understand—"

That was the good part of being there, the look of the Yard itself, so beautiful and dignified, with all the old brick and stone and hard white paths, the green irregularly sloping but perfectly tended grass. And mainly all the faces. The marvelous male ways of walking. The possibilities.

The bad came late at night, when the three boys with whom he shared the suite in Weld had gone to sleep, probably, and he lay there alone, crying like a baby, a mute, dumb baby with an inconsolable erection as he thought, You goddam little Southern queer faggot, you fairy pansy, just wait till someone finds out about you and what you're really like, you'll be punished, sent home for everyone to see. They don't want little boys like you around Harvard, or anywhere else.

Of his three suite-mates, two were from Andover, the other from St. Paul's; all three seemed more adjusted to and less intimidated by Harvard than he—but then, the same was true of everyone else he saw. Pierce and Bradley were both ex– and probably future track stars, real jocks. Pierce planned to concentrate in Gov. (his father was someone important in Washington right now); Bradley thought probably Econ., and then the business school. Paxton Sedgwick, from St. Paul's, was the least jock-like of the three, although the tallest. He was thin and soft-spoken, certainly the least threatening. Paxton wanted to study American History and Lit., a new field of concentration—with a famous and controversial political-leftist scholar. Paxton had read some of Russ Byrd's poetry, which he admired. Or he said he did. But he seemed to know not to ask too much, no dumb questions about what Russ was "really like."

It seemed to Graham that the handsome faces, the tall or small terrific bodies that he saw in the Yard were constantly new, some principle of beauty perpetually renewed. New faces, but also ones that he came to recognize as almost familiar, some that he looked forward to or searched out. There was the dark blond man in the Navy, a tall trim officer, with his Navy raincoat and his hat—and the smaller brown-haired one in tweed who smoked a pipe, or at least always carried one around. And the very slightly plump blond guy in his sailor suit, with a shy, fey look of Peter Pan.

And Graham thought, Which—oh which one for me? Then sternly telling himself, None, not one, you goddam little fool. You're the only little fairy pansy queer at Harvard. Then, mustering what logic, what rationality he could, he knew this to be unlikely; still, that was how he felt.

Bad jokes about people like him circulated:

"Do you know why there're no stairs in Dunster House? It's full of fairies, they fly up and down."

Sometimes, daringly (although he hardly had a choice; he saw no way out), Graham took part in group discussions on this topic.

Pierce said that at his sister's school, in Virginia, some girl had a big crush on another girl; there were intercepted letters, found by some super-wary teacher, saying, according to Pierce's sister, "these really sicky things, about touching breasts and stuff."

Shudders around the room at this shocking revelation: "Girls touching tits—oh, yuck."

What happened finally was that the school expelled both girls; it seemed the only way to quiet things down.

It was Paxton who said, "That seems hard cheese for the one who was just the object of the crush. I mean, she didn't write any letters, did she? She was probably embarrassed."

No one agreed with him—except Graham, who did not dare speak.

The other boys, the Andover jocks, were as one in their view that the girl who was the object of the unspeakable "crush" must have done something herself to bring it on. She must have been asking for it in some way. "I mean," Bradley tried to sum up their joint feelings, "how come the queer one chose that girl out of all the other girls in the school?"

"Still seems unfair to throw her out of school," Paxton muttered.

And Graham, silent, agreed, of course he did, at the same time that he thought, What an incredible ass of a girl to write letters like that! Lord God, girls! He further resolved that if anyone made any kind of a gesture of that nature he would turn them down flat, no matter how handsome they might be; they could easily turn out to be a spy for Harvard, trying to seek out and expel all queers.

It was much easier all around in Pinehill. In his secret heart Graham knew; he knew how he felt and what he was, but no one else seemed even curious about him, in that way. His mother, Deirdre, made excuses for him, although probably she did know what she was doing.

"Graham's in some ways a little young for his age—"

"Graham isn't really interested in girls yet, thank the Lord!"

"Graham is much more advanced in his head than he is in other ways—"

"Someways Graham doesn't favor his daddy at all—"

"I guess I've always babied Graham, starting out like I did pretty much by myself—"

"Graham's always been kind of small for his age, could be that keeps a boy young—"

Sometimes, even, remembering his mother's pretty, silly voice, Graham could still miss Pinehill. He missed mostly the weather there, and the things in bloom, especially in the dirty Cambridge March, when everything was cold and gray and wet. Without meaning. Whereas, in Pinehill, Deirdre wrote (and Melanctha too; he'd had a surprisingly long letter from her), the dogwood had suddenly burst out all over; back in the darker woods it was frothy like fountains, and big creamy magnolia blossoms and the most beautiful rhododendrons of any season ever. Reading his letters and thinking of Pinehill brought quick hot tears to Graham's eyes, even as he told himself, in one of his familiar litanies, You dumb little sentimental fag, you're just lonesome without your silly mum—and horny too.

In her letter, Melanctha also said that Benny Davis, the Negro boy who had been Abby Baird's friend up in Connecticut when they were little kids (and who was supposed to be extremely good-looking now), was coming to Pinehill to visit Abby; they were all wondering how that would work out. Melanctha thought Dolly Bigelow should throw a party for him (joke).

Graham remembered almost nothing of his earliest years, in California. They had not lived on the coast, his mother told him, but quite far inland, in Sacramento. Nevertheless, that ocean was what Graham remembered: a coarse gray beach, at the foot of some crevassed green-gray cliffs, and gentle, small, but very cold waves that had lapped at his bare feet, too cold for wading. "I guess we would've gone over there for a picnic or something," Deirdre told him. "My dad really took to the fishing out there. Although I can't say as I remember any wading days at a beach. California to my mind was really cold, except in the summer when Sacramento anyways was hotter than blazes." Graham did not remember anything hot as blazes, or hotter. He did remember gray, gray clouded air that people out there called fog but that seemed to him more like rain.

Insofar as he had academic ambitions, or intentions, Graham's were not poetic; God knows what he wanted to be (he wanted to be heterosexual—oh Christ! he wanted to be *normal,* hopelessly yearned for just plain normal). He was sure he did not want to be a poet. Well, easy enough, he told himself, just don't write poetry. And, easy enough: just don't do anything sexual with boys—Graham had as yet no clear idea of just what it was that boys did together beyond kissing and touching, touching all over, he guessed; what he thought of when he dared to think of it at all as Mutual M. The scoutmaster at home, Mr. Mountjoy, had told Graham that in France men kissed each other, but he had not wanted to kiss Mr. Mountjoy, who got mad.

However, partly because it worked out with his schedule, Graham took a course that spring called Criticism of Poetry, which required him to read poets he had barely heard of before: Yeats, Auden, John Donne, T. S. Eliot. "What they have in common, at least in my own view, which is to predominate in this class"—a slight twist to his small tight mouth that the class later came to recognize as a smile—"what they have in common is excellence. Also, as some of you have no doubt noted, all are English, except for Mr. Eliot, who became so by adoption, and Mr. Yeats, who was Irish, which is closer than he would have cared to admit." Again the tiny twist, the semi-smile. This professor was short and bald, pale, with intense, burning dark brown eyes—eyes that, Graham imagined, saw everything, even himself; Graham sometimes had a sense of being noticed, observed by this distant and brilliant man, this famous scholar. Which was probably not true, he thought; or it was true that he was noticed, but only because he was there on the second row. (B for Byrd got Graham into many second rows, alphabetically speaking.) He, the professor, was given to discreetly elegant shirts and ties, smooth dark suits (actually all from London), tidy socks, and impeccably polished shoes.

He read aloud, this professor, in a low but penetrating near monotone, a voice that was tightly controlled, but still his passion for the words, the words of the poets, came through.

He read: "And death shall be no more; death, thou shalt die!" and "I will arise and go now, and go to Innisfree," and "April is the cruellest month . . . mixing memory and desire, stirring dull roots . . ."

And, in an apologetic, hesitant way, he said, "I am purposefully choosing the most available, the most popular—the most trite, if you will—of their lines, in the hope that you will be seduced into lifetimes of further reading. Of such glorious pleasure."

Graham was indeed seduced. He left each class in a state of blind euphoria, seeing no one, aware only of those words—and of weather, April, the cruelest month, but so beautiful in its way, in New England.

Alone, as though furtively, he read more and more of those poets. And he developed a special feeling for W. H. Auden, as yet unmentioned in class. On one of the book jackets there was a photograph of Auden, of that long, lined hyper-intelligent, sensitive, witty face. Graham wished that his father had looked like that, in fact that his father had been Wystan Auden instead of handsome American Southern Russell Byrd. His father could never have written, ". . . mad Ireland hurt you into poetry," nor, "We cannot choose what we are free to love," nor, ". . . the distortions of ingrown virginity." Could not have written, very likely not understood. And Graham wondered, Did *he* really understand? When Auden wrote, ". . . honor the vertical man, / Though we value none, / But the horizontal one"—did that mean what Graham believed that it did?

One day, leaving class in the crowd, Graham overheard this exchange:

"Do you think we'll ever get to old Auden?"

"Maybe not. Maybe the old man has it in for queers."

"But he is one. Haven't you heard that? Everyone knows."

Oh, you too, I'll bet. That was what Graham wanted to say, but did not dare. Nor did he dare to believe what he had heard.

The roommates ("suite-mates," as they were called, and in fact each man did have his own tiny room for sleep) all—usually all but Graham—went out to a great many movies at night. "A flick at the U.T., and then a couple of beers at the O.G." was the standard description of an evening. U.T.—the University Theatre, O.G.—the Oxford Grill. Wednesdays were Revival Nights at the U.T.; the films revived were from the thirties, mostly, ten years back, with a few twenties treasures thrown in. They always politely asked Graham to come along, but much more often than not he refused. He said thanks, but he had a lot of reading to do. Or, more honestly, he said that for some reason he had not slept well the night before, and hoped to make up for it that night.

Sleep—elusive, stubbornly eluding him, it seemed. At night Graham's mind announced, I'm busy thinking, I'm remembering everything that ever happened, every place or person that I ever saw, and what they said, and I'm scrambling in a frantic haste over fantasies of what will happen next, beginning tomorrow.

All the sounds of Cambridge made this sleeplessness worse, cars and horns and street shouts, the occasional ambulance or fire truck. A cacophonous conspiracy, preventing sleep.

And not sleeping well on one night did not guarantee a sound night's sleep on the next, nor an early one, Graham found. Sometimes, lying awake, he yearned for the sounds he was used to in Pinehill; only those sounds would allow him to sleep, would lull his troubled head: the tree frogs in the spring, the hum of pines in summer winds, the stray lone baying of a hound. A long train whistle.

Thus, when they all had gone off eagerly to see *Top Hat* (Fred and Ginger were perennial favorites with everyone), Graham was still at home alone. Truly tired, that night he went to bed early, and, amazingly, fell almost instantly asleep.

He woke slowly, sometime later, to the feel of someone in his bed with him. Hands on his back, hands reaching. Strongly aroused but still half asleep, he thought, Another dream, one more wet fantasy. But in the next instant he knew that this was not a dream; it was Paxton, his friend, now holding him, hard. Pressing, pushing in. So that Graham experienced first pain, then an unbearably escalating pleasure. Pleasure that made him suddenly scream before he could stop the sound. But Paxton cried out too—they must be alone, and in another minute Paxton whispered, "It's okay, they're still out. I sneaked back." A little pause. "I wanted you, I planned this. God, I hope I didn't hurt you."

Graham slowly turned around in his arms, and they kissed.

The next morning, though, having met for coffee by appointment at St. Clair's, they spoke very seriously. They both knew what they had done and meant to continue to do—something for which, if apprehended (Jesus, apprehended!), they could both be thrown out of Harvard. And they could be permanently labeled. In many ways ruined, for life.

Paxton's face was dark and narrow, as his body was. A long thin pale face, with a very high white forehead, a long thin nose, and narrow green-gray eyes. A serious (and sensual!)

wide mouth. Very quietly he said, "There's something I have to tell you."

Graham's heart froze as he watched Paxton's face, and waited. As he thought that Paxton was going to say, You know we can't ever do that again. I didn't like it. Let's try to be friends. I have this girl. . . .

But Paxton said none of those things. What he said was, "This is something very serious for me—I mean, what I feel is serious, and I think you too—?"

"Yes. Christ! Yes," Graham breathed.

A taut smile from Paxton, "Well, we have to plan. We can't just meet, any old way—tumble into bed of an afternoon."

Hearing those words, Graham experienced a quick jerk of desire as he thought, We can't? We can't right now—?

"The thing is," Paxton continued, "I have all this money. My grandfather—this trust—this month—I'm eighteen. I mean, I could rent an apartment—"

"I've got some money too."

Paxton smiled. "Well, we're lucky, aren't we?"

For discretion, they did not go apartment hunting together. Paxton simply called a friend of his father's, a trustee of his trust, who just happened to own a building.

"I need a space to go to, it's so hard to study in the dorm," Paxton explained.

"Well, I have this one that should do you fine. If you don't let yourself get overrun with those Radcliffe girls. I hear they're pretty aggressive these days."

"I'll try not to, sir." The trustee too was a product of St. Paul's, as was Paxton's father.

The small furnished apartment was on Walker Street, near

the Radcliffe dorms. "It'll look like we have dates over there." Paxton laughed.

"Well, in a way we do."

Sometimes, before or after love, they met for a drink in the nearby Commodore Bar, which was suitably dark, and a perfectly natural place for a couple of men to go for a drink. There was actually a rather male tone to that bar, at that time; it was certainly not a place to which women (in those days) would go alone. Paxton and Graham often noted at other tables a couple of ensigns, say, or a captain and a lieutenant who did not look like father and son. Friends? Or—possibly—? In any case, it was a place in which they felt at home, although the observance of some caution still seemed necessary: any show of affection was *out.* They should not even appear there together too often. One could never tell.

23

THAT spring Odessa's husband, Horace, discharged from the Navy, stayed around longer than he had ever been known to do, there in the Bairds' garage apartment with Odessa. Sometimes he worked odd jobs around town, but mostly he just worked out in Cynthia's garden. (It was felt in town that the Bairds overpaid Odessa and very likely Horace too: what did Yankees know about treating their help?) Horace certainly did a lot of work for Cynthia, and with resultant magic, although all over town that particular April was deemed extraordinary. Such a profusion of tiny curled pale green new leaves, like secrets, everywhere, and such bursts of tender bloom, white dogwood and redbud trees and pear trees, azaleas and rhododendron. And roses; roses bloomed all over town, although it was generally conceded that Cynthia Baird's were the most various, and striking. "She's got every kind of rose known to man, and some not ever seen before this, not anywheres."

It did not seem quite fair, and her luck, as it was termed, with her garden was mostly attributed to Horace, who everyone knew had a way with flowers like no other gardener, white *or* colored.

It was also attributed to money, and not only what she

allegedly paid Horace. "She must've spent a fortune on that place, the manure alone don't come cheap these days."

Or to Harry's stray weekend visits, down from Washington, when he was indeed observed to spend a lot of time out in the garden.

Or, getting into metaphysics or maybe theology, it was said that Cynthia's beautiful garden was God's recompense for all her bad luck with men, Harry trying to ditch her for that English lady, Miss Obesity, whatever her name was. (Dolly kept this view current, whispering it about, trying not to let Odessa, especially, hear her.)

The one thing that no one seemed to notice, or anyway to say, was that in her garden Cynthia worked her hands to blisters and then to hard calluses with trowels and rakes and shovels, and wrecked her nails—although this was surely one of the truths about her flowers.

Abby, however, home for Easter and observing both her mother's hands and the beautiful, perfectly tended garden, did observe, "Mom, talk about working your fingers to the bone, you've really done it."

Gratified, Cynthia told her daughter, "Nice of you to notice. Harry just asked why didn't I get a manicure. Come to think of it, Dolly asked me the same thing."

"I'm a scientist, an almost-doctor, remember? I observe." And Abby laughed, in her easy, good-natured way.

Abby was either too good-natured or, maybe, too absorbed in her own life to ask Cynthia, What's really going on with my father? Which Cynthia could not herself have answered, even had she wanted to. He came down from Washington on weekends—occasionally, and without a great deal of notice: a phone call on a Thursday, say: "Okay if I come down? I thought, tomorrow?" Once, experimentally lying, Cynthia said, "No, I'm sorry, this weekend's really out for me." But that seemed to be all right too, no questions asked. In fact, they talked rather little, and in a personal way hardly at all. At a much later time, thinking over this period, Cynthia wondered at it, amazed: how could they have said so little, have asked so little of or from each other? At that later time she concluded that it was at least partly out of fear.

And how could they have shared a bed on all those weekend nights and not made love? But that was the truth of it; for months they neither seriously talked nor made love.

A partial explanation for both these lapses was that they were drinking a lot, a *lot.* Harry had some access in Washington to a very good English gin, and French vermouth—less of that, the vermouth, but then the martinis that they drank, and drank and drank were little more than a glass of chilled gin, with a twist of lemon or a tiny pickled onion, and sometimes a whiff of vermouth. And so, on most nights, by the time they went to bed they were pickled themselves, too drunk for love or for significant conversation.

And occasionally, in what talk they did have, small dangerous flashes occurred.

Harry referred to someone called Vera. Several times.

"Vera?" asked Cynthia.

"Veracity. I told you she was in Washington, she has this job—"

He hadn't, actually, or if he had Cynthia had not taken it in, but she told him, "Yes, of course. The Lady V. I suppose you refer to me as Cyn?"

"*Very* funny."

During this period, Cynthia rarely thought about and never heard from Derek McFall. She assumed that he was off somewhere, covering something. (Her interest in world events, like that of many people, had greatly diminished since the end of the war—thus Derek's important broadcasts from Moscow escaped her attention.) Did Deirdre ever see him? Did she travel glamorously to New York or wherever to see him? Cynthia did not know, but she tended to believe that she would have heard of it, in talkative little Pinehill. Dolly Bigelow would surely have said, "Well, that Deirdre Byrd's not wasting much time. No grass growing under that young woman's feet. Off to New York City to see that newspaper fellow, that Derek whatever. Well, she always was some looker. And what you'd call sexy, I guess." Very easy to imagine Dolly saying all that—but in fact she had not.

In this period of her life, though, humiliatingly, Cynthia found herself very moved by trashy songs that she sometimes—well, often—heard on the radio. Disgusting—disgraceful; she felt her blood and her literal heart respond to those throbbing trombones, pulsing drums, sleazy saxophones, and whining clarinets. Such awful music, and the words were even worse. How could she react with such strong and vague yearnings? Not, thank God, for Derek, or for Harry. Just someone. Someone to make her feel less alone. To kiss. She often got up and turned off the radio—and soon turned it on again.

And now she was listening, again, to Frank Sinatra ("This love of mine—") and not to Abby, who had stopped whatever she had been saying to announce, "God, I can't stand Sinatra."

"Me neither," Cynthia lied. "And he's everywhere."

"Well," said Abby, in the tone of one continuing a conversation, "at least we can be pretty sure Dolly won't give a party for him," and she laughed.

In an agreeing way, Cynthia laughed too as she tried to recall exactly what Abby had been saying, and then it came—the (to Cynthia) not entirely welcome news that Benny Davis,

Abby's old (Negro) friend, the former Harvard football star, now an about-to-be law student, was coming to visit. This weekend. Here.

But in that quick following moment of looking at her daughter, Cynthia felt a sudden surge of pure love for Abby, love and pride in her, admiration, some awe, and not a little fear. Abby would not go easily through life, and Cynthia inwardly sighed with this knowledge. Abby was too straightforward, wholehearted, clearheaded; she was warm and generous—all too much for a devious, crooked-pathed world.

Abby was directly and unequivocally pleased that her old friend was coming to see her, of course she was. The fact that he was a Negro, was "colored" as they said down here, and that her home was here, in the middle (bigoted, narrow) South was secondary to her affection for her oldest friend. Being far from stupid, being in fact highly sensitive and aware, Abby saw some complexity ahead, with the visit, but that is what she saw, complexity, surmountable complications. Dolly would not give a party: a joke.

"The thing is," said Cynthia, feeling her way and not at all sure just what "the thing" was, "the thing is, no one's ever had a Negro come and stay with them. Not in this town."

"Not even at the college? Some visiting prof?" Abby's tone was purely judicious, curious.

"I don't think so. But if they did, no one here in town knew, you know? So it wasn't an issue. But if we do—"

Abby smiled, but now her voice was clear and purposeful. "You mean, *when* we do. Mother, he'll be here Saturday. This is Tuesday."

"Of course. You're right."

"Mother, of course I am."

"I was just thinking about Odessa."

"You mean, I should warn her?"

"Abby darling, of course I don't mean 'warn,' but maybe tell her? Let's face it, this will be unusual for her? She could be—embarrassed?"

Abby spoke firmly. "Odessa will be like she is with any guest." She half smiled. "But after all, he did go to Harvard. Compared to Odessa and Horace and their kids and anyone they know, he's rich, and that almost makes him white." She laughed. "Joseph says it's like that with Jews. If you're rich enough, you're not really Jewish."

"I suppose. Buffy Guggenheim in school seemed—" Cynthia had been about to say, "just like anyone else," and then with a small laugh stopped herself. "I guess the truth is I haven't known all that many Jewish people," she said. "Even in Washington, somehow—"

"But now you're getting a Jewish son-in-law, and a bunch of Jewish in-laws. Communists at that," Abby laughed. And then she said, "Speaking of all that, Joseph is really worried and sort of ticked off at his sister."

"Oh?"

"She ran off to Madison after that Ed Faulkner. You know, the Negro soldier who was on the train with Russell Byrd when he died, and then the C.P. almost loused the whole thing up, interfering—"

"I remember." Cynthia had always found the whole story confusing, but of course she remembered who Ed Faulkner was. "How did Susan know him?" she asked.

"From when the Marcuses asked him to come and stay—mostly because he's a Negro, I think. Communists!—they're so irrational. Anyway, Susan developed this big crush on Ed, and when he went out to Madison to school, she pulled together all the money she could get out of her family, borrowed some from Joseph too, and went out after him. She rented a house and everything, said she'd get a job and maybe even finish her degree there. God, with her grades, fat chance. But of course it didn't work out, their living together. Joseph has the idea that Ed never really even liked her very much, it was all in her head. Not his."

"Oh dear." Even as she had listened, though, Cynthia had wondered: How would I ever tell Odessa that story, for example, assuming that I wanted to? How could I tell her anything?

To Abby she said (and she knew that she was really talking to herself), "You know what's really terrible, I've never really talked about anything with Odessa. There's a lot of affection between us, I know that, and I know she feels it too, but we don't talk. I mean, even if I wanted to, and in a way I think I do, there's no way to explain to Odessa about Benny Davis coming."

Abby said, "I know." And then she said, "I'll do it. It'll be easier for me." She laughed. "And I'll tell Dolly Bigelow too. That'll be the fun part."

Feeling clever, not making a lot of the gesture, Abby picked up the big picture of Ben in his football uniform, and said to Odessa, "Did I show you this picture of my friend Ben? He's the one coming this weekend." She had been straightening her desk when Odessa came in to vacuum; in fact, she had been arranging her pictures: Harry, and Joseph, and Ben.

After the smallest pause, Odessa said, "That is sure one handsome boy."

"Well, he's sort of older than a boy. I mean he's older than I am. But we used to go to school together, back in Connecticut. A long time ago."

"That so," was all Odessa said, and then, "All right if I do the vacuuming in here now, or you rather I wait?"

"Oh no, now's fine. I wasn't really doing anything."

"Really no reaction," Abby told her mother. "But does 'boy' sort of mean Negro, to her? If he were white, would she have said young man, or something like that?"

"I truly don't know. I told you, we don't exactly talk. We just exchange essential information like what I should buy at the A&P, and all the rest is nonverbal. For instance, I have no idea what she thinks is going on with me and your father."

"Especially since you don't know yourself."

Startled, Cynthia stared at her daughter. "That's true," she rather weakly answered.

Dolly's hair was now dyed a very dark brown, and still tightly waved in a somewhat out-of-date way. (Abby supposed it to be thirties; it certainly did not look recent, not mid-forties.) In any case, the dark dye job made her carefully-never-exposed-to-sun skin look paler, more finely wrinkled. Older. Abby made this judgment as she also thought, How smart of her mother, Cynthia, not to dye her hair; God knows, she, Abby, never would. On the other hand, maybe blondes like Cynthia (and Abby) could dye their hair so that it didn't show; Cynthia was perfectly capable of such subterfuge, Abby knew, even of a certain duplicity in small matters.

Abby had time for all these and further thoughts as Dolly talked—and talked and talked—about her garden. Her essential message being that Cynthia's flowers far outshone her own. But this took a long time to get out, what with various ramifications, explanations, and excuses. Much of the last, the excuses, had to do with "help," both the hired help and the non-cooperation of the men in her house; namely, Willard, her husband, and the boys. "I declare, if I didn't know better I'd say they were all just plum lazy, the three of them. Willard and Archer and Billy too." She sighed deeply. "It's not like I had the least little help from that Horace, can't even spare me one hour once or twice a week, like I came near to begging him for. And Odessa knows. But I still don't begrudge Cynthia all her lovely flowers, not one bit. She deserves them, she really does."

Abby then just managed to get in, "I'm glad they'll look nice for my friend who's coming this weekend."

"Oh, is this the weekend for your boyfriend? I guess I could say fiancé, since Cynthia's told me your plans. Well, some of your plans."

"No, this weekend another friend is coming. This boy I knew back in Connecticut. He was at Harvard and played football—"

"Well, a Harvard football star from Connecticut! Sounds mighty attractive to me. Maybe even some competition for that fiancé of yours."

How to explain? "It's not like that," Abby began, faced with the smiling, eager Dolly. "We've been friends since we were children, nothing romantic at all. Besides, I'm probably not brave enough. I mean, if we wanted to get married. I did tell you he's a Negro?"

Dolly took this much better than anyone would have

expected—although, as Abby and Cynthia later speculated, God knows how she reported these facts.

Or maybe, they further wondered, a lot of Dolly's quoted remarks were actually invented by themselves by their own imaginations? Dolly was an easy mark for caricature: the dumb Southern bigot. Whereas she was not dumb, as they knew, and maybe not so rigidly bigoted as they thought.

In any case, at this time, the time of her conversation with Abby, all Dolly said was, "Really? A Negro boy? You know I don't think I've ever met one, I mean at a party. In a social way. But you're probably right. It would take a lot of courage to marry one, and maybe not right for the children. But I'm sure you're brave enough for anything, Abigail Baird. You remember that paper on integration you wrote, back in high school? Seemed like you were still just a child, but you said all that."

"How could I forget? I thought we'd all be run out of Pinehill."

"Now, now, folks down here are not as bad as all that. You just shook us up some, that's all. But now, about this fiancé, the friend you are going to marry. Joseph, his name is?"

"Yes, Joseph Marcus. He's Jewish." Abby was not sure why she had needed to add this last. And if it had been a bait for Dolly, as such it failed.

"That so?" was Dolly's comment (for a moment sounding just like Odessa). "Well now, soon as you-all set the date I want you to let me know, and I want to have, oh, just the biggest old party since the war. To celebrate. You promise, now, honey?"

24

THEN, quite suddenly, one day in April the weather changed, and a dark fierce storm blew in. It came from somewhere far out in the ocean, the wild cold Atlantic, the papers and the radio all said. Winds and lashing rain, dark and gray, attacked the small town of Pinehill and other towns all over the state—and the whole of the East Coast, actually. All around Pinehill, the country red clay roads were slick, and red clay washed down from eroded banks on either side of the new white concrete highways, so that they too were slick and dangerous.

Even inside her house, which was warm and dry, Cynthia felt an unease, in that weather, a threat, a sense of danger.

"Looks like somebody up there's angry for sure," was what Odessa said, arriving at a run from across the yard, her raincoat clutched over her head. "No use even trying to use an umbrella in this wind."

Cynthia, meeting her in the kitchen, could only agree. "You're right, this is one angry storm."

"Horace, he real worried over his azaleas, and the rhododendrons he just put in near the pool. But he do what he can to save them."

"Oh I know he will. Odessa, don't you want some coffee? Please take some."

Coming into the kitchen just then, Abby grumbled, "Great weather for Benny to drive down in. God, I never saw such a rain."

"Terrible," Cynthia agreed, and she thought of driving, all those roads, cars skidding across, only she was thinking not of Ben but of Harry. Quite irrationally but powerfully, she imagined Harry—Harry suddenly, whimsically, deciding to surprise them with a visit. Harry heading South in his little pre-war Ford coupe. ("Gas is easier to come by than train tickets, a lot of the time, these days." He had said that more than once.) She imagined the phone call, for Mrs. Baird: ". . . an accident . . . your husband—" She shuddered, realizing with the smallest jolt of surprise that an accident involving Harry, hurting Harry, would be quite literally unbearable to her, she could not stand it. She must not think about damage to Harry, no matter what the weather.

"I have to go over to see Melanctha," Abby announced, over coffee, as Odessa started upstairs with the new vacuum cleaner that in theory did everything. "Honestly, she's getting more than a little nutty about that dog," Abby added, of Melanctha. "She says he's been throwing up, and would I come and look at him. Honestly, it's not as though I were anywhere near being a doctor yet. I'm not a vet, I probably don't know any more than she does."

But Cynthia could see that Abby was somehow pleased. "Maybe she's worried and just wants to see you," she suggested to her daughter, at the same time thinking, If that dog, if River gets sick and dies, Melanctha won't be able to stand it, she just won't, I know that. And at that dark moment, in that dark and rainy, windy day, she believed that Melanctha's dog would indeed turn out to be very sick. She asked Abby, "You're driving over? Be careful, it looks awful."

"Oh, Mother, come on. Cheer up."

Of course she was right. It was just a dark day, on which very likely nothing bad would happen, not to Harry or to Abby, or even to Melanctha's dog, River.

To fight off what she realized as irrational low spirits, what Harry used to call "a patch of blues," Cynthia kept herself busy with small personal and household tasks: her nails, a few letters and bills, the several downstairs houseplants, and the start of a salade niçoise for dinner, for herself and Abby.

By the time the phone rang, around mid-afternoon, she had almost forgotten her earlier forebodings, and even the rain had lifted a little. Only a light gray misting hung over the garden, the shrubbery and the flowers. Still, Cynthia started at the ugly mechanical phone sound, the insistent *brrring.*

Long distance. Collect. For Miss Abigail Baird. But it took Cynthia several long, confused, and frightening minutes to piece out even that much information from the maze of deeply Southern voices.

She tried and tried to get across the fact that Abigail was out, she would be back soon, and she, Abby's mother, Cynthia Baird, would take the call.

She was sure that this was Harry, Harry in some trouble that he wanted to break to Cynthia by way of Abby, and she experienced a colder and colder fear in her veins, reaching to her heart.

Does slow speech indicate slow wits? Certainly these operators seemed most incredibly slow of speech, and of dubious intelligence.

At last, after what had seemed forever, a strong male voice (but not Harry's voice) broke in, saying that Yes, yes, he would like to speak to Mrs. Baird.

He said, "This is Dr. Jefferson," and Cynthia, still thinking of Harry, froze—but even frozen she still reacted to the voice, which was deep and rich, authoritative, and Negro: a Negro doctor, down here? "We have this patient, just came in," he said. "Your daughter's name and address. He's not in good shape—car accident—head injuries—back—"

"But what's his *name*?" Cynthia cried out.

"Oh, Davis. Name of Benjamin Davis."

Although the rain had stopped, wide patches of red clay still smeared the highway, slowing, almost halting cars along the way. The roughly twenty-five miles from Pinehill to the County (Negro) Hospital, in Orange, would take forever.

"I don't dare go any faster," Cynthia told Abby for the fifth or sixth time; she could feel Abby's impatience, her tension, and also her wish to be nice to her mother.

More or less to herself, Abby said, "I just hope we're there when he comes to." She breathed very deeply, breaths that Cynthia could clearly hear. "I mean, assuming that he does."

Cynthia took this in, along with Abby's visible determination to be brave. To be good. And she helplessly looked across at her daughter.

"Melanctha's dog's okay, though," Abby said a little later, with a tiny ironic smile. "She really is sort of nuts—she hadn't even felt his nose. Which was beautifully cold and wet."

"But that's the first thing you do with an animal," Cynthia said. "You feel their noses."

"You'd think. But she hadn't. Anyway, he just ate something that must have disagreed. He'll be fine. Lucky thing. Melanctha's so crazy about him, really crazy."

For several very long and slow cautious miles, they talked about Melanctha in a worried, distracted way: her intense, tangled, and troubled relationship with her father; trouble with Deirdre; trouble at Radcliffe. Seemingly trouble all over, except with River, the dog. Abby and her mother were the two people to whom Melanctha talked most, it seemed, and unspokenly they had agreed that it was all right, not really breaching confidence, to discuss her between themselves.

"She even told me she'd been planning some plastic surgery," said Abby. "Breast reduction. But now she won't. 'River doesn't care,' she told me. I know she was kidding, but still."

"I'm afraid I'm the one who told her about that operation. Buffy had it, and she looked a lot better, easier with clothes."

"I don't know—" Abby said as Cynthia slowed down and braked with great care. "I'm glad she's not going to do it. She could always meet some guy who thinks big breasts are wonderful."

"Easily. Don't most men?"

"I think. County Hospital. I guess we're here."

The hospital was an old brick building, clearly built with some other intention; it had housed a very large and prosperous family, probably, many years back. Now it was shabby, paint long peeled from the high-pillared porch, and it had a swollen look of overcrowding, of lack of money and time for even rudimentary upkeep.

Inside, the impression was the same, with various strong

human emotions added: fear, desperation, and a harried need for haste, goodwill.

It would take forever even to find Ben; Cynthia knew this as they entered and a sweet and pretty but overwhelmed young nurse scanned a list, which turned out to be the wrong one, found another list, and at last found Ben's name and the location of his room. "He's just out of Intensive Care," the nurse said. "Been there a while." Cynthia watched her daughter's face tighten at that news, and she thought: Abby really loves her friend Ben, she always has.

He was in the far corner of a large men's ward, Negro men ("Colored"), their dark heads and faces, many bandaged in one way or another, their arms attached to tubes, hanging bottles, in their high white narrow beds. Ben's head was bandaged, his arms attached to both tubes and bottles. He seemed to be asleep, peacefully, but Cynthia wondered, Asleep or unconscious? Surely there is a difference?

"I'm going to find his doctor. You stay here," Abby whispered firmly to her mother—who obeyed.

Ben's hands were spread, palms down, on the limp white coverlet. Long, fine, beautiful brown hands, against that coarse cloth. Such perfect hands, Cynthia thought: perfect male hands, strong and so—so sensual. She delicately touched the one close to where she stood; feeling its smoothness and mostly its reassuring warmth, she realized that she had not been sure he was alive. But the hand was living, warm. Cynthia felt, or thought she felt, the smallest return of her slight pressure.

"You can tell from the size of a man's hands how big his thing is," a sophisticated Vassar senior had said to a bunch of (probably) virginal freshman, in one of the smoking rooms.

Candida, the senior, was rumored to have slept with five different boys over the past summers, before she was twenty-one. "It's not true about feet. Just hands. And believe me, girls, size counts."

God, what an appalling recollection for her to have just at this moment: Cynthia is horrified by herself. Here she is, standing beside a possibly dying man, her daughter's friend, and thinking about penises, about his.

She let go of his hand and covered her face.

"Mother, are you okay? He's going to be all right, we think." Abby, returning, patted her mother's shoulder—and Cynthia did not explain. (It was an hour or so later that she thought of Harry's hands, which were large, and Derek's, very large. Russ Byrd had rather small hands, for such a tall man. And she thought, Size may be important, but it's not what you remember.)

"The thing is," Abby told her mother as they began the drive home, "they're not sure what's wrong. He is conscious some of the time, and of course that's good. I wished he'd woken up a little while we were there. They need to do more tests." She added, "They've called his mother and she's coming down."

"Where will she stay?" Practical Cynthia had instantly thought, No hotel around here will take her.

Abby gave her mother an appreciative look. "Actually, there's a hotel near the hospital where they often put their visitors, one of the nurses told me. So it must be okay. Not Jim Crow."

Cynthia had been about to say, They could stay with us, but for whatever reasons (maybe guilt about her sexual thoughts) she did not.

The sky had partially cleared; there were bright acres of blue between the gray rain clouds, and sunlight glittered on the wet pine needles, on the trees along the highway, above the high red clay banks.

Abby said, "I'm worried that I have to go back to school on Monday. Could you sort of call and check on him, do you think? I remember his mother, and she's nice, sort of shy."

And then Cynthia did say, "You know, they could both come and stay with me. There're all those rooms, and Harry's hardly ever—"

"That's really good of you." Abby reached to touch her mother's hand, a quick pat. "First we'll see how he does."

25

IN May, on a rare visit to New York—she had left her work there the year before but liked an occasional visit—Esther Hightower became suddenly, extremely, and at first undiagnosably ill. She was rushed by friends to Mt. Sinai, and Jimmy arrived the next day. She was prepped for surgery the day after that, a surgery that Jimmy was told was exploratory. "We honestly don't know what we're going to find in there, but I have to tell you, man to man, I don't think it looks good, from the tests so far."

It did not look good. It was a tumor, advanced and inoperable, metastasized to her liver, and so as soon as she was able to travel Jimmy took her home to Pinehill. To their pretty long-shared bedroom with its lovely garden views. To a full-time nurse and a new live-in maid. To visits from their anxious daughters, and (occasionally) from friends.

"A lot of people seem to think I'm contagious," Esther remarked. "Well, for all we know it is. Doctors seem to know little enough. So maybe they're right. Can't you just see the headlines? 'Dying Jewish woman located as source of cancer outbreak in Pinehill.' Maybe it's a Jewish disease? After all, Freud had it. And what would I have to say to any of them, anyway? I've run out of small talk. Poor Jimmy, all this stuff you have to listen to."

Poor dearest darling Esther, is what Jimmy thought, and later wondered if he should have said. But Esther fought off sympathy. She woke from her rounds of drugs at intervals, angrily, and she glared about, she spoke in savage and sometimes incomprehensible bursts. She raged at everything in the world except her illness.

She looked extremely beautiful, which was another thing that Jimmy thought and did not say. And the phrase "extremely beautiful" was accurate. She had achieved, or reached (God knows through no conscious effort of her own) an extreme of beauty, with her almost translucent white skin stretched taut over beautiful high strong bones, and her burning huge dark eyes.

Some friends came by, but they mostly left their gifts of flowers and cake and homemade jams and jellies and even handkerchiefs, even books—these offerings were usually left at the door with the maid. Or, sometimes, the presents were just left on the doorstep, with scribbled notes: "Hope you're feeling so much better. Don't want to disturb you. Thought you might be asleep. Hope you're feeling better. See you real soon . . . feeling better . . ."

In any case, Esther's perception that people avoided seeing and being with her seemed well-founded.

Curiously, the person who came almost every day, sometimes bearing gifts, as often not, was Dolly Bigelow. She came and talked and listened, and she stayed. And came back for more. She was lively and malicious, affectionate and often funny. She provided a much needed buffer, or neutral zone, for Esther and Jimmy, who had been thrust by this dire illness into an intensity of intimacy with each other that neither could easily bear. If they were, either of them, conscious of this function of Dolly's presence, they did not say so.

What they did remark on was the surprise of being so cheered and warmed and cosseted by Dolly Bigelow—"of all people."

"But I've noticed this before, or I think I have," said Esther, talking to Jimmy over her nighttime dinner tray, prepared by the maid, nice cold pretty suppers of aspic and roast chicken and biscuits and gift desserts. "Though," Esther continued, "I couldn't tell you the circumstances when I found this out. But at real bad times it's often the sort of minor characters in your life who come forth and help the most. While you wonder where your so-called best friends are. Oh, I do remember, it was like that when my daddy died, and the person who really helped us the most was this woman who'd just moved in across the street. She came from South Carolina, and she seemed to be just doing what she thought was right. Of course she was Jewish, that may have had something to do with it. But I mean, for instance, where is that Cynthia Baird?"

Although she had not of course heard the question, it was Dolly who answered it. "I guess our Cynthia's got her hands full with those colored people staying with her," Dolly said. "That Harvard football player boy and his momma. It was sure real kind and Christian of her to take them in, but I don't know, I don't like to think I'm a prejudiced person, but Negro guests in anyone's house is just something I never heard about before, though I reckon it's something they do up North all the time. But that boy being a friend of Abby's, of course, and Cynthia knew him when he was a little kid, of course that makes all the difference. I wonder how Odessa feels about it, waiting on people her own color? Well, you can bet your last dollar we'll never know, Miss Odessa won't be telling anybody anything, she never has."

"She just goes on and on like this little stream," Esther told Jimmy, with an almost happy small laugh. "I think sometimes I sort of drop off for a while. But she doesn't ask for much by way of response. And I'm seeing so much of her, it's interesting. What she said about not being prejudiced. You know, in a way that's true. There is an enormous gap between the prejudice of Dolly Bigelow and the Ku Klux Klan and lynch mobs. Not to mention concentration camps. She's essentially harmless, I guess is what I'm saying."

There was something not entirely right about that argument, Jimmy felt, but he was in no mood to argue, to find intellectual fault, as he might have before she got sick. Now, if Esther felt warmly, gratefully toward Dolly, and was even—often!—amused, well, so very much the better. And much better for Esther to listen to Dolly than to newscasts that described more and more horrifying disclosures from Germany and Poland: the camps, trenches, decomposed bodies in piles. Teeth. It was more than he, than anyone could stand. But especially Esther.

Esther's illness was more than he could stand.

"Well, seems like Miss Melanctha's found herself a job," announced Dolly. "Over to the Bairds' most every day, helping out with the invalid since his momma's gone back up to Connecticut. You-all don't see her going by on account of she uses that back road, road where I think in olden days Russ and Deirdre used to have their clandestines." (Dolly accented the last syllable, making it clandes*tines,* as though French, and somehow more vivid.) "Road goes from up in the woods past Russ's house, up to behind the post office. Easy to get from there to Cynthia's house, as I guess Russ knew when he bought that house for Deirdre. You-all remember? Seems so long ago now, like history. But anyways, like I was saying, there's Melanctha over to the Bairds' house just about every day. With her dog. Reckon that colored boy likes dogs? Lots of them don't, and it's mutual—some dogs just growl and bark at the scent of colored. But I guess it's different with Harvard and all. I don't know what Russ would have made of all that. I reckon he'd feel just like the rest of us, he'd wonder what she does over there all day. Esther, honey, you sure I can't make you some fresh tea?"

"You know what I think?" began Esther. "I'll just bet Germany recovers and rebuilds itself into another big strong terrible country. They'll never go away, those people, they'll come back like mean tough old weeds. And poor old England and France will take much longer and not do so well. They weren't punished near enough, those Germans.

"Does it seem to you that Dolly takes a sort of special interest in Melanctha and the Bairds? I can't quite describe what I mean, it's just that whenever she mentions any of them, her tone sort of picks up. Quickens.

"Oh, poor darling Jimmy, all this must be true hell for you. You sit there listening to me rant. Watching me die."

. . .

Gradually, day by day, Esther was given more sedation. She was almost always asleep, but still Jimmy spent most of his time by her side. And Dolly still came over. There were, increasingly, nights when Esther wanted simply to doze off alone; she would signal this to Jimmy and to Dolly, if she was there, by a nod, a tiny hand gesture, a sort of wave. And by then closing her eyes.

And, sometimes, Dolly and Jimmy then went on downstairs for a nightcap, or whatever.

"I ran into Miss Melanctha at the post office today," Dolly told him. "My, something has sure cheered up that little girl. Well, not so little, that . . . front on her she's got, the dead spit of her momma's, SallyJane's, poor dear sad lady." Dolly sighed piously for the dead (as Jimmy had a terrible foretaste of just how she would sigh for Esther, not long from now). "Anyway, Melanctha not only looked real happy herself, along with that dog, that scamp of a River, she told me that Graham's really liking it at Harvard now. Liking it a real lot. They surely do go to extremes in that family, don't they now? Hating it somewhere, then the next day before you know it they're in love, with wherever. Seems like that Graham has some friend, some other boy, I don't mean a girlfriend, unfortunately, but some young fellow coming down to visit this summer, Melanctha says. Jimmy, do you reckon that Graham—I mean, do you ever think that he could be . . . like that—a boy liking boys more than girls? Oh, that would be something that Russ, that Russ just couldn't—oh, I know he's dead, but still—"

And she burst, literally burst into tears, terrible shoulder-jolting sobs, her hands flung over her face. Jimmy gently patted her back, since that was the part of her nearest him.

He had no idea what to say, and he just kept on patting until the gesture seemed futile, ridiculous, even.

Very slowly, gradually, her shoulders slowed, and her sobs thinned out, and Dolly began to tell him, "I just can't stand it, so much dying. Course I shouldn't say that to you, with Esther—so sick. But Clifton, you know we never did anything much, just a bunch of petting in the car, but I liked old Clifton, I really did. But Russ, would you believe me if I told you that I really loved that man—that true great poet of ours? I did most truly love him, and we did—we went upstairs one night and—we did it, did everything, I was genuinely in love. But don't you think all of us were in love with Russ, one way or another? Though I'm not at all sure he loved us back, and most probably not. I think he loved Deirdre a long time ago, and I guess SallyJane even longer ago than that, though from what I heard it was mostly her idea, and her daddy's, their getting married. And I reckon he loved that Cynthia, Russ did, at least for a while. The way those two used to carry on! But I loved him, in the worst kind of a way."

She had begun to cry again, so that Jimmy could barely make out the next thing that she said, which was, "Russ was in love with your Esther, you know, though she would never give him the time of day. But I reckon that's why, probably. The rest of us were too easy."

Jimmy could not really believe anything that Dolly said. Russ taking Dolly to bed? Doing "everything"? Ridiculous. And Russ in love with Esther, his Esther? Preposterous.

"Well, I'd better go fix my face afore I go on home," Dolly told him, still sniffling. "Else old Willard will really get the wrong idea."

. . .

Going upstairs, Jimmy decided not to repeat any of this to Esther; whatever for? Although she might have got some kick out of the sheer ludicrousness of Dolly's inflamed imagination.

"You know what I'm really glad about?" Esther asked him.

At the moment, Jimmy could think of nothing and so he only smiled, and took her hand.

"I'm really glad you never took on that Los Alamos screenplay project. Way things have turned out, using that murder bomb not once but twice, it would have been a whole lot worse than tacky. Like a dance of Dachau." She laughed, a small croaking sound that was horrible (for Jimmy) to hear. She added, "I don't think Russ would have done it either, finally. Do you?"

"No, of course not," Jimmy lied. Russ had apparently been fairly excited about the project, seeing it as a way of getting back into the swim of things, of proving he was not old, and nowhere near retired.

On a beautiful, dew-sparkling early June morning soon after that, the maid came into Esther's bedroom with the pretty, useless breakfast tray, and found her dead.

Esther had been clear on several final things: she wanted a service in a synagogue, and she wanted to be buried in sacred Jewish ground. None of which was available in Pinehill, and so arrangements were made for Esther to go to Hilton. For good.

The synagogue in Hilton was a quite small new building,

not much frequented by the Jewish students, mostly from New York, for whose use it had been donated by one of their fathers.

To Dolly, the music seemed weird and strange. So emotional, not at all like what you hear in an ordinary church. And no familiar words. The strangeness of it all made Dolly feel even worse, as though after all Esther had been some alien person, not just a friend from Oklahoma who was really just like everybody else, just talked different. It made Esther even more dead, and Dolly found herself crying uncontrollably, crying for all the dead. For Esther, and for Russ. For Franklin Roosevelt, and for Eleanor too, who would probably be the next to go, thought Dolly.

26

DEREK McFall and Deirdre Byrd were in the living room of the Byrd house; Melanctha and River in the study, adjacent. Melanctha had been dozing in what had been Russ's old very comfortable big leather chair, and River slept at, or rather, across her feet; he snored very mildly. This was after dinner one summer night, a dinner at which both Deirdre and Derek had drunk a lot of cold white wine. Melanctha, scared by a couple of drinking-too-much occasions, most memorably at the Deke House, in Hilton, with Archer Bigelow—ugh!—after getting sick that time, she had decided to take care how much she drank. Easy enough, since she didn't really like the taste.

Derek and Deirdre were speaking more loudly than they realized, and Melanctha woke up from her doze to hear: "I don't fall in love. I just never do, it's not my style." (Derek)

"Oh, is that so. You, big old famous you, *you* don't fall in love. I'll bet you don't, I'll just bet. Just what is it makes you think you're so almighty different from the rest of us poor mortal folk who do fall in love? Can you answer me that?"

There followed what Melanctha, listening, heard as a very long pause. Were they facing each other, touching? She could not imagine.

And then she heard the deep, practiced laugh of Derek McFall, who said, "You're some girl, you know that? Southern women are not supposed to talk back, no one ever told you?"

"Lord no, I always gave as good as I got, and I intend to keep it that way."

Melanctha knew this to be untrue. Deirdre had really let Russ push her around, had seemed to encourage it, even. But then Russ was somebody famous, and Deirdre was a lot younger. Derek was pretty famous too, come to think of it. Maybe Deirdre had just had time to figure men out, in the course of getting older? She knew what they wanted?

They were quiet in the living room for a while, and Melanctha assumed they were kissing, or something. Then they began to talk again, but now in whispers. They were probably trying to work it out about where they would sleep, how to go about fooling her, Melanctha. If only they knew how little she cared where they slept, or what they did first. They were both so old, it couldn't be much, she thought. And she *did not care.*

When they went to bed, Melanctha and River, River slept on Melanctha's girlish, ruffled (courtesy of Deirdre) bed. He seemed to like or maybe need body warmth, the warmth of something living next to his long lean body. Melanctha wondered what it was that he missed, a bunch of dogs or was it other humans, his owners before her? Wanting to be his first person, she preferred to think that it was puppies. In any case, they continued to sleep back-to-back, or sometimes River curled against her lower legs. He usually went to sleep first, occasionally giving a wakeful twitch, a snort; God knows what rabbits or squirrels were running through his mind.

Melanctha slept lightly until she heard the bumping, trying-to-be-quiet sounds of Deirdre and Derek coming upstairs together. Not wanting her to know. She thought of going out into the hall to say, "I know you sleep together, I know you make love, or try to, and I don't care, I just don't give a goddam."

Which she of course did not do.

However, she did not want to see them at breakfast, and so as soon as the first sunlight woke her, she got out of bed, rousing River, who followed her into the bathroom where one of his water dishes was.

Downstairs, dressed and hungry, Melanctha fed them both, her toast and coffee, his can of glop for dogs. River ate tidily, always looking around as though to see if someone was checking on his table manners, or maybe if someone was going to take away his food.

After such a rainy spring, the back road was overhung with leafed-out branches, and thick vines twisted among the bordering trees and shrubs. The road was deeply rutted, impassable now for cars, which was fine with Melanctha; she liked the walk, and River needed the exercise. He ran back and forth ahead of her, always checking back with a very light touch of his cold nose on her hand, the tiniest kiss.

It was still early, but Ben always said he liked to see her early. If only she didn't run into anyone she knew in the post office, she could be there in another fifteen minutes.

But there was Dolly Bigelow, dead ahead of her on the

street when Melanctha emerged from the road, as though Dolly had been waiting for her there. River, who loved all people, with no discrimination or prejudice, rushed out to greet her.

"Well there, if it isn't Miss Melanctha herself! Big as life and twice as natural, as your daddy used to say. My, you're looking so pretty in that yellow dress. I always did love yellow, though it does something terrible to my skin—the color, I mean. You're lucky that way, with that nice curly dark hair. My goodness, if this isn't the friendliest dog I ever did see. Get down, Rover, whatever your name is."

"It's River—"

"Such a coincidence, just before I saw you I saw Cynthia Baird just speeding by, like she was on her way to something important in Hilton. Or to the airport, maybe? Speaking of airports, last night I saw that announcer fellow just outside the Grill, that Eric something, or is it Derek? You reckon he could be around these parts again? Used to be a friend of Cynthia's, didn't he? Or was it Deirdre?"

"I guess, I'm not sure. Maybe. Well, I've got to keep on with River and his walk. He gets restless. Real nice to see you, Miz Bigelow."

"Oh, Melanctha. Real real nice. And you give my love to your Deirdre, you hear?"

"Oh, I sure will."

At last, they were able to walk on, Melanctha and River, in the steadily increasing heat and sunlight.

Cynthia's car was indeed not there in the driveway, and so Melanctha walked around to the back of the house, to the kitchen, and there she saw, as she had expected, or hoped, Ben Davis eating his breakfast, by himself.

Sometimes when she arrived, he got up and kissed her, friendly, on the cheek, or on the nose, being funny. Today he just stood up, both being polite and showing off that he could stand by himself now, but he just said, "See? Look, no hands. I'm really glad you came, I hoped you would. For one thing Odessa's been driving me nuts." He laughed. "I think she thinks I'm her long-lost son. Or else she wants me to marry Nellie. I think she worries a lot about Nellie." He patted River, who was licking at his ankle. "And you, River, you think I'm your long-lost brother. You want some coffee?"

"Sure. We saw Dolly Bigelow, coming over. She calls River 'Rover.' "

"I'd hate to hear what she calls me when I'm not around. I'll bet it's not Mr. Davis."

"What a dumbbell." Melanctha poured milk into her coffee.

"No, I don't think she's really dumb, any more than your Deirdre is. They just talk that way. You ought to be used to it."

River was indeed all over Ben, like a long-lost whatever; having finished with Ben's ankles, he settled across his large white tennis shoes, as though to prevent Ben's leaving his chair, just as he often lay across Melanctha's feet.

Melanctha sipped her coffee, and then in a sudden burst—she had not known that she was going to say this, but these sudden bursts of speech or of ideas seemed to occur to her with Ben—she said, "You know what I'd really most of all like to do?"

"No, but lucky you if you do know." His smile was gentle and kind and interested, though, and his tone without irony.

"I'd like to raise dogs. I mean starting with River, I'd like to have generations of dogs, and maybe sell one or two sometimes but only to people I like." She laughed with pleasure at her idea. "Can't you imagine River as a grandfather, with a lot of puppies around who look just like him?" She laughed again. "I was so glad when the vet said he hadn't been fixed."

"The first thing is you have to get him a wife. So he can start on all these generations."

"Oh. Well, I guess I do." Melanctha mused for a moment, and then, more or less from out of the blue, she said, "I think Deirdre and Derek McFall will get married."

"You do? I thought you said they weren't getting along."

"They weren't, and in a way they're still not. But I think they'll get married. It's just a strong hunch, but I'll bet I'm right."

"Probably you are. And they'll go away to live somewhere else and the boys will stay away at their schools and then their jobs and marriages, and you'll have the house and all that land for the dogs."

"Well, that's what I think. Or at least today I do." She wanted to add, And when you get married you'll come down with your wife and children and they'll play with the dogs. But she was too shy with him, still, to say that.

Could you fall "in like" with someone, not in love? For that is what Melanctha felt had happened with her and Ben. She just liked him so much, and part of it was her sense that he liked her too. She liked and trusted Ben; with him there would be no bad surprises, no unexpected jolts of cruelty, or violence. Or sex: he would never start anything like that with her.

When he was first immobilized upstairs, over the course of his recovery, they had talked and talked, so that by now they knew almost everything, or almost all, about each other's lives. Childhood hopes and fears, disorders and early sorrows. Melanctha wished he were one of her brothers, or maybe even her father, which he was certainly not old enough to be; he was only a couple of years older than she was, but she thought of him as someone much older, and wise and strong and reliable. She had had the curious thought: Are many Negro men like that, like Ben? If they are, you'd think more white women would want to marry them. But then she thought, Probably not, it's just Ben.

He said, "I mean, you're lucky if you've even got an idea what you want to do. Ever since I gave up the med school plan, I just don't know." He stretched long legs out in front of him, displacing River. "I'll feel better when I can get some exercise—right, River? Shall I come down and help you with your dogs?" He laughed. "Be funny if I ended up in Pinehill, wouldn't it?"

Before she could stop herself, Melanctha said, "I don't think you'd really like it here. Not for long."

"Probably not." He stretched again. "What I think as of today is that I'll go back to school and get my master's in history, U.S., contemporary. There's already a course called Philosophic Problems of the Postwar World. With a master's from Harvard, I can always get a teaching job somewhere, probably."

In a way, it was too bad that Ben was so very handsome, Melanctha thought. Inevitably that was the first thing that anyone noticed, What an extremely handsome man—Negro man. It had occurred to her that if Ben hadn't been looking sort of awful after his accident, bandages on his head, all that, they would not have got to be friends; she would have been scared off.

"I wonder where Abby and Joseph will end up," Ben was saying. "He seems to be having some trouble with programs in physics."

"Really?"

"You know, dumb stuff about his parents being Communists. I mean, they are, or they were, but what on earth does that have to do with anything? Can you see Joseph giving atomic-energy secrets to the Russians?"

But suddenly they heard, at their ears: "Goddam those Southern idiots anyway." More intent on their conversation than they realized, Ben and Melanctha had not heard Cynthia come into the kitchen. But now they heard her, loud and clear. "Those dumb jerks at Hilton, they won't let me into their stupid law school. 'We're just real sorry, Miz Baird, but we just don't see our way clear to doing like you want. You know, some of the old professors, they're not even sure that a pretty lady like you really wants to be a lawyer. Besides, young as you are, you'd be a tad older than all the others.' Oh, those asses! But I'll show them, just wait till I get my degree at Georgetown, or even Harvard! I think they let in 'ladies' at Harvard, Yale too." Running almost out of breath, Cynthia sat down hard, her face red and what breath she had left coming in short quick jerks. "Oh, I'm so mad!"

"No kidding, are you?"

Ben gently laughed, and for a moment Melanctha thought Cynthia would get madder yet, maybe throw something at Ben. But after a tiny pause she laughed too and gave him a wide smile as she admitted, "Yes, I am, I'm furious. Oh, River, I'm sorry, I didn't mean to scare you."

River had slunk into a corner near the new refrigerator, and now gave them all reproachful looks.

"We've been planning his future," Ben told Cynthia. "He's going to be a grandfather."

She sniffed. "Well, I'm glad someone knows what to do. And how about you kids? What are your life plans?"

Almost simultaneously they said, "We don't know!" and laughed.

27

NOT entirely by coincidence, Ben Davis left for Connecticut the day before Harry came down from Washington for a visit, although Cynthia tried to object. "You've never really seen Harry since you were grown, and you'd like him, I know. Everyone does. Besides, I could take you to Durham to the train and then wait there to meet Harry."

"I'm taking the bus, or I think Melanctha wants to take me. You've been so kind already."

"Well, if Abby insists on getting married, you'll have to come down for that."

"Oh, I surely will. Lord, I'm beginning to sound Southern. My mom's going to be real pleased." He chuckled.

"Well, I hope you'll come back to see Melanctha too."

"I'd like to. But—she's—I don't know."

"I don't know either." Cynthia hesitated, realizing that the topic of Melanctha was impossible between them. How could she say to this very nice, intelligent and extremely kind, and handsome (Negro) young man: Melanctha is a deeply troubled girl, I really don't know if she can have—ordinary relationships with other people. Both her parents, especially her mother—well, really her father too—were sort of crazy.

She could not have said that, and she felt considerable

gratitude when Ben said, a minute later, "She's trouble. I think mostly to herself."

"Oh, you're right!" But even as she was agreeing with him Cynthia had the thought that maybe this young man could be the one to save her, to save Melanctha from herself, so to speak. Of course his being "colored," as they said down here, would make things difficult, depending on where they lived, and why on earth would they live in the South? Maybe Boston, or even California, someplace distant and more sophisticated. Things had to get better along those lines eventually, Cynthia thought—now that the war was over. Maybe Melanctha needed some large challenge in her life.

With a small show of reluctance, Harry said, "I hope you're going to think this is funny." They had just finished breakfast on his first day back, but still sat in an undecided way at the table.

"I'll try." Meaning: Of course I'll think whatever you tell me is funny. I always do, don't I?

But what he said next did not amuse her. He said, "You remember—you remember a Veracity McCullough?"

"Well yes, you must mean Lady Veracity. That does ring a bell." You fucking idiot, she did not say, but that phrase could have sounded in her voice.

"Cynthia, darling, for the thousandth time, I'm *sorry.* But *please,* bear with me. It gets to be funny, I promise."

Coldly, "I told you, I'll try."

"Cynthia, Jesus. We've been through all that. Or I hope we have—enough. Anyway, as I told you, I haven't seen her for a month or so—"

Or maybe a week, was Cynthia's unsaid thought. On the

other hand, could he be telling the absolute, literal truth—trying *that*?

". . . and then she called, and she said that at a party in New York she'd met this man who said he was from Pinehill, and did I possibly know him. And, can you imagine? Jimmy Hightower."

"Well?" But Cynthia knew the large outlines at least of what she was about to hear: Lady Veracity had, somehow, met Jimmy Hightower (contrived to meet, is what Cynthia really thought) and Lady V. was—whatever the English, the English aristocracy, would say, she thought Jimmy was: attractive? all right? possible—a possibility? Whatever, and she wanted to check him out with Harry, by now her dear old friend. (Lady Veracity, Known for rapacity—)

"What does this girlish giggle mean?" Harry asked her.

"Nothing. I'm just waiting for you to tell me all about Jimmy and Lady Veracity."

"Not much to tell. I guess they went out to dinner, and it sounds like they had a really good time. He took her to some very fancy place in New York, the Brevoort?"

"I've been there, it's nice but not all that fancy. God, Harry, *we've* been there together."

"Oh, I thought it sounded familiar. Sorry. Well, the next day Jimmy called me and he sounded pretty excited. Manic, you might say."

"He's been so depressed and sad about Esther. Manic is hard to imagine."

Harry mused, "It's part of the same thing, I think. I mean the same process. Mourning."

"Oh, Harry." She paused, and then said, with conviction, "That's really smart of you. I'm sure you're right."

"The funny part is," and Harry chuckled to himself, "and Jimmy loves this, Lady Veracity is Jewish."

"What on earth do you mean? That's impossible, isn't it?"

"No, it isn't. She is. Some distant offshoot ancestor. What's called a drop of Jewish blood."

"Well, I guess that is pretty funny. Esther would have liked it."

"That's what Jimmy said."

Harry and Cynthia had indeed talked about Lady Veracity, and Harry's connection with her, their "affair," whatever one wanted to call it. Or rather, they had talked around it, around and around. Harry never quite said, I never loved her, I've never loved anyone but you. Although that was implied in everything he did say.

And Cynthia never actually said, I've had a few flings of my own. Although neither did she protest her own fidelity.

Nor did they ever arrive at the question of what next.

They did talk, though, and more or less in their old way, about mutual friends, gossip, speculation. Including about Melanctha.

"I have this fantasy about her going off with that handsome Negro boy. You remember, Abby's friend. Ben Davis. Benny, we called him then."

"I barely do remember. He was just a little kid."

"Well, he's a big kid now, and really handsome. And nice. And smart. He did terribly well at Harvard, and he was accepted at the med school, but then he decided he didn't want to be a doctor. You know, I have this bad intuition about Melanctha, though. I think she's really terrified of sex. Of men. Most girls her age—well, look at Abby, practically married already to Joseph Marcus. And as for Betsy Lee—"

"With those breasts, Melanctha must get a lot more attention than she wants."

"Oh, I'm sure. Poor girl, she hates her breasts. And I think too much attention is why she has that dog. For protection. And he's a sort of substitute for sex."

Harry stared at her. "I'm sure you're right."

They still did not sleep together.

Odessa, the only person who could have testified to this fact, refused to say a thing, although Dolly tried, and tried.

Dolly began, of course, in a roundabout way, or somewhat roundabout. She said, "You reckon Mr. Harry's going to stay here for a while?"

"I couldn't rightly say, Miz Bigelow."

"Well, it must be nice for Miss Cynthia having a man in the house. Not that she's ever exactly gone without." Dolly giggled, with a questioning look at Odessa, asking, Now, has she? But Odessa remained impassive, absorbed in the ironing: Dolly's handkerchiefs and cocktail napkins, often indistinguishable to anyone but Odessa.

"I guess they must be getting on lots better than they did," Dolly next ventured, to an answering silence.

"Odessa, watch out! You're going to scorch that lace!" Odessa had never in her life scorched anything, as the look she gave Dolly clearly stated.

Into the heavy ensuing silence, Dolly plunged yet once

more, and her voice went wrong with the effort—even to herself she sounded strained, and tight. She said, "Nice for Miss Cynthia, having him there in her bed every night."

To which Odessa, still standing accused of scorching, gave no answering sound of any nature.

"I'm just not sure that Melanctha's brave enough for all that." Cynthia spoke in a discouraged way to Harry, one August night, at dinner.

It was still too hot to move, or to think. All day the sun had pressed down, intense, immobilizing. Cynthia, and very likely everyone else, felt as though her brain had melted.

" 'Brave'?" asked Harry.

She made an effort. "Marrying a Negro. That takes some courage still, I think."

"Who's she marrying?"

"Ben Davis. Of course."

"It's not 'of course' to me, it's news. You're saying this is going to happen?"

"Harry, you're so cross. And I don't know. I don't know anything."

By the middle of the night the heat had lifted a little. At Cynthia's window a faint breeze whispered in the light starched summer curtains, a breeze that Cynthia felt just barely across her face and down the single sheet that covered her damp naked skin. In a groggy, melted way, she thought, Why am I sleeping alone? Why hasn't Harry come to my door, why hasn't he asked to move back in with me? Oh, why doesn't Harry love me anymore?

. . .

The next morning cooler air made the local world a little more sane. Waking, Cynthia pulled both the sheet and a light top blanket around her shoulders, and she began to think more clearly and coolly than she had for several days, or maybe weeks.

She thought: Am I really so sure that I want Harry, in bed or anywhere? Couldn't it possibly be Derek that I still want, in spite of Deirdre? Or maybe because of Deirdre, a little.

In any case, she very firmly thought, If and when I make up my mind, I'll tell him. Whichever one of those two it is. Or maybe it's someone else entirely, someone I don't even know yet. But why should I wait around for some man to decide about me?

28

"I HAVE dibs on having the party," was Dolly's loud exclamation on hearing that Abby Baird and Joseph Marcus were "really getting married." This was how everyone put it, as though they had been married in some not real way before, and in a sense they had: "Living together all that time," as everyone said.

"And don't you dare even try to tell me no," continued Dolly. "My darling Abigail, the girl I first met in those long pigtails. Next thing I know, you'll be telling me you're getting married too."

"Dolly, I am married," said Cynthia. "To Harry."

"Well, you could always get remarried. I mean to Harry." She giggled. "I have truly heard of folks doing that. 'Renewing your vows,' is what they call it."

"If Harry and I should ever do such a thing, you'll be the first to know."

"And I've got just the best idea. I'll give the party out in Russ's garden. You know, I've had it all fixed up for the sale. I'd've known Jimmy Hightower was going to be the buyer, I might not have gone to so much trouble, but now it's done, and just the loveliest place for a party."

"But I thought my house," Cynthia objected.

"Now Cynthia, of course your house and your garden are absolutely lovely, but your garden just doesn't have the space that Russ's does. You reckon we'll go on calling it 'Russ's house' after Jimmy's moved in with Lord knows who all? Another family, maybe?"

"Probably—"

"Besides, I stole Horace away from you for all my pre-sale fixing up." Not adding, And so your garden's a little shabby. But that unspoken judgment weighted the air.

What had happened, and all fairly quickly, within a month or so, was more or less this: Deirdre announced that she was tired of living in Pinehill; she wanted to move back to California, where she thought the schools and the *air* would be better for her little daughter, SallyJane. ("A lot Deirdre cares about schools, or air either," had been muttered around the town, along with certain speculations as to more plausible motives. "You reckon that Derek McFall she likes so much could be out there? Seems more than likely to me.")

Melanctha had said, Fine with her, she didn't want this big old house anyway; she wanted a new modern house somewhere out in the country, and maybe not in this state, maybe Texas or Montana, where she'd build some kennels and raise a bunch of dogs. With what Russ had left her and her share from the sale of the house, she'd be able to do that, probably. And all the boys had similar far-reaching plans of their own.

And, not coincidentally, at just about this time Dolly decided to take a job in the local real estate office. "I've been thinking that I need a little more by way of occupation," she explained. "And with the boys gone, and Willard almost retired— And anyway I thought what with the war ended and all, there'd be a lot of house reshuffling going on. Sort of a big-scale game of musical houses."

Saying that, had she known that Jimmy Hightower was looking to buy Russ's house, for which he'd always had sort of a hankering? Possibly she had, and certainly she had known that the new classics professor, coming to replace Willard, had a family and a yen for something "contemporary," a perfect choice for the glass-brick Hightower house (which Esther had never really liked very much).

In any case, the sale of Russ Byrd's house to Jimmy Hightower was a very lucrative coup for Dolly Bigelow, and one whose implications were much discussed.

"You reckon all these years Jimmy's had this private hankering for Russ's house?"

"Seems more'n possible. Something Esther would never have gone along with."

"Russ either, comes to that."

"And how about that Melanctha? You imagine that little old girl off in Montana or Texas either with a bunch of dogs?"

"And maybe a colored boyfriend."

"Now, now, we don't even want to think about that."

"Folks in Montana might be a little more 'liberal' along those lines."

"Bunch of Yankee Republicans, I guess."

"Well, she's a whole lot better off than she would be in Texas, that's for sure."

"Wonder what all Dolly's going to do with that mess of money she got—her 'commission' is what they call it."

"I heard she said she'd take old Willard on a bunch of vacations. England, Venice, Hawaii, all places like that."

"First off she's got to get him retired."

"Oh, she'll manage. Don't you all worry one speck about Dolly. Seems like she's found her true calling at last, in this life."

. . .

None of these moves had actually taken place yet, though. By the time of the party, the Byrds were still in residence in their house, which is to say that Melanctha and Deirdre and little SallyJane were there; all the boys were at their various schools, with Graham still up at Harvard and the others scattered over various Southern schools, including the law school in Georgia, and Annapolis.

However, presumably both Deirdre and Melanctha had been consulted, and both were amenable to having the party there.

One of the things that Dolly did with some of her money was to buy an extraordinary display of flowers, for Abby's party. Flowers everywhere. Now, with late September succeeding a couple of weeks of unremitting, bleaching, drying heat—when everyone in town had given up on gardening, on flowers, and felt not quite ready to start up fussing with bulbs—all over the large, terraced Byrd garden there were the most amazing flowers, in vases and pots. "She must've cleaned out every florist in the county" was frequently remarked, and, a little less frequently, in an undertone, "Sort of strange-looking, isn't it? None of them actually growing in the ground, like real flowers do?"

"The ones in pots are growing," stated Sylvia Marcus, who had a rather literal mind. But she had a lot to contend with that day, poor lady. Her husband, Dan, was up in Albany for some inside super-important Party meetings; he was angry that she had not come along. Never mind that it was their only son's wedding, and that their daughter, Susan, was not there either; she had just started at NYU, so much better for her than Swarthmore, probably. In any case, already she had a serious new boyfriend (but then Susan was always serious; she had been serious about that Negro Army man, that Ed whatever), but this was a nice Jewish boy, for a change. And so there was Sylvia, alone among all these at least superficially nice new Southern people. (God knows what their attitudes on certain basic social issues would be.) Even the Bairds, from Connecticut, were unfamiliar, actually. So—Episcopalian. Upper-crust.

The wedding, which was on the next day, had occasioned a little local trouble.

The Episcopal minister had refused to marry the couple, on the grounds that Joseph (of course) had not been christened. And was not about to be, Joseph said loud and clear. And so the ceremony would be performed by the local Presbyterian minister, known as a "liberal radical," who supported integration, things like that. The rabbi from Hilton, a handsome young man, was to be in attendance; he came to the party and was recognized by everyone as the person who had conducted services for poor Esther. (Jimmy Hightower was absent; he had urgent business in Washington, he told several people, with a great big hinting smile.)

Joseph has never looked so happy in his life, thought his mother, with a small inward sigh. On the whole, a serious man (when he was a small child, Sylvia had worried: should a three-year-old be so intense?), today he smiled, he beamed, all day. It was as though he had decided that it was all right, at least for today, to be just purely happy. He even seemed at ease among all these strange Southern people, though once Sylvia had worried that he was so shy, not friendly and outgoing like Susan (Susan was almost too friendly, too easily) or like his father, gregarious Dan.

When Sylvia thought of Dan, which of course from time

to time she did that day of their son's wedding, he seemed surprisingly remote, much farther away than simply Albany (just as the C.P. itself seemed remote), and she thought: This is the first party I've been to, it seems like ever, where there's no one here from the Party, and the only other Jew is the rabbi, who is even younger than Joseph. She felt a surge of loneliness, of abandonment, both of which she indistinctly blamed on the goddam C.P., which had literally ruled her life, *their* life for all those years. If I can ever get out, thought Sylvia, I'll never go back anywhere near it. I'll have all new friends, nice friendly nonpolitical ones.

Graham and his friend, Paxton Sedgwick, down for the wedding, were dressed very much alike: dark blue blazers with gold buttons, white shirts, striped ties, and gray flannel pants ("You reckon that's some kind of a Harvard uniform?"), but they did not otherwise resemble each other, tall bony-featured Paxton and smallish, pretty Graham. Paxton was universally perceived as being extremely nice, so very well mannered ("for a Yankee," was just not said), and so—so masculine. "How could we ever have worried that he would be—like that? Such a nice good friend for Graham to have, a kind of model."

To Cynthia, Paxton had a very New England face, and his accent, not to mention his name and his clothes, reminded her of boys from a long time ago, at college dances in New England, in long-lost autumns. There was also in the air, on that hot Southern afternoon, a New England autumn smell of chrysanthemums, acrid, sharp; Dolly had splurged on giant blooms, great dark green glass vases of the huge white-petalled blossoms. Looking across the garden and smelling those flowers, Cynthia was visited by a nameless angst, as though she had been displaced from her own true home, wherever "home" was. And she felt a lurch toward old age, and loneliness. Which she instantly told herself was ridiculous: turned down, finally and at last, by the law school in Hilton, she was writing back to Georgetown tomorrow.

"Abby looks even younger every time I see her, you noticed?"

"Sure does, looks a whole lot like that little old girl first moved down here."

"I remember. With the long pigtails, blond. Like a little old Dutch girl."

"And that Yankee way of walking, so fast, with her feet stuck out like a boy's."

"Well, even without those pigtails, she sure looks young. How old is Abby anyways, would you say?"

"Let's see now, she must've been 'bout ten or eleven when they first moved down here, was that in '38 or '39? Or was she twelve or thirteen?"

"I don't know anymore'n you do. Anyways, they got here not long before the war, and Abby was real young."

"We all were, before the war!"

"And now it's after the war and Abby still looks real young, though maybe in another way."

"I should think so! And getting married tomorrow!"

In a way that suggested some plan and agenda, Deirdre walked over to Abby, but nevertheless she began whatever she had to say in a roundabout way. "My, Abigail, you are just the prettiest thing—that blue, with your blue eyes. Too bad you're not wearing blue tomorrow too. So becoming, but I guess it has to be white?"

"No, actually not. My mother thought so too. Cynthia's funny, she said, 'After all, it's your first wedding.' "

"Ooh, that Cynthia. Well, I reckon you'll fool her—"

"I plan to. But I'm not wearing white. After all, we've been living together almost since we first met. No, I've got this wonderful sort of gold dress—even Cynthia thinks it's great."

"Well, I'm just sure it is." There was a pause, Deirdre seemed to be having trouble saying whatever it was that she had intended, but at last she did say, "Since you bring up Cynthia, I had this sort of confession—or maybe just a question—for her."

Standing there in the sunlight, near a row of yellow roses that were placed in tall glass vases, somewhat apart from the others, the two young women had another moment of silence as Abby had a sense—not exactly of *déjà vu* but of an old relationship returned. She was remembering Deirdre when they first met: she, Abby, a pigtailed newcomer, a lost Yankee, and Deirdre, a dark, too beautiful, too young mother, with her little boy, Graham, whom she had to pass off as her brother. And so now she said to Deirdre, in a very friendly, direct (un-Southern) way: "She won't bite. If you want to ask her or tell her something, just do it, Deirdre. God knows you've never been a coward."

Deirdre's delicate chin lifted just slightly at that praise as she said, "I reckon not."

The Deirdre-Derek rumors then must be true, Abby thought; Deirdre was going off to meet Derek in California, and Abby also thought, Well, good luck to her. Poor Deirdre, she doesn't seem to have a lot of sense about men—but then neither does my mother—or does she?

She watched as Deirdre went directly over to Cynthia,

Cynthia so very pretty in brilliant pink (to Cynthia, Schiaparelli pink—to most people down there, "nigger pink," though none of those ladies and gentlemen would have said that ugly phrase aloud).

Deirdre had indeed just said, in a somewhat jumbled rush, that she was going off to California where Derek was. And Cynthia said almost exactly what Abby had thought: "Well, the best of luck, Deirdre. I think you're a really brave young woman. You're not just beautiful. I always have thought that, since Abby first ran into you and Graham down by the creek and brought you home, remember?"

"Of course I do." A wide and beautiful smile from Deirdre.

"I have to admit," said Cynthia, with an answering slightly giddy smile (she had had a couple of glasses of the punch, which was stronger than anyone had yet realized), "I have to admit there was a time when this would not have been such great news. I was missing Harry a lot, and I had a sort of crush on Derek. I was missing Harry," she repeated. And then she added, "Of course Derek's very attractive."

Deirdre laughed. "I guess he knows that."

As Cynthia thought: We've always been so unfair to Deirdre, all of us, including me. We've underrated her. She's so very beautiful, still—or maybe more so, and according to people around here she's sort of lower class. They would never put it that way, of course, just an occasional murmur about how her folks were Baptists and her daddy ran a filling station. She's like a heroine out of Hardy, in a way. Whereas Dolly, who's certainly not beautiful, just barely pretty, Dolly makes jokes about her Baptist cousins so no one thinks of her that way. Dolly is smarter than Deirdre is, but Deirdre is more intelligent—and Cynthia resolved to give more thought to the difference between the two, smart versus intelligent.

And she thought: Russ would never have fallen in love with Dolly (even if she likes to hint that there was something between them), and for that matter neither would Derek.

"Russ could be mean," said Deirdre. "I reckon Derek can be too, but I think he knows what he's doing. He's more in charge of himself, you know?"

"Yes, and you're right."

Odessa had been bribed and begged to come for the afternoon, for the party, for Miss Abigail. She did come, looked pleasanter than usual, Dolly thought. So Dolly tried to approach her.

"Odessa, I've been thinking, and Willard has too, we've talked about this, what with the boys away, looks like for good, and Willard about to retire, I've been thinking on trips, a whole lot of trips, just me and Mr. Willard," she laughed girlishly as Odessa stared down at her, as usual, impassive, unresponsive.

"And what I'm getting to," continued Dolly, "is that that leaves a whole lot of the house, a whole wing with nobody there, and I thought, we thought, that might be just ideal for you, and Horace too. Not any rent to pay, of course not, just you could sort of look after the house, see that the dust don't settle down for good and the silver don't turn black, and Horace could do just a few little things in the garden, I know how he loves those flowers." Somewhat out of breath, she paused.

Odessa spoke almost too quietly to be heard. "Well no'm, I reckon not."

"What's that you say, Odessa?"

"Horace and me, I don't reckon we're studying on moving, not anytime soon leastways."

"Odessa, don't you understand? I'm offering you this nice clean warm big place to live, both you and Horace, for free."

"We got us a place—"

"But Miss Cynthia and Mr. Harry, you don't know what they're going to do, not even if they're still married—"

"No'm, but I do trust them to provide."

"Odessa, I don't understand you. But then most probably I never have."

"No'm, I reckon not."

Joseph Marcus was not quite as happy, as blithe, as his mother thought him to be, nor perhaps as he looked. Deeply happy in regard to Abby, of course—he would have said that: "I'm terrifically happy, *of course,* marrying Abby. I even like her parents, both of them."

But what made him much less happy, what in fact he found profoundly troubling, was a letter that had come to him that morning from a physicist friend, Saul Aaron, a few years older, an instructor at MIT. Joseph's parents and Saul's were old C.P. friends; they had marched together, raised money for Loyalist Spain and the Scottsboro boys together, and so their own boys had always known each other, gone off to interracial camps together. Had always been friends.

Saul wrote, "I predict bad years ahead, and the fifties will be even worse. Not that things aren't always bad for the Jews, as our parents always told us, but as I say, a lot worse."

Well, Saul had always been a gloomy guy; he even thought the new state of Israel was probably headed for trouble. ("The Palestinians will think they got a raw deal, and they probably did.") And Saul did not have beautiful, smart, funny, kind Abigail Baird in his life.

Thinking of Abby, trying not to think of Saul, Joseph felt his inner joy—and peace; Abby made him peaceful, finally, and he smiled again.

"What I think is, people are really going to miss the war—this war," Harry said. He was speaking to Dolly Bigelow, but was very aware that Cynthia stood just a few feet away from him, beside a potted pink rose. The rose blossoms were so perfectly beautiful that they looked false, and the scent was strong, but he could still smell Cynthia's familiar Shalimar.

"Why, Harry, what a thing to say! Whatever can you mean?" There was genuine shock in Dolly's voice: to miss a war, when so many people had got killed and all the rest of them had had to do without so many good things, like gas and steak and Scotch? What would these Yankee Bairds say next!

Harry said, somewhat loudly, "The heroic certainty of it all. The moral clarity. Hitler was bad, we're good. And we'll miss the excitement, the fervor. Wars are *sexy*—"

Smiling to herself, Cynthia thought, Oh, *Harry*.

Dolly had set up loudspeakers here and there among the expensive florists' flowers, and so the music of the day, and nights, poured out across what had been Russ Byrd's garden. Glenn Miller, Tommy Dorsey, Benny Goodman, Jimmy Lunceford. (Lunceford, the only Negro, was the closest to real, great jazz, thought Joseph Marcus, a passionate fan of Louis Armstrong, of Bessie and Lester and Billie.) And the voice of Sinatra (whom Joseph hated), along with Anita O'Day and Margaret Whiting and Dinah Shore (who was not too bad, not as bad as the others). "I'll Never Smile Again." "It Had to Be You." "I've Got a Crush on You." "Where or When—"

All wrenchingly nostalgic, desperately yearning, Cynthia felt. As in the background a chorus of trombones sounded their bullfrog backup. And despite all her awareness that this music was mostly junk—sugarcane, pablum—she felt tears near her eyes.

As—so romantically!—she felt a hand that must be Harry's against her bare right shoulder. He was going to ask her to marry him—again! How perfect, Cynthia thought as she felt the tears gather closer.

She turned to face him, and they both smiled, familiarly, but what Harry said was, "I'm not supposed to tell you this but I have to: you got in!"

Not at first understanding him, Cynthia then thought, Oh, law school. He means Georgetown. And she felt a stab of disappointment, strong and irrational, she knew that. Just what had she wanted him to say? She said, "Oh. Swell."

Why didn't he say at least something about her coming back to live there, to live with him? Deciding that she was not so irrational, she scowled. "Goddam it, Harry," she began.

But whatever diatribe she had had in mind was interrupted by a loud creak from the garden gate, not far behind them. Harry and Cynthia turned to see that the gate was opened by Paxton, Graham's friend, who was standing closest. And there in the gateway was a very tall, thin, hesitant young woman. Shy and pretty. Light brown, a Negro. Who said to Paxton, in a low half whisper, "I'm looking for Miz Odessa Jones—told me she'd be here."

Paxton looked politely blank, but Cynthia cried out, "Nellie!" and she hurried over to where the young woman stood, just outside the gate.

But Odessa got there first. Odessa, seeming to swim out from behind and around Cynthia. Odessa, speaking more loudly and harshly than anyone had heard her before, "Girl, where you *been*?"

But, at the same time, she grasped her daughter, the girl her exact same height, in an enveloping hug that lasted. Then the two women stood apart from each other, and Odessa, now smiling widely, could be seen to be scolding her daughter, but no one, not even Cynthia, so near, could hear the words.

Paxton to Graham: "What on earth was that all about?"

"That young one was Odessa's daughter, Nellie. I guess she's been missing, and Odessa's been really worried."

" 'Odessa?' What a great name."

"She's always been here, she's a great woman."

The two young men exchanged a look of great affection. Of pleasure in each other. Of love.

Some yards away, near a splendid group of potted white azaleas, Abby Baird was explaining more or less the same thing to Joseph, and to his mother, Sylvia. "Odessa is really the greatest," Abby whispered. "She and my mother have always got along, in their way, but Dolly Bigelow—God! explosions."

"Two strong Southern women," Joseph mused.

"Yes, Odessa's stronger, but I'm not sure she knows that."

Odessa was heading into the house, closely followed by her daughter, and everyone could hear as Odessa said, "I've got a whole heap of work to do, and you can help me with it. Never mind if these days you're a secretary."

Happily, Nellie laughed. "Come on, Mama. Secretaries work."

Music blared out over the garden just then. Inappropriately: "Moonlight Serenade," Glenn Miller. The repetitive slow-dance beat, the insinuatingly sweet thin melody winding in and out. Conversation except with the nearest person became impossible. To Joseph, into his ear, Abigail said, "In high school they always played this for the last dance. Escort no break."

"What?"

She explained the system, and Joseph laughed as he told her, "You sound as though you liked all that. How can I marry a Southern belle?"

She admitted, "Well, I sort of did. It was hard not to, really. You know, it even smells like one of those dances here. Gardenias, we all wore them, but I don't see any growing, do you?"

He looked around, "I probably wouldn't know a gardenia from a turnip."

"You know, what Billie Holiday wears on her ear."

"Oh."

Melanctha put her hands over River's ears, such beautiful long brown silky ears. She knew that he didn't like music; he disliked it almost as much as he disliked thunder, and guns. And she was sure that he would especially not like this goopy garbage.

Deirdre, who had always liked this song, tried not to cry. She was reminded of so many things, mostly dances back in high school, all those good-looking boys, lots of them probably dead by now in the war. And Derek somewhere on the sidelines of the dance, cross, superior, and more handsome than anyone.

Sniffing the air, with a tone of discovery Cynthia told Harry, "You know what? I smell gardenias—"

He sniffed too. "So do I, but I don't see any around. What are you wearing?"

"Shalimar, of course. But you know what? I'll bet Dolly's sprayed that tacky Jungle Gardenia all over, it's her favorite."

"Oh, really?"

"It must be, just smell."

Harry said, "Shalimar, the only true scent." He smiled, and as though they were about to dance he said, "About Georgetown, what I mean is, you have to come back and live with me. And be my love."

They both laughed, but then turned to each other and exchanged a quick hard kiss. Assenting.

Watching them from the kitchen door, joyfully, Dolly told Odessa, who was just behind her, "They're renewing their vows! Oh, I just knew it."

But Odessa, though smiling politely, only remarked, "You reckon?"